DIVINE
DESTINY

- The Divine Chronicles Book 2 -

JoAnna Grace

ABW-WJP, LLC
P.O. Box 337
Lindale, TX 75771

2022 Cover Design by Moorbooks Design
Book design by Champagne Formats
Printed in the United States of America

Library of Congress Control Number Data
Grace, JoAnna.
Divine Destiny / JoAnna Grace.
1. Fantasy romance—Greek mythology—Fiction. 2. Romance—Fantasy—Fiction. 3. Sagas—Romance—Fiction.
Fiction. | BISAC: FICTION / Romance / Fantasy. | FICTION / Romance / General. | FICTION / Sagas.
PCN # 2016911674 2016
ISBN 978-1-940460-22-2
www.authorjoannagrace.com

JoAnna Grace

CONTEMPORARY ROMANCES

The Roles We Play

Riverview Romances

Why The River Runs

A River Between Us

PARANORMAL TITLES

Divine Chronicle Series:

Divine Awakening

Divine Destiny

Divine Judgment

Divine Encounter

Divine Pursuit

Divine Deception

Divine Justice

Blake Pride Series:

Pride Before the Fall

Break Her Fall

The Harder They Fall

Divided We Fall

Rise After the Fall

For more information on JoAnna's books, signings, events, and more, Sign up for the NEWSLETTER at http://eepurl.com/B_DM5!

A Note From Jo

Thank you, dear readers, for once again picking up a JoAnna Grace novel. I hope you enjoy it. It brings me great joy to hear from you. Please connect with me on social media:

Facebook: facebook.com/joannagraceauthor
Instagram: instagram.com/authorjoannagrace

Want updates delivered to your inbox?
Make sure you're in the know.
Sign up for my newsletter today! Visit http://eepurl.com/B_DM5

Do you want to help an author?

Leave a review!

Your opinion matters. Every review can help.

Share a link to this book on social media!

Like, follow, tag Jo, and share this book with your friends.

Support Indie Authors!

Did you know that an Indie Author fronts all
the cost of production?

That's right. We appreciate every person who purchases
our books because that's how we continue to produce
more. Independent authors, cover designers, editors, and
formatters work hard to bring readers quality products and
stories they can fall in love with.

Like. Share. Follow. Subscribe. Tag. Review.

It all helps the Indie community!

Share the Love.

DEDICATION &
ACKNOWLEDGEMENTS

I believe that for everything under the sun there is a time and a season. And because of some wonderful people and the grace of God, mine has come.

To my wonderful family: Donny, you have been nothing but supportive even when it was a sacrifice to you. Thank you for all you had to do when I was zoned out in front of the computer. I love you Forever. G,S, & C, Mommy wanted to lead by example. Anything is achievable if you have ambition, dedication, and faith. I can't wait to see you soar!

Mom, you have always been my biggest critic and my biggest cheerleader. I love your honesty, your unconditional love, and how you yell "Go Girl, Go!" every step of the way. I hope I'm half the woman you are!

Cheryl, you are my person. Thank you for everything you have done. Some things I can name—and some are just between us! Oh, and nice sword! Tim, thanks for sharing her. Luv ya buddy.

Brandon, Jelaine, Amanda, and my amazing OWG sisters: You are shining lights in my life. You bless me every day. I am thankful for you all. Forever.

2016 Addition: Jennifer- Thank you for helping me spruce this girl up. I've always been proud of this story, but man, now she really shines. Thanks for teaching me and being my favorite pirate wench!

PROLOGUE

AVERY'S FINGERTIPS NUMBED DUE TO THE ROPES SHACKLING her wrists. They rubbed her raw as she struggled to free herself. The wad of cloth crammed into her mouth captured her cries for help.

"He's here." Jerry smiled and faced the front door.

Wood splintered as a great force knocked it off the hinges and sent it flying into the other room.

Crystals of terror froze in her veins, rendering her motionless. A creature in a black cloak floated across the threshold with an army of men in red military-style uniforms. She couldn't see its face, but she could see the red flesh of its claw-like hands. Black talons stretched out like daggers. There was nothing human about it.

She fought harder against her restraints, dreading what those talons might do to her. No! This couldn't be happening. This couldn't be real. Deep inside the core of her body, something stirred. At first it felt like the roil of stomach acid, but then it spread out into the rest of her body.

"What's up with her eyes?" Jerry pointed at her, his eyes narrowed and darted back and forth between his master and Avery.

"Ah!" said the creature. "She'sss awakening." He took a step back and folded those talons in front of him, as if ready to observe the show.

The world began to spin and shadows crossed her vision. She clamped her eyes shut. Every nerve ending in her body raged hot. Smoke tickled her nose. Something was burning. Something familiar and organic, like wood or fabric. When she opened her eyes, the world had taken on a red tint.

Raw power flooded her body. When she pulled against the ropes this time, they easily gave way.

"Fire Keeper." The demon said in an awed tone. "Incrrredible."

Avery looked down at her body. Flames licked up her skin, tickling her arms and legs, warming her stomach and chest. Her clothing disintegrated, eaten by the fire. Every inch of her body glowed yet her flesh wasn't burning. In fact, Avery had never felt more alive, liberated even.

"Kill her," the demon hissed to his men.

CHAPTER ONE

AVERY'S HOME BURNED IN A RAGING INFERNO. HER ENTIRE WORLD was engulfed in flames. The orange and yellow stretched to the sky in a cry for help as her home lost the fight. Every memory, every texture and smell of home would be gone in a matter of minutes. When the roof collapsed, Avery covered her mouth before the scream could escape. Instead, she buried her head into the neck of the man carrying her through the woods and away from the nightmare she had just experienced.

She sobbed silently and hit her fist against his chest. Though Ryse had promised to carry her to safety, she didn't know if she believed that. Only moments ago Avery had watched him kill mercilessly. It might have been to rescue her, but a normal person didn't wield a sword with such precision and no remorse.

Then again, a normal person didn't burst into flames and incinerate her attackers.

⚜

Ryse's cell phone rang just before the car veered off the interstate to go south. "Ryse," he answered with clipped tone.

"Master," Hammon answered in his African accent. Ryse's second-in-command had been with him for centuries. A fine, loyal soldier, he trusted Hammon with his life. "All evidence of our time here is gone. No one will remember us. Philippe held off the flames so we could gather some of her personal belongings before we escaped. Brenden will continue his ruse as an officer. Cutter will make sure all believe Avery and Frank were killed in a lover's quarrel with Jerry. All other bodies have been taken care of. Yankee was able to get the Lady's dogs out before anyone arrived."

"Good. Everyone will meet up at the safe house. Tell Brenden to stay behind, finish out his job, then get to the Haven. We don't know if the Rogues will come back and I don't want him there if they do."

"Yes, sire. We are not far behind you."

Ryse hung up his phone and cast a quick glance at his passenger in the back seat. She was a mess. He knew beneath the quilt was a bloodied, shaken body and more emotional scars than one woman should have to carry. Her beautiful face was bruised, her cheek was gashed, and tears had cut tracks in the soot that clung to her skin.

His mission had been to get her out safely and calmly. Instead, his presence had alerted the enemy in hiding. Ryse hadn't known how close they had been all along. By the time he found out, there had been no time to explain, no time to coax her trust or comprehension. There was only time to save her and get the hell out.

Jerry had known quickly what Ryse was. Olympians could shield their auras—hide them completely if needed. However, a powerful Olympian like Ryse could not be contained by such magic. Any Olympian within a five-mile radius could sense him even with his aura shielded to the best of his abilities. Jerry, one of the traitors known as a Rogue, knew that if Ryse got too close, his chance to kill Avery would be lost. His success would have been hell for Ryse.

Thank the gods Ryse and his Elites had arrived in time to find Avery alive. What he hadn't expected was to find her on fire, the brilliant flames dancing along her skin and burning away her clothing. She had been ethereal, a red and orange glowing goddess, her long auburn curls floating about her head alive with the fire. He stood paralyzed by her deadly beauty before he fully comprehended what it meant. Helioan fire keepers were rare. It was a good thing Philippe had been there to counteract her heat with his cold.

Her soft voice broke into his thoughts. "Where are you taking me?" He nearly choked at the fear in her words.

"Somewhere you will be safe."

"Those people who tried to kill me, you didn't get them all. There was one that, well, he just *vanished*." She sounded like she didn't believe her words. "How is that possible? How is any of this possible?"

"Their leader had a Teleporter. There aren't many left in our world, but they can transport themselves anywhere in the blink of an eye."

Her voice trembled. "In your world? What world is that?"

Ryse looked back at his charge. "The world of Olympians, Avery, the descendants of the gods. Your parents didn't live to bring you home, but now that I've found you, it's time for you to take your place among us."

"This can't be real. I'm in a horrible nightmare." Avery said, fresh tears dripping down her face. "My friends will search for me."

"I'm afraid not, love." He looked back quickly, then turned away again. "They will all believe you're dead."

He could hear her sobbing and mumbling, see her rocking herself in the back seat. "I'm going to be sick." She grabbed for the handle to open the door and Ryse swerved to stop the car on the side of the road just as she lost the contents of her stomach. Luckily, the interstate wasn't busy this time of night and only a handful of cars passed them. Ryse came to her side, made sure her nakedness was covered and held back her hair.

"Avery, I can make you sleep if you wish." He prayed she took the offer.

"You're going to drug me?" She scrambled to get out of his hold.

"No. No, I swear. I can simply put your mind to sleep so that you have relief from this agony. Please let me help you. Your body needs to rest." He tilted her chin up until her eyes met his. He'd fallen for those green eyes the moment they first connected with his two days ago. "Please. I won't hurt you."

For a long moment she stared at him unblinking. He wondered if her shattered mind even recognized what he'd said. Instead, she dropped her eyes and turned her face away. "Just make it all go away."

Ryse picked her up and laid her down across the back seat, tucking the quilt around her. He placed his hand over her forehead and closed his eyes, praying to the gods. As he spoke the sacred prayers, his hand began to glow with a soft white light and Avery's eyelids slid down. The power of his aura flooded her body. He thanked the gods and watched for a moment as Avery relaxed into a deep sleep. She would need her strength in the days to come. Avery's life would never be the same.

CHAPTER TWO

WHEN SHE FINALLY AWOKE, IT WAS BECAUSE RYSE WAS CARRYING her again. He was taking her up a set of stairs. She heard voices, but none of it truly pierced her mind. A fog had settled and there was no seeing through it.

"I'm Paula, Master. I've set out clothes and food." A woman, portly and graying, followed them up the stairs and into a room. "You may take her straight to the bathroom to be cleaned. I will take the quilt and dispose of it."

Panic curled in Avery's gut at the woman's words. This solitary quilt was the only thing that she had left of her home, her heritage—no matter how unsure of it she was at the moment—and of her family.

"Can you get the blo—stains out?" Ryse spoke before she could remember how to form words. "It was made by her mother. If it can be salvaged, please try."

"I will do my best, Master. The…*stains* look set in." She glanced back and forth between the two. "I will go run a hot bath." Paula scurried off to the bathroom while Ryse sat Avery down in a chair and wrapped her tighter in the blanket.

She watched as he went to the console and fixed a plate of fruit and bagels. Had Paula called him Master? Twice? Why would she do that? What was he the master of?

He sat in front of her and held up a strawberry. "Eat," he demanded. The response was silence, her eyes averted. There was no hunger in her of any kind. No hunger for life or food.

Bowing his head for a moment, his whole face changed when he looked up again. He appeared tired and weathered. "Avery, please," he begged as he lifted the fruit to her lips. Though she could feel the textures in her mouth, feel it go down her throat one bite at a time, she tasted nothing. Half a bagel and a few pieces of fruit later, she turned away.

Paula joined them as Ryse put the plate down. "Master, the bath is ready. Should I stay?"

"No, Paula. The Lady and I need some privacy." He walked over to Avery and knelt down in front of her. "Let's get you cleaned."

Avery numbly went along with him as he unwrapped her from the quilt. Paula had started the shower so that she could rinse off before settling into the tub to relax. Sweet old Paula didn't realize that there would be no relaxation tonight.

The woman took the quilt from Ryse, her eyes wide as she beheld Avery's blood-crusted body.

"My god," Paula said, putting her hand over her mouth.

"You may leave. Thank you for all you've done." His words were kind, but his demeanor was not. Paula caught the admonition in his tone, bowed and exited hastily. Ryse nearly shut the door on her.

Avery stared numbly at the battered woman reflected in the expansive wall of mirrors. It was the first time she had seen herself since she'd gotten home from the bar—before Jerry showed up at her house and brought carnage.

That's when she noticed the change.

Less than twelve hours ago, Avery's hair had been long and wavy, silky brown like luscious dark coffee with hints of red. But this hair was different. It was lighter, redder—more auburn than brown. The difference was significant. The curls were tighter. It felt coarse, dry, and in need of deep conditioning. Only after running her hands through the strange mane did she look at the rest of her skin from the neck down. The vast mirror showed everything to her knees.

Blood caked everywhere—brown, dried, stinking blood. Frank's blood. All the blood one healthy male body could hold. It'd run onto the hardwood floor of her house, soaked into her rugs and felt warm on her skin as she'd told her best friend goodbye. The thought made her dizzy, made her body shake.

"Whoa, I've got you." Rysc caught her in his arms and held her. "It's okay. Shh. Hush, baby," he crooned to sooth her.

Avery didn't realize she had been whimpering. All she could feel were the shattering chills that racked her body against Ryse. Her legs were useless.

"I'm going to help you." The slow oozing warmth slipped over her again, allowing her muscles to unclench and loosen. Ryse held her with one arm and removed his clothes with another. Avery's face pressed against a now shirtless, hard chest.

"Come on, Avery. In you go." He gently shifted her into the tiled shower and under the water.

The hot water flowed over her and she shut her eyes. Ryse began cleaning her with soap. His actions didn't surprise her or anger her; she felt nothing. Ryse was acting as her arms and her mind. Later she would appreciate his efforts, his gentleness and soothing words as he worked to erase the terrors of the night.

When she was rid of the physical evidence of her struggles, Ryse turned off the shower and moved her over to the large round bathtub full of hot water and lavender and rose scented oils. He sat Avery in the middle and then carefully slid in behind her, making the water nearly overflow. His legs went on either side and Avery vaguely noticed that he still wore a pair of boxer briefs.

Two large hands slid over her shoulders and down her back, rubbing her. Then he very slowly pulled her back until she lay on his chest, his arms wrapped around her, their hands clamped together on her stomach. They lowered into the water and stilled.

Avery was aware of the layer of power that sheltered her body. She was going to have to ask him what that was, just not right then.

— · ⚬ · — ►

Any other time, Ryse thought, this would be romantic, sensual, passionate. Avery was naked, lying on top of him, her breasts peeking out of the water along with one arched knee. He'd gotten a full and intimate feel of her body when he had washed her earlier. Had he been a lesser man, he would have been aroused.

As it were, this passiveness terrified him. It was wrong in every way. He used his aura to help her relax, but still Avery would have *never* allowed him such access to her body under normal circumstances. She would have fought back; her southern accent would have deepened with her temper. Not in a million years would she have let him wash her or let him in the bathroom with her, period. Independence defined this woman. He'd seen it in her dealings with customers, the way she handled her friends, in every facet of her life.

Yet here she lay, nothing more than a shell. The silence was agonizing. No words came to him. What could he say to make any of this better? Nothing. There was nothing he could do but love her and hold her and let her know that he was here.

For Ryse, this intimacy was foreign. Touch, closeness with another being, it was usually so difficult. A man raised by Thracians didn't get much coddling. It took all his concentration to process the sensation. Ever since he walked into Avery's cafe, things had been different. He had been different. Every minute he'd spent with her over the last two days had been heaven—and hell. It broke his heart to lie to her about who and what he was. Bounty hunter, yeah, you could call him that. He chased around criminals all the time; they just happen to be Olympians. The plan for last night had been to tell her the truth and convince her to leave town.

Ryse had bonded with her. He'd never engaged mentally with a woman until her. Never wanted to. Everything he knew of caring for a woman, she had taught him in two days. In the short days he'd spent in her presence, she'd coaxed laughter from him and even made him grovel—something he wouldn't have thought impossible. He'd come to care about her café, her friends, the pictures in her home, and her dogs. The stories, rare glimpses of her family and past, were gifts he would treasure forever. They shared laughter, casual touches—things he hardly allowed from anyone. He relished their intimate kisses and longed to be near her, feeling empty without her. She unearthed the part of him he had been missing.

All his many years of immortal life, much more than she knew, had been devoted to his craft. Born as a Thracian warrior, he had a great responsibility to his people. Most of his existence had been spent training to be the lethal blade that he was. Many hundreds of men had died at his hands. It was his job, his heritage and his birth-right as a chosen one to protect his people.

But there were two sides to his coin. The other part of his birth-right was being born the eldest son of earth-bound Deities. One day he would rule the North American Olympian population as his father and his father's father before him. Avery was his gift from the gods. She was his perfect companion, chosen by the heavens at birth and gifted beyond all others. Avery was his soul mate in a very literal way, the gods had proclaimed it.

And his soul mate was broken. Ryse had learned long ago that the past was gone and no matter how much we prayed or begged of the gods, it couldn't change. Oh, how he wished that were not true, though the fact still remained. Now he had to convince Avery to move forward.

Her body shivered once and he knew that they had been lying in the water too long. It was starting to get cool and she needed to be in bed asleep. "I'll get a towel for you, baby," he whispered as she leaned up, letting him get out of the bath.

Ryse knew that she wasn't going to turn and look back at him, so he removed the wet briefs. Provisions had been made for them and that included clean clothes. He dressed in clean jeans, not worrying with a shirt.

Soon, Avery was wrapped in a thick robe with cotton pajamas under it, Ryse combing out her hair. The sun might have been high in the sky outside, but they were getting ready for sleep. A knock tapping at the door startled them both.

"Hey boss, it's me. I have the dogs," came a muffled voice from the other side of the door. Yankee.

When he opened the door, Ryse was nearly toppled by two German Shepherds. They had scented Avery and were anxious to get to their owner. One of them jumped up beside her and nuzzled his nose under her arm. The other came to sit between her legs on the side of the bed.

Avery only stared without recognition of them. For a moment, Ryse's heart stopped. Before he could make a move, Avery grabbed up the dogs and held them both tightly to her chest. New tears streamed down her face as she sobbed. Frank had given her the animals and he'd worked closely with Avery to train them. Castor and Pollux, being the amazing creatures they were, knew that Avery was damaged. Their usual playful nature was replaced with an ominous quiet. They rested against her, completely still, and let her cry into their fur.

"Master," Yankee whispered. "Can I do anything?" He was talking to Ryse, but looking at his Princess solemnly.

Ryse grasped his shoulder. "You have done well, brother. Go rest and I will call for you later."

"You got it, boss." Yankee nodded and left. He knew. All the men knew that Avery was devastated and only time would heal her deepest wounds.

When he walked back into the bedroom, Avery was in the bed curled up with a dog on either side of her, sound asleep. Castor, the bigger of the two, was behind her with his head resting on her waist. Pollux was in front of her, under her arm. Ryse turned off the lights and lay down on the other side of Castor. He said a prayer of thanks for all of their lives as he rubbed the back of the dog until he fell asleep.

CHAPTER THREE

WHEN AVERY WOKE, THERE WAS NOTHING TO INDICATE THE TIME or how long she had been out. The only light came from the living area. Castor and Pollux were both walking around sniffing. Avery could hear the sound of feet pacing in the next room. Quietly she rose and went to use the bathroom. She could hear Ryse on the phone, so she peeked around the corner.

"I know, this is the worst case scenario, but she is too fragile right now. I know, I know, I miss you, too. I'm ready to be home and put this behind us. Okay, I will call you soon. I love you, too."

He clicked the phone off, then looked at it for a moment, a smile teasing his lips.

His voice had been low and intimate. It reminded her of their first conversation in her café.

When he had looked up with his chocolate eyes and dazzling shy smile, Avery was sure she'd never seen such a handsome man. She wanted to stroke the black hair hanging around his cheekbones. No man should have such thick hair. He'd teased her about her sense of Southern hospitality and deep accent. She'd teased back about not being from Texas.

The next day, at her house, they'd shared conversation and kisses that curled her toes. He joined her later at Marshall's bar with her friends, where they danced close and he whispered that he wanted to spend the night.

A revelation hit Avery and knocked her heart into her throat. She found it hard to swallow.

Ryse was on a mission. Getting to her was nothing more than a job. Frank had often talked about the police officers in big cities who went undercover and did anything and everything to achieve their goals. Was Ryse going undercover with her? Perhaps it was a good thing all hell had broken loose before she'd made the mistake of sleeping with him.

Everything that she had ever been told had been a lie. Her parents began lying to her years ago. If they knew that Avery was… *different* and never told her, wasn't that a lie? A lie they were murdered over. Jerry, who was supposed to be one of her close friends, had been nothing but an actor for the two years that she had known him. He'd been a very believable one. Not once in their relationship had she ever doubted anything he'd said. He'd integrated himself into the friendship she and Frank had developed since grade school.

Then there was Ryse.

The moment he walked into her café, she'd been wildly attracted. His presence rendered her brainless and when he kissed her, hot damn. Her insides melted like ice cream in the Texas summer. There had never been a man who made her body sizzle the way Ryse did.

And now she doubted any of it was real for him.

"Avery?" His voice broke through her thoughts. She'd been standing in the middle of the hallway by the door to the bathroom. "What are you doing, baby?" The gentleness of his voice was alluring. But she was not going to be fooled. He'd also been talking to someone else with that alluring voice. "Do you need something?"

The last two words he'd spoken to a closed door. Avery sat on the toilet seat and buried her head in her hands. Last night, or this morning, or whenever it was—ugh, she was disoriented—Ryse had not only seen her naked, but had also bathed her. *Bathed* her! His hands had been all over, washing and scrubbing her. How could she let him do that? How could she allow someone to lay in a tub with her, dry her, and then put on her clothing? It was the cherry on her nightmare sundae. Acid rolled in her stomach and her skin grew warm with blush.

There was no denying now that Ryse had a very intimate look at her body. And, she remembered with utter humiliation, so had his men. She'd been naked after catching on fire. An entire room full of men had witnessed it, their eyes wide with shock but their gazes averted. She shook her head, feeling the blood pool in her cheeks. This only kept getting worse.

After a long twenty minutes, Avery decided she couldn't hide in the bathroom all day. She opened the door to find Ryse leaning up against the wall, his hands in his pockets. He stood up when she came out, gazing at her with those chocolate eyes. They held such concern her heart dropped in her chest.

Avery looked away and tightened her robe around herself. Laid out on the bed were a pair of jeans and a red sweatshirt that looked about her size. She found her toothbrush and hairbrush in a brown leather bag. Personal belongings were so few now. It surprised her how much she longed to be home, even with everything that had happened. Dorothy had it right; there was no place like it.

Except she didn't have a home anymore; that she remembered. Her home had gone up in flames—flames that been released from her body.

"Would you like to get dressed?" He'd been standing right behind her, but she barely recognized that Ryse was in the room. "There is food. Are you hungry?"

She felt something deep within her begin to bubble up. No one had been honest with her—not her parents, not Jerry, not even Ryse. Even now her trust waivered. Every kind word, every touch—was all nothing but a lie? Only Frank had ever been truthful, and he was dead. Hot tears streamed down her face. Her breath came hard and fast.

Ryse touched the side of her neck, his eyes searching hers. "Avery? Baby?"

Baby? *Baby!* How dare he call her his baby! She didn't belong to him. This deceptive man had no right to endearments. With all she had, Avery slapped him. It barely moved his head, but a bright red handprint began to appear on his cheek. His face became full of anger and then…understanding?

"I'm sorry," he whispered.

To hell with his pity. She slapped him again.

"I'm sorry," he repeated.

She hauled back to hit him again because it had felt good. He caught her right hand firmly in his own, so she tried with her left hand. He caught that, too.

"I know you are angry with me," he said, holding her hands tight. "But you have to understand that I never meant to hurt you. You can't possibly hate me as much as I hate myself for letting that bastard get to you, for not being able to stop him from killing Frank. Nothing was supposed to happen to you. We were there to keep you safe."

"You failed."

CHAPTER FOUR

F*RAGILE MY ASS*, HE THOUGHT AS THOSE WORDS BIT INTO HIS HEART. Yes, he'd failed her. He'd failed at keeping her safe, failed at keeping Frank alive, failed at protecting her from the evils of his world until she was ready to handle them. The man inside wanted to pull Avery into his arms, beg for forgiveness, make love to her until she had no doubts left that he cared. But that wouldn't happen. He dropped her hands and stepped back. Not able to meet her eyes, he turned and walked away.

Before he opened the door to leave, he called over his shoulder. "Get dressed. We leave in a couple hours." He left her in the tiny apartment and went to find someone to spar with. Hammon would fight with him. That would burn off some of these *emotions*. They were too raw and he didn't like them a damn bit.

⊷ ⊶

Avery jumped when she heard the knock. She cracked open the door to see a man with curly black hair and hazel eyes. He nodded to her and removed a cigarette from his lips.

"*Principessa*, I collect your bag and dogs." His thick Italian accent evoked the memory of the first time she'd seen him. This man had touched her fire-consumed hand and absorbed the heat of her flames. His hazel eyes had turned white in that moment and his smile told her he gained some sort of pleasure from the act. Right now, he stared at her as an addict would look at a syringe.

"You—you did something to me. How did you put out the fire like that?"

"I am Elementalist. I control *il fuoco*, the fire. I take from you."

"Did it hurt?" Avery asked, hugging her chest, afraid she might have caused another person pain.

"No. It is," he said as he tilted his head in search of the right English word, "is fine. Is okay."

Avery's curiosity pushed more questions from her lips. She could have asked Ryse, but he was intimidating where this man was not. "Do you control other things?"

"*Si*, air." He waved his cigarette holding hand. "Winds. Uh, dirt. Gaia."

"The earth?"

"*Si, si*. And *l'acqua*, water."

"Fire, wind, water, and earth." Avery nodded slowly. What a combination. This man could do scary and amazing things. "What is your name?"

"Philippe, *signora*. I serve Master, I serve you." Nodding once he took another puff on his cigarette. "Come, *cani*." He took her bag and patted his leg to summon the dogs.

They walked out to the balcony that overlooked into the barn. Metal clanging against metal reverberated off the walls. Avery froze, dropping into a crouch to grab her dogs' necks. The tinny, violent sounds spiraled her back to the night of the attack. She flinched at each strike.

"*Signora?*" Philippe looked at her in question. He reached out to touch her, then stopped and nodded. "Is okay."

Philippe walked over to the end of the row of rooms and peered over the balcony into a roping arena. He took a puff of the cigarette and leaned against the wall.

In the middle of the raked dirt were three shirtless men. Ryse was in the middle of two men—a tall black giant and a smaller Asian.

They took fast, swift blows from their swords. For a moment, the scene slowed. Then Ryse gave some sort of command and the choreography sped up.

The three of them were a blur of movements and sparks when their swords clashed. There was no separating the men as individuals. Even though they were of different skin colors, they mixed together in a swirl of vanilla, cream, and coffee. Dust from the arena flew about them in a tornado.

When it cleared, the Asian man lay on the dirt floor, Ryse's foot on his neck. The man was without his sword and trying to push off Ryse's foot. He didn't succeed. Ryse's sword pointed at the black man's neck, indenting the skin, but not breaking it. For the briefest second, their faces were somber, and Avery knew Ryse could have killed them both. Was that what they waited for? Did they fear their master would end their lives as quickly as he did the men who attacked her?

Just as Avery felt her heart shrivel up like a raisin, the three of them laughed. She released the breath she'd been holding and loosened the death grip she had on her two dogs.

"Breathe, *signora*," Philippe said with a smile, blowing smoke out his mouth. "Is fun. *Si?* Hammon." He pointed to the black man, then the other. "Cutter."

She looked down at Ryse, who now stood, gazing up at her. Their eyes met and she didn't try to hide her wide-eyed fear. He was so strong, frightening. Ryse's lips pinched and he scowled. He nodded a dismissal to his men and strode towards the staircase she stood in front of.

Back on solid feet, the other two men bowed respectfully. They were quite the opposite; Hammon had to be around seven feet while the Asian man, Cutter, was about her height, a mere five and half feet. Both wore placid expressions of calm focus, not smiling or frowning, but their eyes held her attention.

"If you don't mind, I would shower before we leave?" Ryse asked kindly. It meant something to her that he asked not ordered.

Her head bobbed once in agreement, as if she would dare tell him no after a display like that.

She watched him disappear into a room. Something clicked in her. The way he was acting, the strength he exuded—it was such a far cry from the sweet man she'd gotten to know and it pissed her off. Who was this guy, anyway? Why should she go anywhere with him?

"Hold the dogs, please." She threw the leashes at the Philippe. He fumbled with his cigarette before grabbing them. "Those things'll kill you." She motioned to the stick hanging from his lips.

"Not likely," he smirked. Philippe took the dogs and walked them down the stairs without question.

Avery barreled into the room after Ryse and shut the door. It didn't hinder her one bit that the shower was running. He would give her answers. She threw back the shower curtain and nearly forgot what she was doing. The steam hit her face right along with her blush and she tried to keep her eyes off the exquisitely sculpted body standing under the hot water. If she let her mind go there, she'd never keep up her nerve. Instead, she pierced his shocked, wide brown eyes with her stare.

"Who are you? I want the truth this time." Her arms were rigid at her side, her hands in fists, her whole body shaking.

Ryse let out a long breath and grabbed the bottle of shampoo, squirting a quarter-sized amount in his hands and running it through his hair. Ryse rinsed the shampoo away. The complete control and calmness he kept made her blood boil in her veins.

"Who. Are. You?"

He took his time answering, turning off the water and drying off first. "My men and I are sons of Ares. We are warriors devoted to protecting the descendents of the gods on earth. It was my job to locate you, protect you, and see you safely to the Haven where you will be taken care of."

Oh, just freaking great. Another loony, because Jerry wasn't enough.

"You sound just as bat shit crazy as Jerry. What in the devil does that even mean?"

A smile played at the corners of his luscious lips. "You do have a way with words, baby." He allowed himself a small huff of a laugh.

"Do *not* mock me!" she screamed at his turned cheek. "My entire life has been nothin' but one big lie. My home is gone, my friends believe I'm dead. The only man that I did trust *is* dead. A group of— of whatever the hell you are is holding me hostage. *My. Entire. Life. Has. Been. Destroyed.* Understand that? So don't you dare mock me!" She'd backed him against the wall, her finger poking into his chest. Ryse took her shoulders and in one swift spin had her pinned. "Get off!" In the back of her mind, she thought she should be afraid.

"Avery, please." He tried to push the hair off her face, but she blanched at his touch. "I would never hurt you," he whispered. "You must believe me. Everything I have done has been for your safety and welfare. If I hadn't been watching you so closely, they would have killed you for sure. They already got too close and Frank suffered for it."

"Died for it. Frank *died* for it."

"Yes, and that was one death that I would give anything to undo, but not if it meant you taking his place. You don't understand right now, Avery. You haven't been educated in what and who you are."

"But you knew all along. Did you say one truthful thing to me before five minutes ago? The other night at my house, the bar when we danced—it was all one big act, right? You said whatever you needed to get the job done."

"I couldn't tell you everything immediately."

"Let go of me," Avery whispered, her will to fight him gone.

He turned away to dress. Avery's eyes were drawn to the tattoo that stretched down his spine. It was a sword with intricate symbols and designs. As she watched, it shimmered and flickered with a soft golden glow.

"Avery, you need to understand something. When I kissed you—"

"Please don't go there."

In the blink of an eye he was in front of her. "No. I want to say this. I have to." He touched her shoulders gently. Warmth radiated from his body. Avery felt the sweet relief and knew this was part of his power, the same power that put her to sleep. "Every kiss, every touch was real."

"You try to sell that Arizona oceanfront all you want to. I'm not buyin'," she shrugged his hands from her shoulders.

Whatever that warmth was, he was using it against her. Reluctantly, he stepped away. There was nothing he could say that would make her feel better about the situation. Her mind was crowded with the emotions of losing the ones she loved and learning the world she lived in was not as stable as she thought. "I want to go home."

"You can't. Staying at the Haven with the Thracian guards is the safest place for you."

"I don't believe this." She sat on the edge of the bed, her brain refusing to take in anything else.

"You will understand soon enough. Right now the mission is to get you behind Palace walls."

There was that word again. Mission. He'd sauntered into her café and pretended to be just another guy from out of town. He'd asked her out, came to her home, and all the while they were laughing it up over her kitchen counter, he'd been on a mission. Trust wasn't something she gave easily, and he'd broken it with every lie of omission.

"Fine." She pushed off the bed and stared him down. "Once we get there, I want nothin' to do with you."

CHAPTER FIVE

AVERY STORMED OUT OF THE ROOM AND MADE HER WAY DOWN THE stairs to the black SUVs. The men standing there were no better than the one she just left. All of them had the same stone façade over their faces. The features might have been different, but they were a united front.

Avery was about to get into the car that held her dogs when Paula came walking up holding a treasure in her hand. "I did my best, Miss, to get the blood out." She handed Avery the folded quilt; the white and pink and yellow pattern looked better than it ever had. "I was delicate with the stitching. Handmade as it is, it's a remarkable piece of art."

She hugged the quilt, the biggest piece of her home she had left, to her chest. "Thank you."

"It's my honor to serve you, milady." Paula curtsied. That was odd.

Avery held the quilt to her chest for the next several hours as they traveled through Mississippi and Alabama, then into Tennessee. She opted to sit in the back passenger seat again, her dogs taking up most of the room in the vehicle. Ryse was at the wheel with the dark skinned man named Hammon beside him. The three others were in a separate vehicle.

When her eyes became heavy, she wrapped up with her quilt

and leaned back. It was such a small piece of home, but its warmth did wonders to her aching body. Her thoughts were not what she would have expected, riding in the car with two strange men to a place that she had never been.

Her mind went to the night before—images of Ryse bathing her, washing her hair, dressing her with such care. The soft thump of his strong heartbeat as she leaned against him in the bathtub and let her muscles rest.

Even in his anger and frustration of today, he was stunning: that long, black hair framing his cheekbones, chocolate eyes searching her soul, a finely tuned body of tested muscle. She didn't know that there could be such a sculpted picture of perfection in reality. He'd been comfortable naked as she watched him shower. Coupling that image with the passion of the kisses they'd exchanged on her couch, her body temperature began to rise. Izzy was right. He was a walking orgasm inducer.

Izzy. Avery had been so brain dead since she'd left with Ryse she hadn't even thought about her best friend. Oh god! Izzy would be crushed. She would never know anything except that Jerry, their mutual friend, had killed her and Frank. Avery guessed it would never be safe to contact Izzy to say she was alive. Their many years of friendship had come to an abrupt and terrible end.

What would Avery do without her? Sweet, bouncy blonde curls, bright blue eyes, perky smile, laughing, flirting, dancing Isabelle. Never again would she see those curls or that smile. Never again would she dance with her on a sawdust-covered dance floor. Never again would Izzy come over and fix her hair or play with makeup like a teenager. She would never hear Izzy tease about her accent or call her bumpkin or hug her again.

To Izzy, Avery was dead, burnt to death in her home. Izzy would mourn her, cry for her best friend just like Avery found herself doing. She was aware of the two men sitting in the front seats but didn't care. Her partner in crime since childhood was essentially dead to her. Another piece of her was gone, leaving a gaping hole in her heart that grew with the realization of each loss: Izzy, Frank, her café, her routine, her home. She squeezed the quilt even harder.

The only thing that brought her an ounce of peace was knowing that their last night together was full of fun and good times. They had laughed and gossiped and shared while Izzy fixed her hair and dolled her up before going to Marshall's bar. Izzy would take care of the café, too. Avery's mother's legacy wouldn't go to ruin in her absence.

It made her wonder what people would do now that they thought she was dead. How had the accident been explained? Did they find the *bodies*? Would she be buried? Jeez, she couldn't fathom it. All those people she knew, the friends she had in town, would they all mourn over her the way she was mourning them?

"Milady?" The deep bass voice of the African man broke into her depressing thoughts. She turned her tear-stained face to look at him. He was holding a white paper sack. "Food," he said, pushing the bag into her hands.

How had she missed driving through the fast food line? She hadn't heard Ryse order anything. The white bag had the red logo of one of her favorite fast food chains. Her stomach craved the sustenance, her body fighting through her grief with all the energy she had. Under normal circumstances this meal would have pleased her palate. Today, however, there was no taste in her mouth, no joy in the flavors. It could have been cardboard she was chewing and it would have tasted the same. Half way through the sandwich she chose to give the remainder to her dogs.

"Was it not to your liking?" Ryse asked as he watched her feed the fries to Castor. He received a mere glance before she turned back to the window. There was no doubting the authority when he spoke again. This was a man who was accustomed to giving orders that were to be obeyed. "You need to eat Avery. You haven't had a real meal in the last four days."

"Four days?" she asked, wondering how long she had been in the safe house.

"Yes, we arrived early Saturday morning and it's Wednesday today." He looked at her, concern in his eyes.

She nodded, sick at the days she'd lost, then turned back to the window and covered up with her quilt, one hand on Pollux's head.

⚊⚊⚊

When they finally reached the portal entrance of the Haven, it was late at night. To mortal eyes, this was nothing more than a gate leading into the woods. To Olympian eyes it was a grand golden portal leading to the Haven realm. The moment the trees blurred and dissipated to reveal the streets of the refuge, he knew he was home, and his entire body relaxed.

"My thoughts exactly, sire." Hammon said, patting his shoulder. Only Hammon dared to touch him in such manner, intimately as a friend. Ryse wouldn't tolerate it from anyone else.

He turned to look at Avery sleeping. "She will be safe now."

The Haven was in an alternate plane, the portal hidden deep in the Tennessee hills. No human would ever behold it without Olympian magic. Houses of its permanent residents were scattered about the hills, and businesses and shops lined the main street. Emerging over the far rooftops was a sight that made Ryse sigh. The Palace. The stone walls had been there for thousands of years. It was a source of steady confidence in a changing world. It stood above the Haven like a guardian angel.

From the back seat came a sleepy yet awed voice. "What is this place?" Avery had wide eyes as she looked out her window.

"This is the Palace of the Deities, Avery. It's your new home." Ryse cast her a quick glance, but her eyes were looking at the massive structure growing in their vision.

The road winding up to the Palace crossed a small bridge that sent signals to the lights of the front parking lot to turn on. The Palace glowed with soft illumination that accentuated the landscaping and lines of the ancient place. He drove around the tear-shaped pond in front of the estate.

The SUV came to a halt in front of the west wing of the castle. As Avery exited the vehicle, her mouth hung open. Her head rose as she followed the arches and curves of the towers and rooflines.

Ryse walked up and touched her elbow. "Avery, baby." That seemed to snap her out of her admiring trance and she flinched.

"Don't touch me." There was no attitude, only a sense of distance in her words. It wrenched his heart in agony to see pain in her eyes.

Ryse wasn't used to being rejected. Over the expanse of his lifetime, he'd only been adored and revered by those around him, respected and feared by his men, loved but accountable to his parents. He found that Avery's spurning was more injurious than any wound given to him on the battlefield.

He squared out his shoulders, lifted his chin, and barked out orders. "Yankee, the dogs. Hammon, I want a report on Brenden. Cutter, in the morning, you and Philippe begin going over all the footage we have of Avery's house, the café. All of it. I want everything we can get on Jerry and who the hell he was working for. Sleep while you can. Lots to do in the morning."

Men scattered at his commands. He turned to see Avery watching with weary eyes. She gripped the quilt in her hands as a child would do for comfort. She examined everything as they walked into a side entrance of the castle. Guards greeted them with respectful bows as they walked down the hall to the grand suite that Ryse had renovated for Avery. More than anything, he wanted his Princess to be comfortable in his home. Having her sleep in his suite and in his bed was a bonus. Eventually it would be their suite together. For now, he slept elsewhere.

Two tall doors of heavy, dark-stained wood were closed, flanked by guards in black suits and a redheaded woman. Ryse stopped to introduce Avery to her Shadow Lady, Nikki. Giving a bow, Nikki smiled at them all. It was one of the reasons Ryse liked her. She was always happy, perky, and gracious with her affections. The perfect Shadow Lady for his beloved Avery.

"Nikki is whatever you need, whenever you need it," Ryse explained.

"I'm so pleased to meet you Lady Avery. It's a great honor to serve you. Would you like to see your room? I have some food prepared and hot chocolate as well. Master Ryse told me it was your favorite." She winked, and Ryse caught the slightest ghost of a flicker in Avery's eyes, but she only nodded.

"I shall leave you two ladies for now." Taking a chance, he bent to kiss her temple. She didn't shy away, even when his warmth touched her. "I'll be close if you need me."

CHAPTER SIX

As much as Avery wanted to pull away from that kiss, even more of her wanted to lean into him, press her head to his chest and breathe in his strength. Instead, she turned her head as he walked away. Nikki smiled at her and opened the doors.

The first impression of the suite was enough to make all other thoughts go away. Grandeur as she had never seen waited inside those doors. Her entire country home could have fit into this place. The ceilings were at least twenty-five feet tall and a crystal chandelier hung in the center of the room. The raised panel walls were a natural glossy maple, the floor a series of marble tiles in hues of soft browns and creams. To the left was the most beautiful bed Avery had ever beheld—far larger than the king size that her parents had slept on. The four large columns holding up the curved canopy were marble with wooden leaves carved in a spiral pattern. All the furniture in the room had been crafted with the same splendor.

In front of her was another set of double doors opening to an opulent bathroom to explore later. To the right of that was a marble fireplace that stretched to the ceiling. Beside the fireplace, the wall curved and was covered in thick dark red fabric. "What's behind there?"

"Oh! The windows." Nikki walked past the sitting area and pulled a thick golden rope to open the curtains. The parting drapes revealed a balcony behind a curved wall of floor-to-ceiling windows. From the balcony, Avery had a view of the lake surrounded by acres of gardens and cottages in the distance. The glittering lights and moon reflecting off the water of the lake gave it an enchanted feel.

"I kept them closed thinking you would want some privacy when you first arrived," Nikki said, admiring the view. "It's the best view in all the Palace."

"I like it. Leave them open."

"Yes, miss. Would you have some hot chocolate now?" Nikki motioned to the wingback chair facing the marble fireplace. "I can put the quilt on the bed for you." Nikki held out her arms.

"Thanks." Avery gave her the quilt and the moment Nikki touched it, it disappeared. "What did you do?"

"It's on the bed." Nikki gave her a look of confusion. Sure enough, sitting on the bed was Avery's quilt.

Avery's eyes widened. "How did you do that?"

"It's my gift, one of them. I'm a conjurer. I can create or move inanimate objects."

She smiled and poured a glass of steaming hot chocolate into a goblet. Avery sat in the chair and watched the fire dance. She thanked Nikki for the drink and sipped the warmth inside her body. Unlike the food she ate earlier, this she tasted.

"It's good," she said, taking another gulp.

"Thank you, miss." Nikki winked and went to a set of double doors to the left of the fireplace—the bathroom. "Would you have me to run a bath?"

"I can do it."

"Oh no, miss, that's my job." She ducked into the bathroom and Avery heard the water running. When she emerged, Nikki headed over to a dresser in the far corner of the room. Removing clothing from the drawer, she went back into the bathroom.

"Alright, miss. You have fresh pajamas in the bathroom for when you are done with your bath. There is also a tray of fresh fruit by the tub. Is there anything else you desire?"

Avery's mind was blank. "Um, where are my dogs?"

"Castor and Pollux are being bathed. They will be fed and walked before being brought here to spend the night. I have set out beds for them over here," she said as she pointed to the two large dog pillows sitting behind the gargantuan canopy bed. "Though I am sure they will end up sleeping with you."

"You're rather chipper for this time of night, or morning," Avery said, taking another sip of the delectable cocoa.

Nikki sat down on the arm of one of the couches, laughing. "Sorry. You don't know how happy I am that you're here. I've been waiting for years." She shook her head. "Now I can do what I'm trained to do."

Nikki was very beautiful. Not in a stunning way, but a girl-next-door kind of way. Her medium height was complimentary to her small frame. She had striking red hair that was slicked into a pony-tail, which hung over her shoulder and down to her belt. It stood out against the black turtleneck she wore. All her attire was black: black pants, black shoes. Avery wondered if black was standard color around here or if she was some sort of ninja like Ryse and his men.

"What *are* you trained to do?"

"I take care of you, no matter what that involves. If you need a maid, I am your maid. If you need to go to the village, I am your chauffeur. If you need information, I am your Google. Whatever you need."

"And if I need protection?" Avery asked.

"Then I am your bodyguard. Until one of the real soldiers gets there, anyway." She laughed. "I am trained to fight, but I'm nothing compared to the Thracians."

A yawn escaped Avery's mouth and Nikki hopped off the couch. "Come, take your bath so that you can relax. It's been a long day for you."

CHAPTER SEVEN

NEARLY AN HOUR LATER, AVERY FOUND HERSELF ALONE IN THE palatial suite and unable to sit still. Nikki's apartment was next door. As promised, Castor and Pollux were delivered to her in pristine condition. She was happy to see her boys looking so good. They sniffed every inch of the room while Avery did some exploring of her own. Everything she could need had been provided. The dressers and cabinets of the bathroom were full of essentials.

"These people put Wal-Mart to shame," she mumbled to herself as she closed the final cabinet. Catching a glimpse of herself in the mirror, she examined the new tint of red in her hair. At least it had kept its curls. Twisting one of the locks around her fingers, she left the impressive bathroom.

The wall of windows that drew her attention. Beyond, the world outside was not what she thought any longer.

"How are you feeling?"

Avery was startled by the voice that greeted her. She hated how jumpy she was. "Ryse!" She clutched at her chest and closed her eyes, wishing the sight of him didn't flutter her heart. "What do you want?"

"I thought I would check on you." He leaned against the alcove wall that housed the double doors to her chamber. She stayed across the room by the warmth of the fire.

"I'm just looking around." Her arms crossed over her chest, Avery let her hair fall to shield her face, and her blush.

"Do you like it?"

It's magnificent. But she wasn't about to admit her awe. "It's nice," she whispered.

"You should rest, Avery."

"I can't." She stepped away from the fire and sat on the arm of the couch closest to her. Ryse walked over and took a seat on the other couch. "You said something that bothered me." She recalled the orders he was barking out when they first arrived. "Something about watching the footage of my café and my house. What did that mean?"

The look that Ryse gave her made her want to go stand in the fire. It was stone cold, matter of fact. "We bugged your house and your café. You had a tracer on your car and taps on your phones." His words were a swift punch in the gut. Without batting an eye, he continued, "It was necessary to watch over you. I won't apologize. It was an appropriate invasion of privacy."

Avery stood up and paced in front of the seating area. "An appropriate invasion of privacy? You've been stalking me? What in hell's name gave you the right to do that? Is all this about Jerry? Because he was some sort of crazy voodoo-wielding killer? Why didn't you just come tell me straight up instead of spyin' on me? I still don't understand why me? What the hell did I do that you'd go through all the trouble?"

Ryse leaned his elbows on his knees and interlocked his fingers against his chin. "I had to learn about you and the people around you. Brenden was sent in weeks ago. I couldn't come until we knew for sure—"

"You bastard. Don't you have any limits? How could you invade my life like this? You lied to me, manipulated me into trusting you."

"Avery, I was planning on telling you that night. I was going to come to explain everything, get you out of town. That was the plan before we realized the sentinel we were after was Jerry."

"So you were gonna kidnap me?" she clarified.

"The plan was to get you to safety—one way or another."

The air left her chest. "Oh yeah? Well, this little plan of yours has unraveled so nicely as is." It was a low blow, but she was so angry her body was beginning to shake. "No one has explained anythin' to me. No one can explain why I'm even here—beside the obvious Avery's-a-blowtorch incident."

"Be realistic, Avery." He stood to face her. "If I had come up to you and started talking about what powers you had or if you say, burst into flames when you get angry, you would've had Frank serve me with a restraining order." Avery flinched at the mention of her lost friend. "I admit, things have not gone smoothly, but I can't help that now. What's done is done. All that matters now is your safety and happiness."

"Happiness?" She let out a snide laugh. "Is that your idea of a joke?" Ryse pressed his lips together and said nothing. "Do you think all of this," she waved her hands around at the immaculate room, "will make me happy? Is it all a bribe? Is that what it is? A gilded cage is still a cage, Ryse. Am I your captive and this is my consolation prize?"

"Absolutely not." His brows furrowed in insult.

"What's in it for you, Ryse? What do you get by having me here?"

He pursed his lips and dug his hands in his pockets. "That's not a simple question and there is not a simple answer. But I promise you will get just as much if not more benefit from being around your own people."

Avery ran her fingers through her hair in frustration. He couldn't answer her question and that let her imagination roam to all the worst of possibilities. Thankfully, before she could dive into the thoughts of being some sort of concubine, Ryse spoke.

"Avery, you must understand, there are some truths that I had to protect you from until the time was right. You have a whole new life ahead of you." Ryse stood and touched her cheek. "I can't wait to show it to you—if you will allow me."

A whole new life. The words seemed to resonate deep within her. A small spark, a flame no larger than that of a match flickered to life. Hope. It was hope she felt. Once the emotion named itself, things changed. She looked into a pair of eyes so deep and rich she dreamt of their beauty. In that moment, the sting of his deception didn't hurt as badly. He had made a valid point. If a strange man had come up to her in her café and began talking about the things she had seen in the last couple of days, she would've considered him crazy.

Yes, she thought it was going overboard, a complete invasion of her privacy and it had made her mad. But buried deep within the grief and loss was the hope that what he was saying was true.

"Get some sleep, baby. I'll be back in the morning." He bent to press his lips against hers. Avery instantly felt the electricity. From the first time he'd kissed her, when she believed him to be a normal guy, until now, knowing he was a powerful warrior, nothing had changed. Currents of heat and desire rippled throughout her body. Warmth flooded her extremities and her heart fluttered in her chest. This was what confused her most, this unexplainable, undeniable magnetism that connected her and Ryse together.

When he pulled away and left her standing by the fire, she looked around the spacious room and felt more alone than she could have imagined. After everything that had happened, the thought of being left without protection scared her more than the thought of being with him.

"Ryse!" she called to him as he walked down the hall from her room.

He turned to look at her, his face illuminated by the moonlight coming through the windows of the hallway. "Yes, love?"

"I—I um, I don't want to be…" She stopped, looking at the floor, ashamed of her weakness. "I'm sorry. Never mind." She rubbed her temple.

The warmth of him flooded her senses. She'd felt this warmth before. It was familiar to her, comforting in the most intimate of ways. It was the sensation of swimming in a cold river, then basking on the bank in the sun, the slow gentle heat chasing away the water's chills. "I'm here for you, Avery," he whispered in her ear.

"What is that? That warmth?" Her eyelids became heavy and her shoulders relaxed.

"My aura. Every Olympian gives off energy based on their powers and gifts. I've been shielding mine so that you don't get overwhelmed. This is but a taste of it." He picked her up and cradled her in his arms. "Come. I'll help you rest."

Ryse set Avery in the bed and helped her get comfortable. Warmth radiated from his hand where he touched her cheek. She welcomed the coming peace. But there was one thing she had to know before she drifted off. "Did you really want me, Ryse? When you asked to stay the night with me, did you want me or was it just part of the job?"

"I want you more every moment I'm with you, even when you are hitting me." He chuckled at her quiet gasp. His smile would be her undoing. It made her stomach twist. "Go to sleep, Avery. I'll watch over you—forever."

⚊⚊· ⚬ ·⚊⚊

Avery drifted off to sleep and Ryse watched her body relax into the pillows. Her beauty was staggering. In his eyes, the gods had created perfection. The new color of her hair glistened under the soft lights. Flecks of copper and strands of brown mixed together, giving it definition. He couldn't resist the urge to move one soft curl from her delicate face. She didn't stir. All of her features fascinated him: the curve of her ears, the lines of her chin and cheek bones. Much like her father's people, her skin was slightly brown, as if she had a beach tan. Her lips arched in the middle a bit higher than most. The bottom lip was plush and silky, bitable. Long, dark lashes fanned out over her cheeks. There was movement under her eyelids and he wondered what she was dreaming about.

The sensation of her touch was still so new to him. Never in his long life had he allowed another person to make such contact. Touch in general was personal, warm, and affectionate. For a Thracian Master, this was not allowed. Had Ryse been born to a typical family and possessed only the Thracian genes, touch would have been limited. But knowing that Ryse, a Deity and Master of the Thracians, would need touch to ground him, his mother kept him from becoming a cold, hard stone. It had worked to some extent. Ryse favored his mother's attention but no other. Handshakes were acceptable from most, but nothing more. Touch meant forming attachments. Attachments caused problems, especially since part of his job description included the title of Executioner.

Giving in to temptation, he leaned down and put his face in the mass of curls that spread out on the pillow. Her intoxicating scent filled his head—it was pure ambrosia. The sensation washed over his body, wreaking havoc on his restraint. It took all his control not to crawl into bed, lock his hands on the curves of her hips and pull her tight up against his arousal. By the gods, if this was how her *scent* affected him, what was he going to do when her aura was unblocked? How would he keep his composure when her full energy and power was released? Even more, how was he going to keep every other Thracian male in this Haven from jumping her?

Technically, until he marked her as his own, Avery was free game. The thought of her denying him for another was dreadful. What worried Ryse even more was that he was not the only Prince in the running for a mate. His younger brother was also a contender, though Hayden would never go after a woman that Ryse had claimed. Ashton, the European Prince, was already trying to pry his way into court. Last night, Ryse had learned that the sister of the Prince had already arrived at the Palace. A spy and distraction, Ryse had no doubt.

Caressing the cheek of his angel, he feared for her. He might have rescued her from the jaws of the enemy, but there were still sharks in the water.

CHAPTER EIGHT

AVERY'S FINGERTIPS NUMBED DUE TO THE ROPES SHACKLING HER WRISTS. They rubbed her raw as she struggled to free herself. The wad of cloth crammed into her mouth captured her cries for help. Hot tears streamed down her face. In front of her knelt Jerry, staring at her with an evil grin. Thick, red blood dripped from the knife he held. The knife he had used to repeatedly stab Frank. Frank choked on the blood clogging his throat and she longed to help him, to stop the pain. Pooling blood spread beneath his body.

Avery screamed into the gag and fought against her bonds. Her ankles throbbed under the rope that tied her to the chair.

Why was this happening? What had she done to deserve this? And why Frank? What had he been doing wandering around her house at night, anyway? Now he was dying.

"He's here." Jerry smiled and faced the front door.

Wood splintered as a great force knocked it off the hinges and sent it flying into the other room.

Crystals of terror froze in her veins, rendering her motionless. A creature in a black cloak floated across the threshold with an army of men in red military-style uniforms. She couldn't see its face, but she could see the red flesh of its claw-like hands. Black talons stretched out like daggers. There was nothing human about it. Behind him, touching his cloak, was a short bald man in long robe.

"She's done nothing so far." Jerry spoke to the demon. "But she's one of them. Otherwise the Thracians wouldn't have come."

"I sssenssse their Massster," hissed the demon. "Ssshe must be ssspecial." He approached Avery and she squirmed to get away. His solidity waivered, as if he wasn't completely whole, or perhaps he would disappear with a heavy wind. Evil surrounded him in a thick cloud. He reeked of acid and her stomach revolted. "Sssuch a wassste." Lifting a talon to her cheek, he scored a thin slice into her flesh. Then he leaned in to flick out a serpent like tongue across the bleeding cut. "Deliciousss."

"May I have her first?" Jerry asked. "I've been waiting for two years to screw her." He reached down and grabbed himself. "Doesn't matter if it's before or after she's dead." He leered at Avery. "But I do like it when they fight back."

How could she have been so wrong about him? She'd cooked this sick bastard dinner, for heaven's sake. Now his words made her choke down her own vomit.

The cloaked head tilted as it studied Avery. She tried to make out a face, but he was nothing but shadows in the dimly lit house. "I think I would enjoy watching that."

She fought harder against her restraints, dreading what those talons might do to her. No! This couldn't be happening. This couldn't be real. Deep inside the core of her body, something stirred. At first it felt like the roil of stomach acid, but then it spread out into the rest of her body.

"What's up with her eyes?" Jerry pointed at her, his eyes narrowed and darted back and forth between his master and Avery.

"Ah!" said the demon. "She'sss awakening." He took a step back but not in fear. He was observing.

Something was wrong within her. Liquid heat flowed through her veins until she felt like a volcano ready to erupt. The world began to spin and shadows crossed her vision. She clamped her eyes shut. Every nerve ending in her body raged hot. Smoke tickled her nose. Something was burning. Something familiar and organic, like wood or fabric. When she opened her eyes, the world had taken on a red tint. The gag fell out of her mouth and she roared like a beast.

Raw power invigorating her body. When she pulled against the ropes this time, they gave way and fell to the floor.

"Fire Keeper." The demon said with an awed tone. "Incrrredible."

Avery looked down at her body. Flames licked up her skin. Her clothing disintegrated, eaten by the fire. Every inch of her body glowed yet she wasn't burning. In fact, Avery had never felt more alive, liberated even.

Jerry's brows rose to his hair line. "You never said anything about fire, boss."

"Kill her." The demon hissed to his men.

There was a tickle in her thigh. A bullet melted against her leg. Avery brushed it off and without a second thought, tackled the demon.

He clawed at her and fought against her hold, but his talons went right through her. When his black cloak caught fire, he pushed away and reached for a small bald man. The instant they touched, the two disappeared.

Jerry advanced on her. She glanced down at Frank's body. Jerry had done that, and now he was trying to kill her. Avery reached out on instinct and grabbed Jerry by the throat. His eyes bulged out of his head. The fire that licked up her body spread to him. But she didn't let him go until he was fully consumed. Then she watched him scream with satisfaction.

"No, Avery!"

"Avery!"

Her eyes popped open and she saw Nikki on the bed next to her, her hands on Avery's shoulder. The poor woman was about to have a panic attack. Her red hair was loose about her head. Avery had disturbed her sleep.

"Are you alright, milady? You cried out."

Nikki helped her prop herself up in bed. "I—I think so. It was just a bad dream."

"Do you wish to talk about it?"

Avery offered a smile. "You don't want my nightmares, Nikki."

"I am your Shadow Lady. And sometimes, that means walking with you through dark places." Nikki crossed her legs. Then she closed her eyes and held out her hands. Avery didn't think now was the time for meditation. But then she saw the steaming cups of hot chocolate Nikki had conjured. "Please, tell me. Perhaps speaking out loud will make them seem less real."

Avery thought twice before recounted her nightmare. This woman was a stranger and she worked for Ryse. Why trust her? There was something in her eyes, something that begged for trust, for the right to bear her burdens. The sad fact was Avery had no one else and she needed to unload on someone like she would've vented to Izzy.

Nikki held her hand, kept her hot chocolate cup full and stayed attentive. The problem with this nightmare was that it wasn't simply something her mind conjured to scare her. They were memories of the night her life shattered around her. When she told Nikki about how Frank died, her voice cracked. By the end, Avery's head was laying in Nikki's lap. She sobbed and Nikki stroked her hair long into the morning hours.

"Milady, if you wish, I can fetch Master Ryse. I know he can ease your mind and—"

"No!" Avery blurted out before she realized she was protesting more than necessary. "I mean, he's had a long day. No need bothering him."

Nikki's lips pinched together and she said nothing else of Ryse.

CHAPTER NINE

E VEN AFTER NIKKI LEFT, AVERY COULDN'T SHUT HER EYES. THE demon in the black robe still haunted her thoughts. Instead she pulled a chair over to the wall of windows and stared out at the gardens. They were so beautiful in the light of the rising sun. Whatever this world was, at least it held some beauty.

Castor and Pollux played at her feet. They acted so naturally it made Avery feel at home.

Nikki came back shortly, freshly showered and changed into a light blue shirt. It complimented her hair that was once again pulled into a plait at the back of her neck.

"Mornin'." Avery crossed her arms in front of her and walked to the edge of the patio. Beyond the immaculately manicured gardens was a lake half surrounded by forest. Peeping up over the trees on the far end of the lake was the roofline of several buildings.

"Here you are." Nikki handed her the cup of coffee and a friendly smile crossed her face.

"That color looks good on you Nikki." Avery sipped the coffee, knowing Nikki would be pleased at the compliment. And she was.

Delight glowed across her face. "Thank you, milady! I could say the same for you. The green brings out your eyes." When Avery smiled at her, Nikki beamed. The girl was downright lovable.

"The Master comes." Nikki quickly went to the door before

there was a knock. Avery saw her bow. The exchange between Nikki and Ryse was muffled. Nikki turned to speak. "Master Ryse would like an audience. Are you receiving?"

Avery ran her hands through her hair and took a deep breath. She mouthed to Nikki, "Do I look okay?" and her Shadow Lady nodded. Avery motioned for her to let him in.

Ryse came through the door and Avery's heart sputtered. They locked eyes and everything in the room faded away. He was dressed casually, his black hair was slicked back but rebellious strands fell in his face. Avery had to hug herself to keep from reaching out to fix it.

No man should be so sexy. Ryse was tall and broad, his body pure muscle and yet when he held her it was soft and welcoming. Though he towered over her, she felt perfect in his arms. She wanted to touch him again, feel his body pressed up against her and their lips moving together in sync. The desperation surprised her. How could she crave him like this after such a short time? She cleared her dry throat and averted her eyes.

"Nikki, bring some breakfast to the lanai. I think the Lady needs some fresh air." Ryse commanded.

"Yes, Master." The redhead scuttled off to her task.

Ryse held out his arm and motioned Avery to the patio. "Did you sleep well?" He put his hands behind his back and Avery wondered if he was resisting the same need to touch.

"For a while. I had a nightmare." Avery shrugged it off. "I guess after everything that's happened, it's to be expected, right?"

"You should have sent for me."

Avery turned her head to see his face. His tone had been hard. "And what would you have done? Killed a phantom?"

His face fell, his mouth went slack. "I only meant—"

"I know." Avery waved a dismissive hand. About that time Nikki came out with a large tray of food. "It's fine. It's over. Poor Nikki listened to me cry for hours on end and I'm fine now."

Nikki tentatively touched Avery's arm. "And I would happily do so again should it bring my mistress comfort." The two women shared a smile. Nikki was the type of person Avery wanted as a friend. And after last night's bonding, they were well on their way.

Ryse inclined his head to her Shadow Lady. "You have my gratitude."

"It is my honor. I shall take the dogs for a walk while you dine." Nikki bowed and left them to their meal.

Ryse pulled out a wicker chair for Avery then seated himself. Knowing she needed the nourishment, Avery picked a strawberry off the plate. Her hand knocked into Ryse's. He was going for the same berry. The touch of his skin sent an electrical arc between them.

"Do you feel that?" Ryse picked up the berry and lifted it to her mouth. Avery could hardly concentrate to take a bite. Her eyes were drawn to where he licked his lips.

Ignoring his question, she asked her own. "Last night, when I asked you what you got by me being here, you said it was complicated. How complicated? And why do I get the feeling that this attraction is part of that complication?"

Ryse's chest rose and fell as he took in a deep breath. "Are you sure you want that answer just yet?"

"Ah, hell." Avery curled up her knees to her chest as if that could protect her from whatever was to come. "I'm not gonna like this, am I?"

He chuckled and started, "Lifetimes ago, when the gods decided to leave the earthly plane, they chose leaders from their descendents to stay in their stead. Six in all. The gods poured into these men the blood of their veins. These demigods were named the earthly Deities and had the partial powers of the gods. Each of the Deities was charged with the task of ruling the Olympian descendents and keeping their existence secret to the growing mortal populace. To help each Deity control and rein in his people, Ares, god of war and punishment, allowed his Thracian descendants to remain on the earth and serve as law. As time went on, the Deities and Thracians took control and looked after all Olympians. But the kings grew restless and lonely, needing companions.

"Looking around the heavens, Zeus, master of all Olympians, found only one group of goddesses that could do what was needed. The Graces, or charities, as some called them, were women of great character—goddesses of beauty, charm, nature, fertility, merriment, festivity, and creativity. Combining their blood, and adding in some of the blood of specific gods and goddesses, Zeus created the first generation of Divine Graces.

"The Graces did exactly what they were created to do. They brought peace, happiness, and tranquility to the Deities. They also brought forth heirs. It is the only way a Deity can produce a legitimate heir. Over time the Graces became more powerful and connected to the gods than the Deities they were created to serve. In the last few hundred years, the Graces became more like Oracles, interceding between the earthly Olympians and the gods.

"Besides Divine Graces, there are only two other beings on earth that have the power to evoke the blessings of the gods. One is the Grand Deity. He is appointed by Zeus to be the leader of his peers. The other is the Thracian Master who is in direct communication with Ares."

"That's what you are, the Master?" Avery recalled how everyone addressed him.

"I am." Ryse sat still for a moment and Avery wondered what he was thinking about. "My mother is a great Oracle. She has seen in her visions that the time has come for a new pairing of Deity and Divine Grace."

"And you think, what? That I'm a Divine Grace?" Her heart was in her throat and pounding like a bass drum.

"When you were born, your father had a vision. He was a Promethean, an Oracle, like my mother. He saw you being killed as an infant, so he and your mother ran. They kept you hidden in the mortal world, kept your aura shielded. Your father also bound and shielded himself making it nearly impossible for an Olympian tracker to find any of you. On the day of your parents' deaths, your father used the last flicker of his life to alert the Olympian world of their location."

"If my parents were descendents of gods, how could a car accident kill them?"

Ryse couldn't meet her eyes. "They were assassinated by Rogues, Avery. It was nothing as simple as a car accident. And your mother was human. Your father was one of the few Olympians who mated with a mortal. Before he left the Haven, your father was a fairly famous man among us. He was an Oracle of insurmountable talent. Unlike my mother, your father could call up visions as easy as you might call your dogs. It was foolish of him to think that he could live outside this realm and never be recognized. And with all Oracles, there is a price to having such knowledge."

Avery's entire past had just come into clear understanding. So much made sense now. As a child, she had assumed that all fathers knew their children the way hers did. Nothing slipped past him. He knew every time she even attempted to sneak out. He knew when she stole money from his wallet to buy a ticket to the movies. Once, her father even knew she had a fight with Izzy before she said a word. She never had a chance.

"I imagine they were watching you for a while, Avery. Exactly like we had to. You never exhibited any sort of gifts or aura so Rogues couldn't justify your murder. It's considered below any Olympian to take human life for no reason. There is no honor there, not even for rogues and rebels. Since they had no evidence against you," he hesitated, opened his mouth to speak, stopped and started again. "They figured if they raped you, you wouldn't be valuable to us."

Avery froze. Her heart skipped a beat, then came to thundering life. Only a handful of people knew about that and Frank had taken her secret to the grave. Tears threatened to spill. Her arms tightened around her legs. There was no way she could look at Ryse. She averted her eyes and tried to breathe deep. "How did you know?"

"It is a common misconception that if a Grace is impure, she cannot be mated to a Deity. The rebels immediately defile any woman they suspect of being a powerful Olympian."

"You said I was shielded." She wiped her face, looking out at the gardens. "Does that mean they hurt me for the hell of it? I was barely twenty years old." Her parents had died a short two years before. Though a decade had passed, the pain returned anew with all this information.

"I wish I could tell you differently," Ryse whispered.

Avery closed her eyes and more tears tumbled down her cheeks. She put her forehead on her knees and covered her face until she could hold her head up.

"What made them come at me again? Why was Jerry there? Hadn't they done enough? I'm *defiled,* as you say. What good am I?"

"The gods meant pure of heart and spirit as well as body. A woman whose innocence is taken is still pure of heart, Avery. You didn't willingly give yourself."

No, she hadn't. She just happened to be the woman stupid enough to let a man use her telephone when he claimed his car was broken down. "Why now?"

"Because of me," Ryse admitted, his jaws clenched. "My aura is much too powerful for any magic or shield to fully hide. Jerry felt my presence and that was all the reason he needed to attack."

"So if a bunch of rebels could track my father, why couldn't you track him? Why didn't you come sooner?"

Ryse took a deep breath. "Right before your father's death when he used his powers, Hammon felt the spark. It was so quick, so minute that he barely caught it. It wasn't enough to pinpoint your location. Hammon said it was nothing more than someone turning on a flashlight in the middle of the ocean for a few seconds. All we knew was that somewhere down south, there was a cry for help. We began searching for every registered Olympian we could find. When that came up blank, we looked into all the activities of the rogues. Where was their presence the greatest? Who was moving about? Our spies dropped a hint that a woman of interest was in Texas." He looked up at Avery. "Your father would have to pick one of the largest states to hide in. We had been all over when my mother was given a vision of a woman with green eyes who owned a coffee shop. So we began looking at the records of female business owners. We came as soon as we could.

"You're a priceless gift among our people. Only you can mate with a Deity Prince and produce an heir. Only you can intercede for our people and only you have the complementary powers to help a Deity rule."

Avery took deep breaths to calm the panic that was rising inside of her. Her brain wasn't ready to process everything Ryse was telling her. "I don't have a choice in this at all, do I?" she whispered, a sick feeling in her stomach again.

"No one will force you into anything."

"And if I say no?"

Avery watched his face. It was all the answer she would receive. Ryse looked away from her, his jaw clenched, nostrils flared. His brows dipped low when he looked back at her and repeated, "No one will force you."

The words he didn't say were the ones she heard the loudest.

CHAPTER TEN

MENTAL OVERLOAD WAS A MILD TERM FOR WHAT AVERY FELT. Even though deep in her mind and heart she was grieving, mourning the physical death of Frank and the psychological death of who she was, there was a faint acceptance of this new information.

Throughout her entire life Avery had always been a little different from others. Since her twenty-second birthday, her body hadn't aged. It changed with diet and exercise, but she hadn't *aged*. At nearly twenty-nine she should have signs of aging most women fight their entire adult lives. It wouldn't have even been rare to find a gray hair or two, but she hadn't. For the first time in her life, the feeling of being different made sense. She *was* different.

Now she had a position to fill and she wasn't quite sure how Ryse fit. Was this the end for them? Though they had shared a degree of passion and a few intimate moments, it didn't mean he could continue to be with her since his job was done. He had said over and over that his objective was to get her to the Haven. Perhaps she should be angry that he showed her such affection. But then again, maybe it was as compulsorily for him as it was for her.

"Ryse." It was a prayer whispered reverently.

"Yes?"

She looked out over the gardens. "I never thanked you for what you've done for me."

"There's no need."

Of course not, Avery thought. He was just doing his job, right?

"You helped me get out alive. No matter what happens, I will always be grateful."

Nikki, who was standing out of viewing distance, cleared her throat. "Forgive my interruption, but the Peaen is here to examine the Lady. He waits in a suite upstairs."

"The what?" Avery asked, looking curiously at Ryse.

"The physician."

Avery sat up and pulled her wild mane to one side of her neck. She didn't like the idea of some other-world doctor examining her. Ryse must have picked up on her discomfort by the way she hugged her arms around her stomach.

"Nikki, arrange for a female physician."

"Yes, Master." The delicate footsteps of Nikki's retreat worried Avery.

"She doesn't have to do that. I'll be fine."

"No, no males should touch you unless you are inviting it." His firm tone kept her from arguing.

◄ ─ ·　　ᴏⁱᵒ　　· ─ ►

Only a couple hours later Avery was done with her check up. The lovely woman barely had to touch her except to take a couple vials of blood for genetic testing. Rubbing the bandage on her arm, Avery left the suite and waved to the Peaen woman.

Ryse was nowhere to be found. The Palace was huge and expansive, so she figured she could give herself the grand tour. Hoping she didn't get lost, she wound through the maze of rooms and doors. Going downstairs, she found her way to the main floor of the house. An overwhelming pull led her to the solarium. Ryse's voice boomed from the room and the disturbed tone of it caused her heart thump in her throat.

"Damn it, Salina! Get your hands off me!" There was ice in every word.

"Ryse, come on, love." The sultry English accent was thick with sexual desire. "I know you've missed me."

"No, actually I haven't thought about you in decades." His cruelty bruised even Avery. Her head said to leave, her heart said to stay.

"Now, now, Ryse. I know you have been under a lot of pressure lately. Why don't you let me give you a massage? I know how you enjoy it when I stroke—"

"Enough!" he said. That tone made Avery look around the corner of the wall where she was hiding.

Bad idea.

Avery peeked in time to see a leggy blonde with her hand angled at his crotch. The red mini skirt, tight black halter, and black high heels were a thin cover to her real weapons—large breasts, hour glass figure, and plump ass. She had bright red lips, dark shadowed eyes, and flawless skin. Long hair fell in straight sheets down her back. Her eyes were full of seduction and that seduction was focused on Ryse. It was a wonder the poor man was still standing. Salina was dirty sex in stilettos.

Ryse shoved her hand away with no form of finesse. Fury was all over his face.

"Is this about that *girl* you brought in here? The *waitress?*" she said the last words as a curse. "Is she the little Grace you've been searching for, love?" she scoffed.

Ryse walked away from her and looked out the window. "You're walking on thin ice, Salina. What are you doing here, anyway?" The growl in his voice was something Avery had never heard. It actually scared her that he took such a tone with a woman, even this woman. He had murdered in Avery's presence, but this was far more disturbing.

"My family is planning a visit. I thought I would come early and spend some *quality* time with you. Might have thought twice if I knew I would be so ill received. You know how much your approval means to me, Ryse. It hurts that you might not think fondly of me. After everything that has happened between us, it would kill me if we couldn't be...friends." She let her fingers trail along his arm. "Besides, I want to get to know this little Grace. I've never met a real *farm girl* before."

In a flash, Ryse had her by the neck and pressed up against the wall. "Do you attempt to play me, Salina? Do you think I didn't feel that telepathic push?"

Showing no signs of fear though he was nearly choking her, Salina answered cool as a cucumber. "What do you mean? I would never try to—"

"Do you also suggest me a fool?" he snarled. She remained stone-faced. "You had better watch using your treacherous mind games on me, woman. I have no patience with you. And if you so much as harm a hair on Avery's head or put one hint of thought into her mind, I will punish you as the gods have given me right to. Not even your royal blood can save you from my wrath, Salina. Remember that."

Before Ryse could release her and walk out of the room, Avery turned to sneak away. The last thing she wanted was to try and tangle with this new side of the deadly warrior. Unfortunately, when she quietly turned to leave, she was face to face with someone unexpected.

CHAPTER ELEVEN

S URELY AVERY'S EYES HAD DECEIVED HER. THERE WERE NO SUCH things as angels, yet here one stood. Cascading from her head was a waterfall of white blond hair. Silver-streaked curls swirled down to her waist, spilling over her shoulders and down her back. The satin lavender dress she wore flowed in a continuation of her locks. Striking eyes were nearly the same pastel shade as her dress. Delicate cheeks and pink lips displayed no smile for Avery. Instead, she motioned with her head for Avery to follow.

This had to be the Divine Grace Ryse spoke of. From her sure footsteps to her high-held chin, she emanated confidence and power. Seeing as how Avery was caught spying, she didn't think it wise to argue.

Avery was led through the halls and into a room that was decorated so feminine it had to be personal space. The large bed in an adjoining room informed her that she was in the private master suite. The walls were a warm vanilla cream color with a rose pattern that was so faint it looked antiqued. It seemed to be the theme of the room. Thick cream and pink colored curtains framed the windows. A couch and two wingback chairs were in the middle of the room facing the white rock fireplace.

"Please sit," a melodic voice whispered to her. The words were not cold, but not overly warm, either. "Would you care for tea?"

"P—please." She took a seat by the fire, suddenly feeling a chill. At her acceptance, another lady began serving them. "You're a Divine Grace."

The angel sat and accepted a delicate china cup on a saucer. "I am. My name is Dynasty, you may call me Dyna." Those lavender eyes looked at Avery for a long minute before she spoke. "Salina is a snake, Avery." She let the full force of her words sink in before she continued. "The child practically slithers when she walks. It is such a shame that my eldest and dearest friend had to produce such a reptile for a daughter. But her mother, Filene, and I have been close as sisters since we were girls. That has been many centuries ago. I can promise you, the apple fell quite far from the tree. Charles, Deity of Europe, is a good man with a good heart. Ashton, their son, will make a fine Deity one day." She took a deep breath.

"Why are you telling me this?" Avery set down the cup before her shaking hands spilled the hot tea.

"Because you are not the only one who witnessed that exchange and I can feel your anxiety, Avery darling."

"They have history," Avery said, gazing at the fire.

"Yes. She beds men for sport. I'm afraid to say the girl had her fangs in him at one point, many decades ago."

The tone of her voice made Avery look into those interesting eyes. Dyna was clenching her jaw. Her back was straight as a board with perfect posture.

"How deep?"

Without even a thought she replied, "Not deep enough to keep him interested when the morning sun came up."

Avery flinched and closed her eyes, trapping the tears that wanted to escape. How could Avery ever compete with a woman as gorgeous as Salina, reptile or not? Ryse might have seemed upset with her today, but at some point those seductive curves Salina wielded as a sharp blade had appealed to him.

It hurt more to realize it wasn't her right to be jealous. Avery wasn't intended for a Thracian Master. She was intended for a Deity Prince. That didn't stop her from caring.

"He seemed very angry with her." If she focused on his anger, Avery might not cry.

"Salina is out for power. That is why she seeks my friendship, why she seeks my sons' beds." She casually laughed. "It's a shame, really. Salina is such a pretty girl." Dyna tilted her head and looked at Avery, who was suddenly self-conscious. "I don't know why I'm telling you all this. All you need to understand is that Ryse detests her and you shouldn't be upset about their altercation."

Avery found herself absently rubbing her own neck. Dyna was the mother of the man she was supposed to be mated to. It probably looked terrible that Avery held such an interest in Ryse.

Dyna stood and went to gaze out a large window. "My husband and I are very blessed. Never in the history of our people has a Deity couple been gifted with two sons." She looked over her shoulder but Avery said nothing. So there were two men in the running for her hand? "Typically there is only one son to take his father's place and there is never any question about the inheritance. All other children are female. My second born son, Hayden, is a miracle. He has gifts the like I have never seen in my centuries of life. Nothing is forgotten from his brain. Hayden documents everything and has become a remarkable historian. Our race is lucky to have someone who knows our traditions as he does."

"You're very proud of him," Avery said, wondering where this conversation was going. Was Dyna trying to sell her on Hayden?

"I am proud of both my sons. I have one whose skills are of the mind and one whose skills are of brute strength. That's not to say one lacks where the other prevails." She paused for a moment.

"I knew your parents. Did you know that?" Avery shook her head at Dyna. "It was a short time but I do remember your father and his visions. It's a shame about them. My heart breaks for you. I wish they had lived to see the woman you are and the Grace you shall become." Avery couldn't reply, her mouth felt cemented shut.

Dyna met her eyes in an intense gaze. "Would you like for me to set your aura free, my child?"

"I—I don't know." Avery hated the way she stuttered when she got nervous. "Will it hurt?"

"Only a smidgen. I want to do it gradually over a series of sessions with you. If I free an aura as strong as yours without warning, we would be flooded with Thracian warriors trying to mate you!" She laughed, a carefree sound like orchestra music.

"Mate me?" Avery sat up straighter. "I'm supposed to be with a Deity. Why would a Thracian want to mate me?"

"Legends say the gods created the desire between Thracians and Graces to solidify their loyalty. What begins as a physical attraction to an unmated Grace turns into respect and allegiance upon her union with a Deity. It is not uncommon for Thracian soldiers to be somewhat obsessive with an unmated Grace. It is in their blood, you could say."

Avery slumped back in her chair. Well, didn't that put the last few days into perspective? Ryse was not simply a Thracian warrior, he was the Master of the race. Of course his attraction to an unmated Grace would be far more potent. Every kiss, every touch was based off a biological response programmed in his brain to guarantee his loyalty. She was right. None of it had been real.

She rubbed a hand over her aching chest. Aware that her future mother-in-law was still there, she held back the ocean of grief that threatened to drown her.

"Letting a fraction of your aura loose at a time, while teaching you how to shield it, is much safer." Dyna's voice snapped her back to the moment. As much as she wanted to bury herself in feelings of Ryse, she had to focus. "Do you feel comfortable with that, darling?"

"Yes. I just, um, I need some time to think. That's all."

"Of course, my child. Forgive my impatience." Dyna smiled warmly and reached out to pull Avery to her feet. They held hands as Dyna's lavender eyes connected with hers. "We are so happy to have you here, darling. I've always wanted a daughter and my heart rejoices in your arrival. You are beloved already." Dyna leaned in to kiss each of Avery's cheeks. "If you need anything or desire to learn more about what we are, I am always available to you. My excitement over another young Grace is consuming." Dyna laughed and Avery swore she heard bells. "Whenever you are ready, my child, we shall set your mind and your aura free. Then you will truly experience all this life has to offer."

Even while Avery accepted Dyna's motherly hug, her heart was breaking. Being a Grace didn't scare her nearly as much as the thought of telling this woman she couldn't marry one of her sons. And it didn't erase the pain of knowing Ryse did not truly want her. He said it was real for him, and perhaps it was. But now Avery knew the truth. And she wished she had never met Ryse.

CHAPTER TWELVE

VERY MET A VERY QUIET NIKKI OUTSIDE DYNA'S ROOMS. NIKKI
followed Avery outside before directing her to the gardens.
Castor and Pollux had been playing with some of the staff's
children but came running when they saw her. Avery felt terrible for
not giving them any thought since this morning, but it had been an
eventful day so far.

Feeling guilty, Avery found a walking path that ringed the lake
and wandered off into the forest around the Palace. It seemed the
kind of path that would take a while to walk and give her time to
think and let the boys run. Little did she know that she would not
be walking alone. Coming down the path in her direction were two
men.

It was obvious that one was a man of power. Even the dogs lowered their heads the closer he came. He had black hair highlighted
with gray around his temples. The gait of his walk suggested purpose even in such a casual setting. His features were hard but strik-
ingly handsome. Brown eyes locked on her and her heart stopped.
She had seen those eyes before.

"Lady Avery," he said in an accent she couldn't place. The man
with him, a subordinate, bowed to her. "Finally we meet. I am Troy
Castille, the Grand Deity. I apologize for neglecting to come to you
sooner. The time of your arrival was late and I did not want to in-

trude on your settling in. I hope your accommodations are satisfactory?" He absently petted the dogs that sniffed him.

"Wonderful. Thank you." Avery's throat dried up. She didn't need to be a genius to figure out this man was the closest thing to a god she would ever behold. As a Master Thracian, Ryse had been overwhelming. This man, this *demigod*, made her knees weak and her eyes lower to the ground.

Troy looked around and saw only Nikki a few paces behind her. "Nikki."

"My lord?" She curtsied. Avery wondered if she should have done the same. Damn.

"Do you walk alone?"

"Yes, my lord."

Troy took in a deep breath, rubbed his short beard and focused on Avery again. "Even in my refuge, you should have an escort. An unclaimed Grace is a commodity that causes Thracian males to lose their faculties."

"I only wanted some time to think. I'll go back inside." Avery sighed, needing the sunshine and fresh air. The dogs would have to run without her.

"Nonsense. I shall walk with you. Perhaps I might shine some light on the dark thoughts in your mind." He offered his arm to her and she took it with a shy smile. "Gabrele can keep Nikki company while we walk."

The other man nodded and dropped back to walk by the Shadow Lady. They gave Avery and Troy a large berth before setting off on the path behind them.

"Something troubles you?" Troy asked softly.

Avery huffed indignantly then she remembered she was talking to a man one step below the gods. "At this point it would be easier to talk about what doesn't trouble me. The list is shorter."

"Speak your mind, child." Troy's voice was not commanding, but pleading.

"It's like I've fallen asleep and can't wake up. But I don't know if

I'm having a great dream or a nightmare of epic proportions." Avery felt a compulsion to bare her soul to Troy. It made her wonder if this was part of his powers. "I look back and I think, none of this can be real. I was attacked by a man that had been my close friend for two years. I *knew* Jerry. I cooked for him and watched movies with him. We went bowling together and he fixed my leaking sink. He was Frank's partner. They spent hours upon hours together and Frank never doubted his act. Neither did I. I think of all the times he could have killed me and it boggles my mind. He never once let on, never gave himself away as anything more than a good old country boy."

"You gave him no reason," Troy said, patting her arm. "If Ryse hadn't come to collect you, Jerry might have lived the rest of his life in your town watching you for signs of your powers."

"That's a nauseating thought."

"There is no telling how long they would have had him assigned to you. But we will never know."

"I guess I should be grateful Master Ryse showed up." Avery felt the need to use Ryse's formal title with the Deity.

"But?" Troy asked with raised brows.

Avery waved off his inquiry. "Nothing." Avery didn't want to tell Troy that she had foolishly fallen for a man she couldn't be with. "I'm still learning the aspects of auras."

Troy took this opportunity to school her. Avery was drawn to his voice and watched his face as he spoke. "Auras are but ripples of our emotions and powers that emit from our souls. They indicate the strength of an Olympian. Peoples of diluted blood have diluted powers resulting in weak auras. A Grace such as you should rival Dynasty's aura."

"Magic and auras creating physical responses." Avery shook her head and pulled away to cross her arms over her chest. "That's not exactly what I want my marriage to be based on." This might not have been the smartest thing to say to Troy. But he needed to know Avery didn't want to enter into any kind of relationship if it wasn't built on a foundation of love and trust.

Troy spelled it out for her, "Initially, every relationship is based on physical attraction, Avery. Think logically. Would you want to sleep with someone who physically repulsed you?" Avery reluctantly shook her head. She knew were this was going. "Humans call it lust. They base their version of love on what they feel in the moment. This person makes me happy, this person is behaving how I want them to, so I feel love for them. But they are selfish creatures and many do not understand the real meaning of the word."

"Do you mean that you don't feel love for your wife?"

Troy's head jerked back. "On the contrary. I feel a great amount of love for my wife. Among all the gifts the gods have bestowed upon me, my mate is the greatest. Dyna makes every breath worth taking. She is the reason I am the man I am. I would do anything to please her." Troy looked down at Avery, who had stopped walking and was gawking at him.

"Most men don't talk like that." Avery went mushy inside hearing such a masculine man admitting such profound things.

"Most men are fools." He chuckled and tapped her on the nose. Troy took her hand and placed it back in the crook of his arm. "And to be honest, I would not voice such things to others. You, however, need to understand the type of commitment and devotion a Deity gives to his Grace. It is the same devotion you should expect. You see Avery, love is a verb, not a noun. It is an action, a daily choice made between two people. It is not a state of mind that one can float in and out of. It is not a destination to be traveled to. It is stone thrown into a pond, the effects rippling out. You do not have to know every detail about a person to love them. Compatibility is vital; do not misunderstand. A cow and a whale should not mate. A person must decide if they are compatible with another, then make the daily decision to love that person no matter their faults and quirks. Dyna has often frustrated me and I, her. But never once have I decided I didn't love her because we didn't see eye to eye."

Avery thought it was a shame Troy was already married. If there were a way to clone him, she would have done it. If the gods had truly created a mate just for her, he would be like Troy in many ways. "But the gods created her to match you, right? Doesn't that take some of your choice out of the matter?"

"Perhaps, if you want to see it that way." He shrugged casually.

Avery crinkled her forehead. What other way could it be seen? If the gods create two pieces to a puzzle that interlock, those puzzle pieces can't fit together any other way. Where is the free will in that?

"I feel blessed that the gods created Dyna for me. Unlike my sons, I did not have to search for her. My lovely Grace was all but handed to me. And the moment we met, I was caught in her beauty, her strong heart, and her fierce dedication to serving the gods with all she is. I praise the gods still for every day she is by my side." Troy leaned in to whisper, "...and in my bed."

Avery blushed and giggled. "Men, you're all the same."

Troy's laughter billowed into the air. "Just you wait, sweet Princess. You will thank the gods one day, for they make a Deity and Grace compatible in every aspect."

Avery and Troy talked until they had circled the lake. He was wise and kind. Their conversation touched on everything from her parents to his duties as Grand Deity. Avery learned much about royalty and the responsibilities of the title. It helped her understand how very special being a Divine Grace was. It made her feel good to know that even though Troy ruled the Olympian world, he still made time for her—just like her own father used to do. No matter what work needed to be done, no matter how busy he was, Avery's father had always set aside a time of the day for his daughter. Oh, how she missed that man.

"Well my child, it seems we have come full circle. Shall we go again?" Troy put his arm on her shoulder.

"No, I know you have stuff to do. I'm sure I've kept you long enough. You have a country to rule after all."

Troy smiled, which softened his bearded face. "I will always have time for you. Even a throne is no greater legacy than one's children." He touched her shoulders affectionately. Avery couldn't resist, she leaned in and allowed Troy to hug her. "If ever you need me, I am here."

"Thank you, Troy."

"Go, have some time to yourself. Stay in the gardens and I will make sure none bother you." He left her to the morning air. Though Troy had helped her feel better about everything, she was still overwhelmed. Peace was found in a tunnel made of arched stones and wood supporting a thick wall of purple blooming wisteria. Castor and Pollux found their young playmates and ran off. Avery smiled, sat on an iron bench, and put her elbows on her knees. Dissecting the newest information she received, she let her mind sift through the morning's conversations.

CHAPTER THIRTEEN

THERE WAS NO TELLING HOW LONG SHE SAT THERE—LONG ENOUGH to notice a change in the sun's position. It now was straight overhead. Only part of her brain was aware of Nikki being discreetly hidden in different places around the gardens. Her stomach rumbled, so she took it as a sign to get her mind together and go back to face Ryse. She stood up and turned back the way she came.

A familiar blond was leaning against one of the stone pillars holding up the pergola of purple vines. He was talking to Nikki, who gave him a bashful smile before she bowed her head and disappeared again. Then he turned to Avery, looked at her with those bright blue eyes and a thin smile on his face. He was wearing jeans and a black leather bomber style jacket.

"Lady Avery," he addressed her with a bow.

"I remember you. You're a cop. Or at least you pretended to be." This man had played a part in the last days of Frank's life and as much as she wanted to dislike him, she couldn't.

He smiled. "Yes ma'am. Sorry about that. My name is Brenden. Ryse assigned me to watch Frank, knowing the rebels would get to you through him. You mind if I sit with you for a moment? I'd like to talk to ya." His accent was so familiar it felt like a breeze of pure Texas air had blown past.

"Your accent?"

His grin made his face younger. "Grew up in Dallas. You and I have some things in common." Her voice gone, she nodded and sat on the bench again. "I have the newspaper from your hometown." He pulled the folded paper from his jacket. "There's a nice write-up in here. I suggest you read it somewhere private. It was quite moving." He handed it to her. "You might frown on this, but I sort of took something from Frank's house. Thought you might want it." He handed her a picture. "She was at the memorial service."

Avery looked at the picture of Frank's sister smiling as she kissed her brother, who had his arms around Avery. There were never three happier people in that moment. "Heidi took it hard, didn't she? She loved him, god how she loved her brother."

"She gave a beautiful eulogy for you. Izzy spoke, too. They had your services together, since no one could track down any family for you and all of your friends were the same. No caskets or anything, obviously. There was a great picture of you and Frank taken at the Officer's Ball last Christmas. You were wearing the—"

"Black velvet gown." Avery said, feeling a numbness spreading through her again. "Frank was wearing his uniform. He looked so good in his uniform."

"He was given a formal send off. The whole town showed up to y'all's service. Not a business open in town." Brenden rubbed her back as he spoke. Avery wondered if he even realized he was doing it. Frank had often done the same thing when he comforted her. "Avery," he said, running his fingers through her hair and cupping her cheek, "I got in a couple weeks with him. Frank was a good man. He was honorable and just."

"I know," she said, drinking in those bright blue eyes and short curly blond hair. If Avery had been normal, if she had been human, she might have married Frank. Now she knew why those romantic feelings never took root. Her soul had been waiting on its match.

"He loved you, very much. All he talked about was his Avery. The things you guys did together, the funny things you said, the way you are with people—he adored it all." Brenden wiped away her tears with his thumb. "You should celebrate that friendship and let it free you from this guilt. Frank willingly gave his life for you because he knew that you were destined to be a Deity. He might not have known the name, but he knew the potential."

"Why did you do this for me?" she asked, leaning her cheek into his hand.

"Because I can…sense people differently than the others." His jaw clenched and his next words were stressed. "That's why I was sent in first. I was supposed to be able to sniff out the bastard who was stalking you. I couldn't. And because of my inability a good man, a man that loved my Princess, died. His life was sacrificed therefore I owe you a life. Since I cost you Frank, I offer myself."

"What?"

"Avery, this won't mean much to you, but you remind me of my sister. She was a beautiful person and—" He paused and rubbed his temples. Avery could tell this was a hard subject for him to talk about. She touched his knee and gave him a comforting smile. Brenden straightened his back and took a deep breath. "I'm giving you my oath, *blood* oath, as a Thracian warrior that my life will be devoted to your safety and well-being." He swallowed and those big blue eyes seemed to turn into a child's gaze. "If you will have me."

"You should at least let her be informed of what a blood oath means, little brother." A third voice carrying a heavy New York accent came from behind them. The man they all called Yankee was walking up through the gardens to the other end of the flowery tunnel. He was dressed similarly to Brenden; the only difference was the style of leather jacket. Yankee's racer jacket had a red band around the shoulders. He was fairly tall, not as attractive as the man beside her, and intimidating as hell. His brown hair was so short it was nothing more than fuzz on his head.

Brenden stood to face this fellow Thracian. "What do you want, Samuel? We were having a private conversation." There was steel in Brenden's voice as he called his comrade by his given name. Avery stiffened and she glanced around for Nikki. There was something about Yankee that made her nervous.

"Oh, I can see that," he said, removing his sunglasses. His eyes were full of something Avery couldn't name, but felt angry. "But before you go off on a mission of honor and shit, you need to make sure this woman knows that blood oath is a lifelong deal. The Princess might also need to consider that as an Elite, you answer to Master Ryse and his permission to this *union* is required."

Something about his tone set Avery off. "Something tells me you're not giving such helpful advice out of the goodness of your heart," she said, standing beside Brenden, her shoulder barely touching his.

Yankee looked at her through grayish blue eyes. His expression turned amused. "You're right. See, little brother here is one of the Elites, one of the five most deadly men on this planet aside from the Master. And if he swears his life to you, that means that our team is down a man." He played with the sunglasses in his hands. "Just thinking that you should clear this with the boss man first."

"Brenden," Avery said, looping her arm through his, "walk me inside please. I'm getting hungry."

"I need you to stay and chat with me, little brother," Yankee said. "Princess, your Shadow Lady is right around there." He pointed over his shoulder. "She can walk you in." None of it was less than a nicely worded demand.

"Go on, Avery." Brenden's eyes were locked with Yankee's. "I'll visit you soon."

$$\text{---} \quad \text{---} \quad \text{---}$$

"What the hell were you thinking, Brenden?" Yankee said as soon as Avery and her Shadow Lady were out of earshot.

"Screw you. You think because you outrank me that you can run my goddamned life? And you can kiss my ass, pulling that shit in front of Avery." Brenden's blood was about to boil. Yankee was an obnoxious prick when he wanted to be. And he always wanted to be when it came to Brenden.

Yankee closed the distance between them and put his hand on the side of Brenden's neck in an aggressive manner. "Listen to me, little brother, and listen good." Gray eyes met blue as they stared each other down. "First of all, Ryse is trying to help her get *over* her recent past and here you go being a fucking boy scout with your souvenirs. What do you think she's going to be doing all night if not crying over those memories and thinking about the man she was in love with? You think that's helping her get over him any? It's not." He tightened his grip. "Second of all, when I walked up, your hands were all over her. You better count your damn lucky stars that it was me who saw you and not Ryse. I heard he ordered a female doc because he didn't want another man's hands on her. Imagine what he would do to you if he caught you with your arms around her. You know how he is about touch."

He pushed away, causing Brenden to step back. "You are an Elite because the Master sees what you are capable of." Yankee pointed with his glasses to the training grounds and boarding houses of the Thracians. "There are hundreds of men that would love to take your place. Don't throw it all away by being fucking idiot." Yankee slipped on his glasses and walked away calling back over his shoulder, "He's called a meeting. Now."

CHAPTER FOURTEEN

"Nikki," Avery said with a determined tone, "I need a kitchen." She always did her best thinking when she was cooking. Baking, more precisely. At that moment, she had a lot to think about.

"Lucky for you, milady, we have the best kitchen in the Olympian realm," Nikki smiled at her happily. There was something too knowing about that smile. "Feel like making a cake? I love cake."

"Do you like chocolate cake?" Avery raised one brow.

"Is there any other kind?" Nikki was giddy as a child. Her constant good mood was infectious.

"Lucky for you, Nikki, I make a mean dark chocolate cream cake." Avery and her Shadow Lady linked arms and Nikki murmured something about being in love.

After one look at the Palace kitchen, Avery decided this world wasn't such a bad place. The octagon was designed for efficiency and productivity. Every surface was shining stainless steel or a chopping block. Even the cabinets had a commercial feel. Opening each cabinet, Avery saw all the tools of the trade: pots, pans, utensils, mixers, and grinders.

Avery listed off to Nikki the various ingredients and tools she required to bake. "I need flour, cocoa powder, baking soda and baking powder, salt, butter, white sugar, and vanilla extract. I'll also need two mixing bowls and a Bundt pan."

She brought some water to a boil.

Avery could feel Nikki watching. Finally she asked, "Do you wish to talk about it?" She handed Avery the salt. Nikki tilted her head and smiled. How could Avery resist?

"This conversation is confidential, right?" Avery asked. Nikki nodded and crossed her heart. It reinforced how innocent the dear girl was. "Then which part do you want to know about?" Nervous and without anyone else to vent to, Avery rambled off. "The part where I caught some chick named Salina rubbing up on Ryse, or the part where Dyna caught me eavesdropping, or the hour long walk I took with Troy, or the part where Brenden brought me the newspaper with my obituary? Oh, and then there's the part where he offered to be my warrior before Yankee called him out on it. Did you know his real name is Samuel?"

Wide-eyed and speechless Nikki gawked at her. "Um, yes and how about you start from the beginning." She laughed.

"Well, let's see here." Focusing more on the baking than on the story telling, Avery rattled about her day. Even though she knew Nikki had been around for most of it, her Shadow Lady had given her privacy and had no idea about the details. The courtesy was appreciated.

Nikki's big brown eyes followed her every move. After Avery covered the encounter with snake-witch Salina, Nikki gasped. "She tried to touch him? As in *touch* him?" Nikki's scandalous inflection on the one word nearly made Avery grin. Her little redheaded friend was apparently sheltered. Avery nodded, completely pissed again about the whole ordeal. "But Master Ryse doesn't tolerate touch from anyone outside of his family. I was shocked to see him so free with you. No offense," Nikki added.

He doesn't like to be touched? The statement made Avery think back to all the numerous times Ryse had freely made contact with her. There were a lot of times he had touched her face or back. Her entire naked body had been in contact with him in the bathtub, and he didn't have any trouble rubbing her down when they kissed.

Waving one whisk-filled hand at her, Avery brushed the situation off and began beating the ingredients to pour into the Bundt pan. After all, he was Thracian, she was a Grace. It was nothing more than biology. "It's probably for the best he's put some distance between us today. I seem to have no control of my hormones around him. Is that part of the aura or Grace thing?"

"Sure is. Just wait until your aura is released from the shields. You two might never make it out of the bedroom." Nikki giggled and blushed an even deeper shade of pink.

"Nikki!" Avery looked around to make sure they were alone. She leaned in to whisper, "How can you say that?" Nikki blanched, her face losing all color when she caught Avery's disapproval. "I'm supposed to be with some Olympian Prince. Not Ryse. You shouldn't even joke like that."

Nikki's pretty face contorted into a mask of confusion. "Avery, Ryse *is* an Olympian Prince. He is the eldest son of Troy and Dynasty." She tilted her head like a curious puppy. "Didn't you know that?"

The room began to spin. "I thought he was a Thracian?" Avery's heartbeat sped up and her breath caught. Could this be true? Was all her worry and fear over nothing?

Nikki spoke slowly. Her eyebrows arched high on her head. "Master Ryse is a Thracian. But he was born of both bloodlines. Ares and Zeus blessed him with their gifts. He is both Deity and Master, the first of his kind in all our race's history. In fact there is a great deal of controversy over his joint heritage and Hayden's existence—Lady Avery?"

Avery didn't hear a word she said after 'he is both Deity.' She had stumbled back and hit the refrigerator.

"I need a minute." Avery choked out. Her mind was racing along with her pulse.

Ryse was her Deity.

Ryse was her mate.

It wasn't only his Thracian blood that attracted him to her. Holy shit, what a revelation. All along the electricity between them was because the gods had created them to be together. Ryse was hers! She didn't have to leave him to be with someone else. She didn't have to hide how much she was attracted to him.

It explained why she was so drawn to Ryse, why leaving his side was painful even when she had been angry at him. Dynasty saying both her sons were anomalies, the way Troy's eyes had seemed so familiar, the surge of jealousy when Avery saw Salina touching Ryse. Every kiss, every touch had been more than just a Thracian's breeding to protect an unmated Grace. Ryse belonged to her and she belonged to him!

But—

"Why didn't he tell me?" Avery mumbled. In her mind, it was an obvious answer. He didn't tell her because he didn't want her to know he was available.

"Avery? Are you well?"

She looked up. Nikki's eyebrows were scrunched. "Yes, I'm fine."

"Then tell me what happened next? When did Her Majesty find you?"

Avery picked up the story from Ryse pinning Salina up against the wall by her neck. Asking no questions, Nikki listened intently to every detail of the visit with Dyna. Dyna hadn't mentioned Ryse at all when she was talking about her sons. Did the whole family not want her with Ryse? It was the same when she had talked with Troy. No one had mentioned Ryse and Avery as a pair. Was it possible he wasn't a candidate after all?

It wasn't until Avery mentioned Brenden that Nikki perked up even more.

"So while I cried, Brenden held me and listened." Avery poured the mixture into the pan and put it in the pre-heated oven while she talked. "That's when he offered to be my warrior. I don't even know what that means. Yankee showed up and made it out to be some big deal and made Brenden stay behind to 'talk' to him."

"Oh dear! Brenden *held* you? How?" Nikki's excitement deflated. There was no denying that Nikki had feelings for him. Avery had caught the way Nikki kept looking over her shoulder as if Brenden would come in at any moment.

"He put his arm around me. Like this." Avery walked over to her cooking companion and draped an arm on her shoulders. "It was a side hug. No big deal," she tried to assure Nikki.

"Avery, that is most certainly a big deal." Nikki began washing the dishes they had used. "A Grace is like no other being in our world. It's more complicated than a hug, Avery."

Nikki then had to explain to Avery about how auras worked. Most Divine Graces are born and raised in a Haven. The main reason is to monitor how others react to their auras. As a Grace, Avery's aura appeals to every race of Olympian. "You are practically running around a den of hungry lions with steak in your pocket. That's why Troy was so troubled when we didn't have a guardian today. The Thracians both wish to protect and mate with you. Some think it is a primal instinct to reproduce with an Olympian of championed blood. There have been Graces in the past who gave up their calling to pursue Thracian soldiers."

"Ah, hell," Avery said, wiping off the countertops. "Is there a book on this crap I need to be reading? No one mentioned that. I'm glad I didn't immediately say yes to Dyna this morning when she offered to set my aura free. I can't handle more than one crazy male at a time. Now I have to worry about sendin' mixed messages to Bren. Great!" She scrubbed the countertops with frustration until the metal shined under her hand.

"And let there be no doubt in your mind about this, milady: Thracians are a crazy brood. They are sought out as children and taught from their teenage years in the arts of war and death. Very much like the ancient Spartans, but with the potent blood of Ares running through their veins. Our Master Thracian is the craziest one of them all," she said in hushed voice. "And yes, there is a book on it."

Nikki flopped out her hand expecting the book to fall from the sky. That's close to what happened. The book seemed to materialize right before Avery's eyes. Nikki grasped it and sat down on one of the bar stools. She opened up the pages and searched for a moment.

"So cool," Avery said in amazement.

"Books are easy." Nikki's eyes searched the pages. "You should see me fabricate a vehicle. That's tricky."

"Are there at lot of you in the world? Conjurers?"

Nikki's shoulders slumped, something she did when she was unhappy. "No. Our numbers dwindle by the decade. We are less than one hundred. My parents were quite disappointed when I enrolled as a Shadow Lady instead of remaining hidden and having a litter of babies." Avery realized how very valuable Nikki was to the Olympian people. It also made her realize how lucky and privileged she was to have Nikki as a Shadow Lady.

"Ah, here it is." Nikki began reading from the passage, "'The origins of the Thracian race can be traced back to the days when Ares, god of war, walked among men. It is said that the god took on the name Thrax during this time. In the early development of the armies, the Thracians were known to be bloodthirsty and predatory. They sought out those who would threaten or reveal the existence of Olympians and destroyed them with ferocity. Their war-like ways and expertise in combat soon earned them the reputation of protectors and guardians of the Olympian people. To cross them was instant death with no questions asked. The Master Thracian passes down and carries out all sentences of traitors—'"

"Wait," Avery stopped her. "Ryse is an executioner?" The very thought terrified her right down to her bones. Though she shouldn't have been surprised. He had dispatched the intruders who attacked her with practiced skill.

Nikki's expression said she understood why this would distress her Lady. "Why, yes, Avery. That is a part of his job. Zeus would never leave such a task to anyone else. There is a system that has to be followed, but in the end it is his job to—"

"Kill people." Avery's stomach soured again. The more she learned about Ryse, the more she doubted their relationship was possible.

"Had he not the ability to do so, those men who attempted your capture would still be out there. You should be glad to have such a man protecting you the way that he does."

After a moment of quiet, Avery began to move again. Using the same ingredients, she put her hands to work on something else. Nikki kept reading from the book, but Avery only half-listened. Her mind was working again and her hands never stilled. Every few minutes Nikki would ask if she needed help. Avery kept her at the books, though. There was so much she had to learn and this seemed like a great way to do it. Avery cooking. Nikki reading.

CHAPTER FIFTEEN

SITTING AROUND A RECTANGULAR TABLE IN A SECURE CONFERENCE room was the Elite team. At the head of the table was Master Ryse. To his right was Hammon. This man, straight from the pages of ancient books, was a pillar of loyalty and steadfastness. Hammon was one of the two team members that were not Thracian born. That didn't mean he wasn't as deadly as his comrades. But his skill was tracking, not killing.

To the Master's left was General Gyrfalcon, named for the animal he could shift into. Falcon acted as General of the American Legion of the Thracian Army. Not many Thracians showed signs of age until they reached several centuries old. The sideburns on his face had gray hair mixed with the black, as did his small beard. The crow's feet stemming from his slate blue eyes were deeper than most. Falcon was tall, slender and hard looking; a man who had seen too much death in his day.

Around the table sat the other Elites: Cutter, the telepath and sword master and other non-Thracian; Philippe, whose powers were element based; the master of hand to hand combat-Yankee; and his newest Elite, Brenden. All of these men were the cream of the crop. These warriors sat at this table because they were the best of the best and had sworn loyalty to Ryse as Master.

"Tell me what's going on," Ryse commanded. His eyes landed first on the General of his army.

"Master." Falcon nodded. "Things have been fairly quiet since you left. Only one problem came up. There was a teenager openly using his telekinetic abilities in public. College kid. He was dealt with and warned. Only minor mental clean up was necessary to those who witnessed him. Training goes as necessary for the men. I've been corresponding and synchronizing with General Gastone about a possible visit from the European Deities."

"Were all the men who accompanied the European *Princess* checked over properly?" Ryse's stutter of the royal term for Salina received a couple throat clearings from his men.

"Yes Master, though she was rather insistent that her two personal bodyguards not have to go through the process. She claimed that men General Gastone assigned to serve her personally were immune to the tests of others in her security."

Ryse rolled his eyes, a habit he'd picked up from Avery. He absently wondered how his sweet Grace was doing. "Fine. Keep an eye on them. I don't trust anyone or anything that travels with her. I trust Gastone's judgment and loyalty, but Salina has," he paused for a moment, "means of persuasion."

"Something tells me you aren't talking about her telepathy." Yankee snickered under his breath. One raised brow from Ryse ceased his chuckles. Pissed off Ryse was not prone to appreciate his usual antics.

"I want no one and I do mean *no one* from her security team or maid staff anywhere near the west wing of this Palace. Do you all understand?" Ryse made eye contact with each of them. "The timing of her arrival is anything but a coincidence and I do not want to take any chances. None of you are to be around her. Your minds are too valuable."

"Aw, thanks boss," Yankee piped up again.

"Yankee." Ryse narrowed his eyes. "Since you seem to be in such a talkative mood. Please tell me you have something for me that I don't already know."

Cocky as always, Yankee pushed a file towards General Falcon. "Jerry was actually named Carter Patrokovich. Before he was assigned to Avery, he was on another girl who turned out to be nobody. His job is to get close to the females, and sleep with them or kill them if they have any power at all. According to my spies on the inside, he thoroughly enjoyed his job. He siphons information via touch. We're pretty damn lucky that Avery had no clue about anything Olympian related."

"By keeping her ignorant," Hammon said thoughtfully, "Her parents kept her safe."

Brenden leaned forward, elbows on the table. "What about the Teleporter?"

"Top tier." Hammon would have recognized his level of power. "Once he was out of the house, he was gone to me. But I've begun a search throughout all the registered Teleporters. I'm hoping to track them all since there are so few. I will find him, Master."

"Form a team. I don't want you personally doing this. Your presence is more valuable here. My mother informed me that we should be prepared for many visitors soon. She's had a vision of all the Deities gathering, though she doesn't know what for. When the time comes, Falcon, I want you to assign a liaison for each of the separate Deities' security. I know that all the Generals will want to talk to you directly, but I want you to delegate the tasks. My gut tells me this will not be a happy family reunion."

"Yes, Master. I have competent men who will be more than able to handle a flux of security measures."

Ryse looked the much older man in the eyes when he delivered the next comment. "Seeing as how the men in this army have not only the Elites, but me as their teacher, I will not tolerate any Thracian soldier to be less than perfect. We are the epicenter of the Thracian world and when my fellow royals come into this Haven, they expect to be safer than any place on the planet. If we have any soldier that is less than perfect at this point, they will be put elsewhere, not on guard duty. Understood?"

"Yes, Master." Falcon took the order like the dedicated soldier that he was. He was a General for a reason. "Might I make a suggestion, sir?"

Ryse nodded.

"Perhaps a word from their Master would help reiterate the high standard they are set to."

"Will do." He then turned his attention to the other Elites. "Next?"

The men continued with their meeting for the next hour. Millions of Olympians around the world depended on this rock solid rule of Thracians to keep their secret. The armies of warriors worldwide were deeply infiltrated into the human society. Their soldiers occupied positions in many police departments, government offices, and military rank in every country of the globe. It was crucial for Olympians to be protected on a local and worldwide level. The pyramid of soldiers was vast, all leading to one point—one man who acted by direction of the gods. The Master Thracian.

That man checked his communications device that dinged with the receipt of a message. Ryse hated technology, but even he had to admit that cell phones were handy.

Ur woman is n the kitchen. She's cooking. U've got to c this!

Ryse drew a breath and closed the device. "Meeting adjourned."

He stood up to make his way out of the conference room. Now that the official meeting was over, everyone seemed to relax. They had sorted through a lot of issues. An air of confidence was back. "You men hungry?"

— ⋅—⋅ ⋄⋄ ⋅—⋅ —

Prince Hayden sent the text message and walked into the kitchen to introduce himself to the new girl. It was completely unfortunate that she was good looking and already claimed by Ryse. He would have to live with the hot sister-in-law jokes for the rest of his existence. It would be great ammunition to use against his big brother.

Hayden smirked, thinking about pushing Ryse's buttons. His brother was way too serious way too much of the time.

"Well, well, well." He grinned as he made his way to the bar where Nikki was sitting. "It looks like I'm just in time."

Flashing a huge smile to Avery, he was surprised to see her jaw drop at the sight of him. The Princess held a batter-laden whisk mid stir in a bowl of chocolate goo. Her face was complete incredulity.

"Seen a ghost, Lady?" Hayden laughed quite used to getting the reaction from people who meet Ryse first then see his near twin-like face.

"Holy crap! You're his Mini-Me!"

He couldn't help his roar of laughter. Nikki giggled.

"Never heard that one before. Austin Powers, right?" Hayden propped himself up on the nearest stool to Nikki and grabbed one of the many delectable treats that lay scattered in a banquet on the countertop.

"I'm so sorry. I don't filter my mouth well and the distance from brain to tongue is too short." Avery's entire face turned red. "You must be Prince Hayden. I'm Avery, the moronic ass." She held out a hand.

Hayden took her chocolate covered fingers and stuck one of them in his mouth, overly pleased with the gasps from the ladies. Avery's eyes were about to explode, her mouth hung open at his audacity.

He flashed a wicked grin. "Delicious. Make sure you tell Ryse I did that. It will get under that thick skin of his like crazy. Such a stiff." Hayden winked and shoved a brownie in his mouth.

"I think you and I are going to get along like bees and honey." Avery laughed when she finally remembered to breathe. "That was a heck of an introduction, darlin'."

"I know I won't forget it anytime soon and it wasn't even my finger." Nikki giggled and fanned herself.

Hayden turned his face to the exquisite redhead sitting beside him. Two light brown eyes gleamed at him. He asked, "Your turn?"

"Such a flirt!" She shook her head and rolled her eyes.

Hayden shrugged and smiled innocently. "What can I say? I like the ladies."

"Nikki, you think you can conjure up some rain boots?" Avery asked. Nikki tilted her heard questioning in silence. "'Cause the bullshit's getting real deep in here."

"Ouch!" He grabbed his chest. "You wound me, woman! I might have to eat another one of these brownies to survive." When he reached for the platter of rich chocolates, Avery smacked his hand. "What?"

"Have you had dinner yet?" Avery put her hand on her hip.

"I'm game for whatever you can whip up. It's been decades since this kitchen has seen anyone in it but Valarie. It's going to be worth every broken dish and four letter word she'll throw around when she sees what you've done in here." He laughed, sneaking a chocolate cookie.

"I didn't think about that," Nikki said with complete soberness. "Oh, dear!"

Avery was lost. Her eyes darted between him and Nikki, "Is she going to be mad?"

"You can bet your cute bumpkin ass she will," Hayden huffed. "My mother might rule this Palace, but Valarie rules this kitchen."

The Princess put down the bowl she had been steadily whipping up. "Well, now hold on one minute." She furrowed her brow, hitched her hip, "I'm kind of a big deal around here, right?" Nikki and Hayden both nodded, hiding grins. "So can't I tell her to put her temper on ice and shut up until I'm done cookin'?"

"You know, Avery, I do believe you are getting the hang of this whole royalty thing." Hayden laughed when a smug look of happiness crossed Avery's face. This girl was just what Ryse needed. In fact, she was just the fresh face they all needed.

CHAPTER SIXTEEN

I T WAS ALL SHE COULD DO NOT TO STARE AT THIS SMALLER, LIGHTHEARTED version of Ryse. She and Prince Hayden had instantly hit it off. He was carefree and openly flirtatious with both her and Nikki. From what Nikki had been reading to her previously, Avery assumed that Hayden could afford to be the high-spirited, buoyant version of his brother. He had none of the pressures that Ryse did. Hayden might have come across as a nonchalant playboy, but the intensity and strength of his family legacy was there, too, right below the easy smiles and free flowing jokes.

The physical resemblance was uncanny, especially his face. The first time Ryse had come into the café, it had nearly knocked the breath from her lungs to look at him. He was ruggedly beautiful, a man from her most sensual dreams. Hayden was more Hollywood beautiful; his black hair was longer than his brother's and touched his shoulders. There was no facial hair on him, like Ryse. They shared the same big brown eyes that could melt a woman.

The major difference between the two brothers was their size. Ryse was a broad six foot four. Hayden was a few inches shorter and leaner. The second-born Prince was in no way the lesser of the two by any means. What Hayden might have lacked in physical size, he made up with his magnetic charisma, something that Avery couldn't really say about his older brother. While Hayden seemed to attract people, Ryse was his polar opposite.

"Gross! I have to stick my hands in raw eggs?" Hayden questioned, as Avery gave him a lesson in how to fry chicken. He frowned at the yellow slime.

"You're about as functional as a screen door on a submarine. Get your hands in there." They all laughed as the pretty boy dipped his clean hands into the eggs with a chicken breast, then rolled it around in the breadcrumbs. Nikki peeled potatoes and Avery helped them both.

That's how Ryse and the rest of the Elites found them. Most of their faces were familiar by now. There was the Italian smoker, Phil-something. Hammon was quite unforgettable. Cutter, the small Asian. Yankee. Then there was Brenden, a guy with a face straight off the Disney Channel. He was a comfort compared to the new man with them who instantly made her skin crawl with primal fear. He gave the impression of being much older than any other person she had seen around the Palace and yet his physique was distinctly that of a seasoned warrior in his prime. He had grey streaks in his hair, wrinkles around his sharp eyes and on his forehead. His muscles were thick and no less intimidating than the younger men. There was something very predatory about all of Ryse's Elites and this man was no different. Each of them seemed to hide an animal simmering below the surface of their human faces.

But even these men with their interesting features could not keep her eyes off Ryse. Simply seeing his face made her heart pound. Her skin shivered in excitement. Those piercing eyes locked with her gaze immediately. A cocky, possessive grin barely revealed itself on his lips. Oh god, his lips.

Either he was warming her with his aura or the kitchen was getting much, much hotter. Forgetting everyone else in the room, Ryse walked over to her and put a proprietary hand on her nape and left a kiss on her forehead. She felt so much in the touch: possession, comfort, safety, passion.

"Be careful," she said, using what coherent thought she had left. "I have eggs on my hands." When he stepped back from her, the only sound in the kitchen was the bubbling of the oil as it browned the chicken. Avery was suddenly aware of all the eyes watching. The blood gathered in her cheeks and she stepped away from him. Recalling how he had told Salina how he didn't like to be touched, Avery wondered if this act of affection shocked the Elites as much as it did her.

Thankfully, Hayden spoke up before she let her mind linger on Salina. But what he said was even more blush worthy. "Oh, for the love of Aphrodite, get a freaking room! I'm trying to cook here!" This seemed to snap everyone out of their trance and a few of the men laughed.

"Hayden, the thought of you cooking turns my stomach," Brenden teased as he leaned over the bar to watch the Prince batter up another chicken breast. His eyes kept flickering over to Nikki.

"Hey, look at my teacher." Hayden smiled sinfully sweet. "I've licked her fingers and touched a breast."

Silence again. *Ah, hell.* Ryse went rigid by her side and she saw Nikki swallow a tennis ball down her throat. Hayden chuckled and kept at his task clearly pleased with himself for causing trouble.

"He did *what?*" Ryse said, replacing a hand on the nape of her neck. The gesture was firm, but not overly so.

"He means chicken breast," Avery spit out quickly. "Your brother is trying to yank your chain, darlin'." She gave it her best accent to distract him. "I guess he thinks it's funny to risk his life at attempting a joke."

"Hell yeah," Hayden preened. "Just look at him. He's seething. It's perfect!"

The young man's laughter calmed the situation. Even stiff and solemn Hammon grinned at the two siblings. He, Philippe, Cutter, and the new soldier had taken a casual seat at a breakfast table. Yankee was leaning against the wall, grinning.

"Because you are my brother, you get that one for free." Ryse then did the unexpected and pulled Avery's neck to him. He rubbed her nose with his and whispered, "Mine" before kissing her. Avery could hear a couple of the men chuckle, Nikki giggled, and Hayden made some catcalls and repeated his line about getting a room.

Avery was breathless and disoriented when Ryse released her. The shock on her face was evident and earned her a sly grin from Ryse.

Avery leaned in to Ryse's body. "Hayden should piss you off more often if that's the result." She tried to clear her head of the tantalizingly sensual fog of his kiss. He kept the contact at her neck. She assumed it was to make a public claim to his men.

"Don't encourage him. He does it enough on his own." Ryse punched his little brother on the arm. Hayden puckered his lips and made a kissing noise in return. Then, he winked at Avery.

"You remember the rest of the men, right?" Ryse said. "Yankee, Cutter, Hammon, Philippe, Brenden." Ryse pointed them each out. Avery nodded to each. "This is General Falcon. He is—"

"Commanding Officer for the North American Thracians. It's a pleasure to meet you, General." Avery said with a smile. Ryse's hand tightened on her nape while the General made direct eye contact with her.

"The pleasure is all mine, dear Princess." He stood to formally bow as he spoke.

Yankee moved to sit beside Nikki on the bar stools. "So, peeling potatoes?" he said picking up a knife and a spud.

"Jeez, Yankee." Brenden rolled his eyes. "I hope to hell that wasn't your version of a pickup line. That was smooth as a cheese grater." Brenden took a seat beside the blushing girl. "Go away," he waved off Yankee.

"Watch it, *mutt*." Yankee delivered the punch line with a glare and a cunning grin.

Ryse turned to Avery and asked if she could fix enough for the rest of the men and she was most happy to do so. It put her in her element, cooking for a lot of people. It was very entertaining to see

Cutter, who was aptly named for his knife and sword abilities, show the rest of them how to peel potatoes. He had two, six-inch knives that were moving at speeds her eyes could not follow. He sliced potatoes into paper-thin sheets and Avery put them into the frying oil spices.

"I must say Cutter, you're very handy to have around. That slice and dice job would have taken me three times as long." Cutter nodded and saluted her with a knife. "But I have to know, where do you hide those knives?"

He simply smiled. Avery figured she didn't need to know after all.

Minutes later, the ladies set out the food for all the men. Philippe smirked at her affectionately when she asked him to put out his cigarette.

A dish piled high with fried chicken was quickly plucked down to only a few pieces. The fried seasoned chips were devoured as fast. Nikki filled glasses with ice and drinks. Conversations were replaced with compliments on the food that Hayden took with no humility. It made her laugh.

For a nostalgic moment, Avery felt a sense of home. She watched the men sitting around the table. Some teased, some talked, and some nodded while chewing. Hands moved with sentences and eyes shone in understanding. Many times she had observed her café the same way she did this group of men. Food brought people together and bonded them on a foundational level. It gave her a sense of pride to know she had the power to produce such a scene with her skills here in this new life.

Before sitting down to her own plate of food, she walked over and gave Ryse a kiss on the back of his neck. The wink she received in return was all the payment she would ever need. Avery spent the afternoon learning about each of the men, laughing at Hayden, taking pride in how much chocolate Nikki could put away, and trying desperately to convince herself she could acclimate to this world.

"What in the name of the gods happened in my kitchen?" The outraged scream cut through all the talking and laughing going on.

"Oh, dear," Nikki whispered under hear breath. "That's Valarie."

Avery watched the plump woman walk in with an armload of groceries. Valarie was another striking redhead and her face was dotted with freckles. Her olive colored eyes widened when she saw the inhabitants of her messy kitchen.

"My apologies, your Majesties. Might I ask who is responsible for this *mess?*"

"That would be me." Avery slid off her bar stool and walked around to grab a bag from Valarie.

The lady furrowed her brows, looking down her nose at Avery. "And you are?"

Avery was taken aback by her tone. She had gotten nothing but respect and kindness since she arrived, and this woman was not continuing on that track. "Well I'm—"

"Valarie, Valarie, Valarie." Hayden intervened just as a very protective Ryse rose from his seat. "Why don't you and I take a walk?"

He looked at his brother and waved him off. Ryse nodded and then took his seat before his quick temper could get the best of him. Avery didn't meet the eyes of the woman who was now being escorted by Prince Hayden into a butler's pantry. Avery looked instead to Ryse. He motioned for her to finish her meal. Since she didn't feel like rocking the boat, she obeyed.

The kitchen phone rang and Valarie came out of the butler's pantry with Hayden to answer it. "Yes…yes…I shall hurry," she said into the receiver and looked at Avery. "Pardon my previous disrespect. You, milady, are welcome in my kitchen at any time."

"As long as I clean up my mess?" Avery smiled.

"Even then. Right now, I have to prepare the English Lady her meal."

"You mean the European Princess?" Avery said glancing over at Ryse. "By all means, Valarie, let me help. The Princess can try my chicken." Avery jumped up and fixed a plate full of food including some of the brownies she had made. Hopefully Salina choked on the food.

Nikki whined, "Don't give away the chocolate." Brenden put his brownie onto her plate and she was happy again.

Thirty minutes later, while Avery was cleaning up, much to the maid staff's surprise and Ryse's aggravation, one of the staff working Salina's room brought back an empty plate. "The Lady sends her compliments to the chef. She says the brownies were delicious."

Valarie looked over at Avery with one lifted brow. Avery smiled brightly then said, "Please tell the Lady that the meal was compliments of the *farm girl*."

That comment abruptly ceased the conversation Ryse was having with his men. He turned in his chair to face her. Tension suddenly thickened in the room. Ryse stared at her as if he were a predator getting ready to pounce. She continued to tidy up the already immaculate kitchen.

"Avery." Never had her name been said with such power behind it—and restraint. Suddenly, all the Elites had somewhere to be. Brenden gently tugged Nikki out of the kitchen with the rest of the group.

Ryse stood and slowly walked over to her, took her by the arm. "I think you and I need to speak."

CHAPTER SEVENTEEN

RYSE WATCHED AVERY CLOSELY. SHE SAT ACROSS FROM HIM IN THE living area of her room having no problem holding his stare. Not many people could do such a thing. He was a pro at intimidation, had spent centuries perfecting the art. But Avery sat there with her arms casually resting on the chair, her legs crossed, chin up and eyes glued to his. The confidence was turning him on. If they didn't have something very important to discuss, he would have been all over her.

"Something you need to tell me?" He mirrored her body language.

"No, darlin.' What has you in such a mood?"

Damn he loved that sexy southern accent. And it distracted him for a moment. Which was probably what she intended. Ryse gave a growl. "You didn't pull the term 'farm girl' randomly out of your vocabulary, Avery. Explain yourself."

"Why are you angry with me? You were the one with One-Trick Barbie's hands on your crotch."

Ryse blew out a huff of air, let his head lean back against the chair. "Salina did not touch my crotch and what the hell were you doing there anyway?"

Explaining how she came across him and Salina, she told him

what she had overheard. "I didn't mean to eavesdrop but you can see why the conversation held my attention."

Ryse waved her off, finished talking about the subject. "Ancient history."

"Why didn't you tell me you were both a Thracian and a Deity?" Her tone held firm, but he caught the slightest hitch in her breathing.

Ryse looked back into her eyes. "Pardon?"

Her chin lifted. "Why didn't you explain to me that you were also a Deity Prince? I've been walking around all day thinking you had seduced me to get me here. And now that I was safely behind Palace walls you were done with me."

By the gods! How could he have left out such a detail? He thought back to their encounters, the good and bad. Had he not made his intentions clear? For the life of him, he would never understand the female species. "Is that why you're angry? Because I didn't formally claim you?"

"Formally claim me? Like I'm a tree and you're the dog. No Ryse, that's not why I'm angry." Avery rose from her chair and began pacing about the room. He couldn't have been more confused. He groaned with a deep breath just as she launched into him verbally. "I'm angry because you forgot to mention a vastly important detail about yourself. One that changes the course of my life. I'm angry because if I am somehow betrothed to you and not someone else, Salina's actions are twice as aggravating. Especially since she knows you have a Grace."

"Avery, love, I think you are blowing this all greatly out of proportion." Ryse rubbed the bridge of his nose. He wasn't used to dealing with people arguing with him. How did his father get anything done? "I apologize for assuming you knew about me—"

"That sounds so sincere, thank you very much." Sarcasm dripped off her words. She rolled her eyes and turned to the fireplace. What the hell did she want if not an apology?

When she looked back, the moisture in her eyes nearly killed him. "You know what I really don't understand?" Avery crossed her arms over her chest. "The rules 'round here are sexist shit. Your laws state that I have to be pure, having never willingly had sex with another man, but you get to run around screwing at will?"

"That's not what it says." Ryse leaned over to rest his elbows on his knees.

"And how would you explain it then? I'm pretty sure that you and the blonde bombshell did more than have afternoon tea while talkin' politics and yet no one's accused you of being *defiled*."

Damn. That was a fair enough. And yet he didn't have a good answer. Rubbing the bridge of his nose again, Ryse closed his eyes and tried to figure out what to say. "Avery, I understand your confusion. You have a valid point." He spoke slowly and that only earned him dirty look. "But I will not attempt to explain my entire past to you. There is far too much of it. Salina and I had a one-time thing many decades ago. It was a mistake and it meant nothing. Do not make it more than it was."

Avery's eyes widened, her nostrils flared and her mouth dropped open. Shit.

"Get out," she ordered as she picked up a couch cushion and threw it at him.

Ryse gawked at her. "What is wrong with you?"

Her shocked expression and passionate anger were beautiful. How could he be thinking how amazing she was when they were fighting? "What's wrong with me? Are you serious? For a demigod, you sure are dumb. Leave. I'd prefer to be alone." She turned her back and looked at the fire. He could see the tension in her shoulders, feel the anger radiating off her.

In a blink he was behind her, hands on her shoulders, lips to her ears. "Avery, baby."

"Oh no, you don't," she said, brushing him off. "Don't try to order me around like some dog and then get all sweet on me now. I'm not one of your soldiers."

"I realize that, Avery. But you can't possibly be jealous of that— that troll."

"I'm not blind, deaf, or dumb. That woman is no troll. Why are you trying to make light of this?"

"Why are you trying to make it more than it was? I detest her. She's nothing."

Avery rounded on him and he tried to keep his hands on her body. "Any more *nothings* you want to tell me about?"

With an exasperated sigh, Ryse stepped away. "Believe it or not, Avery, no. By the gods, you women are so damned maddening. Why waste the energy?"

Avery glared at him. "You should really stick to bein' the strong *silent* type."

Ryse knew he'd royally screwed up, though he wasn't precisely sure how. Avery was pissed. There was no bother trying to argue with her when her accent was this heavy. He didn't want to leave, but she made the decision for him.

"Good bye, Ryse. I'm sure you can make your way out the door." Avery went out to the balcony, effectively dismissing him.

CHAPTER EIGHTEEN

AVERY HUFFED AROUND HER SUITE. NIKKI HAD COME IN AFTER RYSE left, but she stayed out of the way.

"Don't do that," she pointed a finger at Nikki. "You don't get to hide under that I'm-just-the-assistant blanket. You're my only friend and you have to give me advice."

Nikki tilted her head over to the side and sighed. "Avery, relationship advice is far beyond my scope of expertise. I've never had one."

"What?" Nikki was beautiful and funny, and a true delight to be around. Avery had seen how Yankee and Brenden—even Hayden—had been flirting with her today while they ate. Especially Brenden.

Nikki shrugged. "Yes, I am a twenty-eight year old virgin. Much like you, so you can't make fun of me."

Her words were a lighthearted joke, but for some reason they tore Avery apart. She was nothing like Nikki. Avery was not a virgin. And that is what upset her even though she hadn't known it until this moment. She collapsed onto the couch, head in her hands. Fat tears dripped down her face.

"Oh dear!" Nikki threw her arms around the Princess. "I'm sorry. What did I say? I was trying to tease but I'm not much good at it."

Avery inhaled a shaky breath. She met Nikki's eyes and gave her a sad smile. "Eight years ago, my choice was taken. I was twenty and much like you—never had a real boyfriend, never been past second base with a guy, and hadn't ever wanted to. I chose to be alone. I chose to be single, didn't have to be. I did not, however, choose to give up my virginity." Anger permeated her words as she remembered the sickening torture of that day. "They took it," she sneered. "My innocence was stolen by the filth of the earth, for no other reason than to keep me from powers I might or might not possess." She blinked back the moisture from her eyes. "Then we have Ryse, able to have sex with a woman completely of his own free will. No sacrifice on his part whatsoever. Hell, seein' the woman he had slept with, he dang sure enjoyed it. The thought of sex doesn't churn his stomach, doesn't make him physically sick with memories." She leaned her head back, closed her eyes and took a deep breath. "The thought of a man's hands on me made me nauseous," she turned her face to Nikki. "Until I met Ryse."

"May I speak candidly, Avery?" Nikki rubbed her knees as they sat on the couch together. "Without the fear that my words might leave this room?"

Avery wiped the tears from her eyes. "I don't have anyone else to tell, Nikki. In case you haven't noticed, I don't have any other friends."

"Then I am very lucky that you have chosen me." Her hazel eyes gleamed with pride. "From what I understand, when Salina propositioned Ryse, he had lost one of his Elites. The man had been with Ryse since his childhood, over two centuries worth of companionship. I don't know too much, only that the death of him hurt Ryse deeply."

"Do you know how he died?" Avery whispered.

"No. No one speaks of it. But you can imagine what the murder of an immortal could do to someone. She came to him when he was weak, Avery, using her magic as a poison. Salina is a telepath. She can put any thought into a person's mind. Perhaps we will never know if it was by her telepathy or by his own pain that he allowed her into his bed." Nikki stopped talking and lifted her head, listening. "Brenden comes now to bring you the dogs." She stood up and fiddled with her ponytail, straightened her clothes as she went to answer the door.

Avery caught the flirtatious look they exchanged before Nikki's eyes went to the floor. Castor and Pollux ran into the room and jumped up on Avery. The story would have to wait for a better moment.

⚊⚊ ⚬ ⚊⚊

Damn women. Ryse paced the floor. He had ducked into a suite right down the hall from Avery, not wanting to get too far from her but needing to be alone to think. Over and over, he sorted through Avery's words. What did he do to make her act like this?

Damn Salina. Given the permission from Ares, he would love to rip her a new one.

As if courting Avery wasn't going to be hard enough with all her trauma from home, now he had to worry about Salina using her telepathy to manipulate the situation. Her presence alone had caused Avery to be troubled.

This was why he had embraced the Thracian side of himself and not the royal. There were no emotions, no feelings, and no intimacy in being a soldier. When he spoke, his words were obeyed without question. The only men who were ever allowed to contradict him on anything were the Elites and his Generals around the globe. Even then, if the gods told him to do something, there was no one that could stand in his way.

But this woman—this woman frustrated him. She argued and challenged him even in public. Avery was stubborn and mouthy and hard-headed...and...and...He let out a sigh and sat on the bed. She was exactly the kind of woman the gods knew he would need, because a mouse would annoy him even more. If Avery obeyed him like a lifeless robot, he wouldn't be as entertained and enthralled as he was.

Her jealousy over Salina did anger him, but it also made him feel special. If Avery didn't have feelings for him, she wouldn't have cared at all. But she did care. He cared.

So what was he doing sitting on his ass? Why wasn't he going to claim what was his?

Stalking into the Avery's bedroom without knocking, he found her and Brenden sitting on the couch, holding hands. Brenden jumped to his feet at seeing Ryse.

"It seems that I have interrupted something." Ryse stared down Brenden until the boy's eyes fell away in submission.

"I was just leaving," Brenden said firmly. He turned to Avery. "We can continue this conversation later. Good night."

"Thank you," she said, touching his forearm before he left.

The movement caught Ryse's eye and he felt the fury build up inside of him.

"For everything."

Everything? Just what had Brenden done in his absence?

"It's my job, milady," he said stiffly.

"No," Avery smiled. "It's more. Thank you." Then Avery shifted her gaze to Ryse.

"Goodbye, Brenden," he said while looking at her. "I will see you in the training pit in the morning."

Brenden's form went rigid and he stopped mid-step, lifting his chin, jaws tight. He spoke through strained throat and clenched teeth, "Yes, Master."

Ryse nodded towards the door and Brenden obeyed the unspoken order. Then he focused his attention on Avery.

◄ —. ₒ°ₒ .—►

Gods help her, he was spectacular. Even in his pique, Ryse was a vision. Every movement was so controlled and full of purpose, glorious in its intimidation. Avery stood completely still as he paced in front of her, a lion sizing up the potential meal on the other side of the glass cage, his eyes never leaving her.

Keeping her chin up, she crossed her arms around her chest and blew out a breath. "Why are you lookin' at me like that?"

"How is that?" The way he could keep such a calm tone when her whole body was shaking pissed her off more.

"Like you're ready to rip my head off. Who do you think you are, rushin' into my room?"

His eyes narrowed as he looked at her and his lips twitched. "Who am I?" he said. "Baby, you do have a lot to learn if you can't answer that question."

With every step he took towards her, she took one back until she hit a wall. "You don't own me, Ryse. I'm not your toy and I'm not your puppet to pull the strings."

"Oh, you've made that abundantly clear by your actions today, my love." He was less than a breath away from her now. "What was Bren doing in here?"

She could hardly breathe. He was so close, exuding pure male sensuality and strength. His hard body only inches from her. Damn he smelled good. "He brought me the dogs and some things from Frank's place that he thought I would want."

"None of that explains what he was doing with his hands on you." Ryse reached up to play with one of her curls. The nonchalance of it didn't seem to fit the moment.

"I don't have to explain anything."

"Oh, but you should. Because if you don't, all I can do is make assumptions. And do you know what I saw?" Avery swallowed hard at the hint of cruelty in his voice. "I saw one of my men trying to be more than a soldier to my woman. I saw his hands on her and his body much too close. Do you know how very suspicious that makes me?"

"Jealous much?"

"Yes," he said, taking her by the nape and angling her head up, "I am."

"Well, join the club, darlin'." Avery grabbed at the collar of his shirt. She wanted to pull that collar, drag his lips to hers and kiss him with all the passion she was feeling.

Ryse furrowed his brows and scowled at her. "Is that why you had him in here? To make me jealous?"

"No. But I'll take it. You think you're the only single man around here?" Ryse released her and took a step back as if she had slapped him. Gathering what courage she had left, she put on a tough face. "You think you can order me around all the time? Don't you think I've got the right to be pretty pissy with you? How do you think I feel, or do you care?"

"Of course I care!"

"Do you? Because if you gave my feelings a moment's thought, you might realize exactly why I'm angry." She didn't even care that hot tears were leaking from her eyes. "I've never been given a choice about any of this. No one gave me a choice from the time I was born. My parents made the choice of what kind of life I would live, my parents chose to hide this whole culture from me and because of that choice, they're dead. You chose to bring me here, chose to take me away from the life I knew, chose to claim me. Jeez, you even chose my damn room! I've had no say at all. I didn't even have a choice in losing my virginity!" she screamed. "Your gods and those against them chose it for me!"

She slumped into a chair. Ryse stood in silence. The look on his face was pure defeat. Perhaps it was shock. Avery had never yelled at anyone so violently.

"Most people always remember their first time. Some might say they were too young or with the wrong person or even that they wished the setting was different, more romantic." She laughed bitterly. "All I remember about my first time was that, up until a week ago, it was the worst day of my life. I never understood why I didn't date, never wanted any of the boys that came calling. I was saving myself for a man I didn't even know existed.

"Then they came for me. And I didn't know why it happened. Why me? I didn't understand any of it. One minute there was a nice man asking to use my telephone, and the next he was on me. I've never felt pain that bad. For years I felt dirty, like I could wash and wash and never be clean. I can still smell him. I remember every detail about his face and the clothes he wore, his breath." She closed her eyes, wishing she could erase every memory of that day. "After a while, I came to terms with it. I became thankful that it happened to me instead of some other innocent girl in town. I would look at some of my customers and think *at least it wasn't you*." Her eyes met his. "But you, you had a choice, Ryse. You knew about me. Maybe you didn't know me by name, but you were educated about the gods' plan. You made your choice and you don't get to be angry with me for being hurt about your decision. If there is one thing that I will have under my control, it's how I get to feel. Don't punish me for that."

Ryse hadn't moved a muscle. Slowly, he stood and walked over to the fireplace, braced his hands on the mantle, and stared at the flames dancing off the wood. Avery watched him for a long time before he finally spoke.

⚊⚊⚫⚊⚊

"I was weak." The painful admittance was against everything he had ever been taught. Weakness was failure; weakness caused men to die. But what kind of a man, what kind of a husband would he be to her if he didn't sacrifice in this moment and admit his sins? Precious Avery had shared her soul; he could do the same. "Andreas, my first Elite and closest friend, back when I had friends, was murdered in front of me. We were tracking a band of rogues that had grown in number. Most of the rogues that band together cause no actual threat. Most are too fearful of the gods to do any real damage. But this group was nearing the hundred mark and it was time to take care of the rebellion. Resistance and questions are permitted, tolerated to some degree. But outright defiance is not.

"Ares spoke to me, told me it was time to remind people that the Deities were the lips and eyes of the gods on earth and those who opposed them would be killed. That's what we went to do. I took

Andreas and three other men. We're Thracians, that's all we needed even against one hundred. All of the rebels were eliminated and we were picking up the mess when one of the men we thought dead rose to his knees. He pulled out a gun unlike anything I had ever seen and pointed it at me. Andreas saw and took the bullet, jumping at the bastard before I could react.

"The gun was the only one we found. We searched each body. There was only the one. It was a dart gun full of poison. It ate him, disintegrated him before my eyes." In all his years, Ryse had never seen anything like it. Never had such a weapon been created. It shook everyone to the core. The immortals might have been in human bodies, but they are hard to kill. Ryse wouldn't have believed that mighty Andreas could be taken down so quickly and so easily, or so gruesomely. "I was mourning him. Andreas had been my friend and my second in command. His abilities with the sword were unparalleled on this earth. Even Cutter paled in comparison. More than that, he was an amazing person. Beloved by all that knew him. You would have taken to him. He was very cheerful, similar to Bren. And he would have eaten you up." He smiled at the thought of how Andreas might have reacted to Ryse being mated such a spitfire. The teasing would have never ceased.

Ryse's memories went south when he thought about what happened next. "Salina came to me in a moment of weakness. I was broken and had let my emotions overcome me. I don't remember how she convinced me. I wish I could say it was her mind tricks or the wine, but I think that would be a lie. My anger turned my heart bitter. In that moment of doubt, I gave in to her." He looked at Avery, who was watching him intently, her face giving him no sign of what she was thinking. "I am not proud of that night. But I learned something after that, many things actually." His people looked to him for strength and for the guidance they needed. Allowing his emotions to get the best of him had been a temporary failure to everyone. His life was devoted to the protection of his people and when he took his eyes off his destiny mistakes were made.

"What had happened to Andreas was beyond my control," he continued. "A true accident that no one could have prevented. Mourning my friend was not the weakness, but being ruled by my emotions was. I vowed that my temporary state of mind would not rule my long-term actions. Until you came along."

He laughed as he sat on the couch and rubbed his face in his hands. "You've changed everything. You irritate me, make me jealous, defy me at every turn, allow men in your chambers. Everything about you goes against the grain. You make me weak."

CHAPTER NINETEEN

VERY'S HEART BROKE FOR HIM. SHE KNEW ALL TOO WELL WHAT it was like to have your best friend murdered before your eyes. And she too had made an emotionally based decision to murder Jerry. Was her sin so different than his? They had both done horrible things in the name of despair.

"I'm sorry, Ryse. I wish I knew how to be the Grace you need."

Ryse stood and took her hands to pull her up. "Avery, my love, you already are. Every moment I was away from you today was miserable. I'm sorry about Salina and I swear to you, I will be rid of her as soon as possible. This is your home and if you do not want her here, then she will be told to leave."

"It's not only her, Ryse. I'm simply not cut out for this."

"You were made for this, for me," he said, pulling her forehead to his. "I can't let you go so please don't make me try."

Avery moved out of his grasp, not able to face him. "You don't own me, Ryse. You can't act like I'm your toy and you don't want the other kids on the playground to play with it."

Ryse grabbed her hand and twirled her back towards him. "Well, you see, my love, you are very much mine to play with, and I will be very upset if the other children play with you," he said with that mischievous grin that crumbled her resolve. He nuzzled his face in her neck and she felt that blissful warmth of his aura blanket them.

"I am very protective of those that are mine. You cannot ask me to change that. It's in the very fabric of my mind."

She touched the side of his face, marveling in the way he could dissolve her negative emotions with one look. "I understand. And I respect the fact that you're so protective. But there is a fine line between protective and overbearing. It might be okay with your men, but not with me. Like today with Valarie, you don't have to fight those battles for me. If I'm supposed to be your partner, I might as well exercise my backbone. And Nikki told me that you freak out about touch. But just because I touch someone or let 'em touch me, it doesn't mean it's anything *sexual*."

"So you and Brenden?" he questioned.

"First off, Brenden is head over heels for Nikki."

Ryse's eyes widened, his jaw went slack like he was thinking. "How do I not know that?"

Avery shook her head. "Never mind. Brenden said I remind him of his sister. He didn't say how, but I gathered that she was—well, that she and I have a similar history. I survived and she didn't. Brenden asked to be bound to me."

"What did you say?" he asked.

"I didn't think it was my call. Ultimately he is your man, right?"

Ryse nodded. "It would make me very *relieved* to have one of my Elites blood bound to you as a guardian. If Bren values you as he did Meg, there is no one that could be more devoted to you aside from me. I will see to it in the morning." Ryse looked into her eyes and ran his fingers through her hair. "By the gods, you are the most exquisite creature they have ever created." He pressed her body close to his. "I promise to be a man worthy of you."

"So you do want me as your Grace?" Avery asked in a whisper. "I thought you didn't tell me about being a Deity because you didn't—"

"Don't even say that." Ryse put his forehead on hers. "It was an oversight. Nothing else. I guess I'm used to everyone knowing who I am. Forgive me, my love?"

Avery nodded, unable to find her voice through the relief that crashed over her. She snaked her arms around his neck and held him for a long moment. "Can we be done fighting now? It hurts too much." Avery squeezed his massive form closer. She could barely wrap around him yet they fit so perfectly together.

His body relaxed in her arms. With a laugh, he kissed the top of her head. "That is the best idea I've heard all day." Ryse bent his head and pressed his lips to hers. Oh, how she had feared she would never get this chance again.

She put everything she had into that kiss. What started out as slow and easy turned into fast and furious. After removing her ponytail, Ryse held her head firm, his other hand on her lower back. Her fingers tunneled into his long silky hair. When his tongue traced over her bottom lip, she gladly opened her mouth and allowed him inside. The taste of him was decadent and she wanted more, so much more.

Ryse reached down and caressed her bottom, lifting until her legs wrapped around his body. He took them to the couch and sat down, Avery straddling him. She felt his warmth and decided to figure out exactly how that worked. "Didn't you say that you were shielding your full aura from me?" Avery could barely concentrate when his lips moved to her neck, his hands slipped under her shirt to smooth over her back.

"Mmm hmm," he murmured against her heated skin.

"What if I wanted to feel more?"

"You sure you want to do that?"

Avery bent her neck, giving him more access. "You won't hurt me."

"Pain and pleasure are very similar feelings, my love."

Her eyes were suddenly blurry. "I'm not scared."

The sensory tidal wave crashed through her body. It made each breath deeper, made her heart race, and every hormone in her body took notice. Had she not already been sitting, she would have collapsed. Her body melted around him, conforming to his frame. Every particle in the air seemed to be electrified with his power. His essence was heavy against her and yet wrapped around them in a stimulating current that made her whole body tingle and squirm. "Wow," she said, closing her eyes to focus on the sensual force of it all.

Ryse spoke with his lips brushing against her neck, "And that's only about an eighth of my mental shields down."

Avery considered the possibilities of that. If this was but a fraction and she was aching for him, how would she react when she faced the full force of Ryse Castille? She kissed him again and mentally let go, if only for the moment, of everything else. Right then, she wanted to enjoy the lips of this beautiful man underneath her. Ryse kept his aura opened and the weight of it was welcoming. She could feel him, feel his arousal and warring emotions. When she recognized it for what it was, she understood he was holding something back.

"What's wrong?" Avery said, prying her body out of his arms. She pushed stray hairs out of her face.

Aroused Ryse was a picture she never wanted to forget. His lips were red from their kiss, his hair tousled from her hands. He was panting. He closed his eyes for a second before focusing on her. "As much as I would love to take you over to the bed and make love to you, I can't. You're not ready for that yet."

"Oh," Avery looked away and felt blood rush to her cheeks.

"It's more than just sex, Avery." Ryse held onto her face, made sure she looked up at him. "When a Deity and his Grace first come together, it's the final step to mating. You receive your gifts and the gods give us their blessing. It can be overwhelming." He stroked her hair. "I want to make sure you have no reservations when that time comes. Once you come to bed with me, there is no going back. We will belong to each other for eternity."

Avery nodded, unsure of what to say.

Ryse gave her a kind smile. "We have only just met, my love. There is no rush. Our courtship can take as long as you wish."

Her heart was glad to hear his reassuring words; her hormones, on the other hand, were not. But as much as she wanted to jump Ryse and not let him surface until the next morning, she was not ready to marry him. "If you can't take me to bed, why don't you take me on a tour instead."

Ryse nodded, tipped his head and then kissed her again. When the time came for them to be together, Avery had a feeling it was going to be the best night of her life.

Ryse showed his beloved all over the castle and the gardens. When they went to the stables, Avery found a horse that she just had to ride. She claimed it was the most beautiful animal she had ever seen. Ryse's heart swelled with pride. The black Friesian stallion was his horse.

They went for a ride through the hills around the Haven. Castor and Pollux ran their legs off. It made Avery happy to watch them, so naturally Ryse was growing fond of the boys. Their afternoon seemed to stretch on as they explored. All the while they talked and learned one another. Ryse hadn't spoken so many words in his life. But Avery was very curious about Olympian culture. For the first time since they met, Ryse felt like he was making real progress.

Avery listened to Ryse explain why he thought Salina was a distraction or a spy. She agreed that they should keep their enemies close, but he sensed her agitation about it. He laughed when she called Salina the snake-witch and then laughed even more when he found out that Dyna had somewhat coined the term. Avery told him all about her talk with his parents, especially with his father. The time they spent together walking around the lake had meant a lot to her. He tensed when she talked about Brenden's arms being around her in the garden earlier that day, but said nothing when she mentioned something about Hayden with fondness.

In his mind, he knew that Avery was nothing like him when it came to touch. She showed her affection freely and constantly held his hand or his arm. He was learning, but it would take time. And Ryse did enjoy touching her. When she mounted the stallion and sat in front of him, he reveled in the way his arms wrapped around her waist, the way she rested her head back on his shoulder. Yes, touching Avery was a marvelous sensation. One he thanked the gods for.

In his heart, he feared that she would need more than he could give. Ryse had limited his touch for a reason. Not too many people knew what his touch would do to them and he intended for it to stay that way. Unlike him, Avery had nothing to lose by contacting others. But his touch could be dangerous.

That night, he carried Avery to their suite. She was exhausted and he could feel her energy seeping away. He deposited her onto her bed, kissed her forehead and turned to leave.

"Stay with me," she pleaded. "I'll behave, I promise." She crossed her heart and gave him a sexy smile.

Ryse chuckled and shook his head. "Oh temptation, thy name is Avery." But he could no more deny her than stop his heart from beating. They changed clothes and Avery cuddled up next to him in bed. "Good night, my love." He sighed as he relaxed, his Princess tucked into his arms.

"Night, bay-bee," she said with yawn.

The corner of his lips pulled back. By the gods, she was enchanting.

Before he slept, he prayed to the gods, thanking them for the woman in his arms, her life and the life they would have together.

CHAPTER TWENTY

AVERY STOOD IN THE SHOWER, LETTING THE EXTREMELY HOT WATER roll down her back. Her arms were stretched out as she leaned out the tiles. Gratitude had to be given to the person who designed this shower. It was an entire corner of the bathroom. The triangle of floor to ceiling tiles and showerheads had an unlimited supply of hot water and floral smelling shampoos.

"Mind if I join you?" Ryse stepped into the shower, not waiting for her response.

"I, um, guess not." She turned her back to him, self-conscious of her nudity. Yes, he had seen her naked and she had seen him. But things were different now. Avery lathered up a sponge and wash herself to distract from the butterflies inhabiting her belly. Ryse seemed to be completely ignoring her as he washed his hair and cleaned himself. Only when she had to reach for the shampoo did she turn to see him shaving at the mirror built into one of the tile spaces. She met his eyes for a moment and thought about how she had awakened this morning.

Sure that she was in a dream, Avery moaned at the feel of lips on her stomach. When she blinked her eyes open, she found Ryse lying between her legs. His hands were on her hips, his lips grazed her stomach and sides.

She'd giggled and ran her hands through his hair. "Well good morning to you, too." He nipped at her belly and tickled her.

His brown eyes shifted up to hers. "Your shirt was pulled up and I couldn't resist. Your skin is very—bitable."

Avery's body coiled tight. The look in his eyes was anything but playful. Her breasts grew heavy and with every kiss she became more and more aroused. Ryse's lips traveled north. He pushed her shirt up inch by inch until his fingers brushed the underside of her breasts. Under his touch her skin heated and tingled.

She buried her hands into his hair and urged him up upward. He willingly came, pressing kisses to the lower curve. When his mouth closed over the taunt peak, Avery arched off the bed. The thrill pushed her further into his hot mouth. Ryse closed his hand over her other breast and sensation swamped her. The suckling on one side, kneading on the other, combined into pleasure she had never known.

"Perfection," Ryse whispered as he switched breasts.

Avery felt his aura. It pulsed heavily with his need. His whole body was pulsing. As he merged their lips, his weight pressed her into the mattress. She cradled him between her hips and felt the extent of his desire. It was a shame that they couldn't take it any farther; she wanted him with bone-deep desperation. And she could feel how badly he wanted her.

"Ryse?" she panted, her whole body tingling from his touch. All she received was a grunt and his lips sucking on her neck. "Why are you torturin' me?"

His head popped up and his brows dipped down. "Torture?"

"You said we can't be together and yet you're teasing me like this. It's almost cruel."

"Well, I would never want you to think of me as cruel—or a tease, for that matter." With a wicked grin on his face Ryse slipped down her body and nestled his shoulders between her thighs. Avery had never been driven so mad in all her life.

As she stood in the shower and thought about what had happened next, her body heated up. Her cheeks flushed and she had to turn away from Ryse. She wasn't familiar with all the gods, but when Ryse's mouth was on her, she had cried out to them. It seemed silly to be shy now. But she was.

"There are warm towels for you, my love." Ryse kissed her

shoulder before exiting the shower. Avery had to take a few minutes to get control after he left. The attraction she had for Ryse was all-consuming. It made it difficult to think of anything else.

Pulling the towel around her, she stepped out of the shower to see Ryse slipping on a pair of pants over his boxer briefs. With his back turned, she saw a full view of his tattoo. The giant sword going down his spine was a work of art. It was instinct to reach out and touch it. With one finger, she began tracing the curves and symbols. The areas she touched glowed golden then faded. His skin sizzled under her finger. Ryse glanced over his shoulder.

Avery felt his aura open more. The sensation of two invisible hands on her shoulders made her gasp. Kneading her in the lightest way, they massaged down her back. The heat of his aura made her body melt into his. She laid her face against his strong back; her head fit right beneath his shoulder blades, a place that had been molded for her. She wrapped her arms around him, placing her palms on his chest. He took in a sharp breath. A smile stretched across her face and she kissed his back in several places.

"Your kiss is a brand on my skin," he said softly as he laced his hands over hers.

"As long as it's markin' you as mine." Avery kissed him once more and pressed her face to his back. "Nikki told me about your tattoo. It's pretty amazing that Ares drew it himself. Will you mark me when I'm yours?"

Ryse turned and took her by the hand. Together they sat on the chaise lounge in the bathroom. Ryse pulled her on top his lap, her legs on either side of him; her towel stretched and pushed up to her thighs. The towel was the only barrier between her and complete nudity as she sat on his lap. Ryse liked her in this position. She would remember that.

"I would mark you today if I knew without a doubt you had made up your mind about me. But there are still questions in your eyes." He pushed back a damp curl from her face. "I will wait until all uncertainty has left."

"I'm not *that* uncertain." Avery blushed. To prove her point, she bent to brush her lips over his. What was meant to be a simple kiss soon became two mouths tangling together. Before it went too far, Avery turned her head so that Ryse's lips moved to her chin. "How exactly does this mating thing work? How do you mark me?"

"Inside and out." He pressed a kiss to her collarbone. Holy Crap! "First you are branded with my mark."

"As in cattle brand?" She was appalled.

Ryse laughed against the skin of her neck. She shivered. "No, it is a tattoo—a smaller version of mine. My Elites and Generals have theirs on their right shoulders."

"So I'll have a tattoo on my shoulder?"

Ryse peeked up at her from under those thick black lashes. "No. I think yours will be right," he said as his finger skimmed the upper rim of her towel along her chest before pulling the towel down and nearly exposing her left breast, "here." Ryse kissed the spot over her heart.

Dizziness came over her as she tried to catch her breath and slow her erratic heartbeat. Her eyes nearly rolled back in her head at the feel of his lips on her. "Th—then what?" she stuttered.

Ryse fisted his hands in her hair and pulled her lips down to meet his, burying his tongue into her mouth. When he pulled away, they were breathing hard, hearts racing, and hormones raging out of control. "Damn." Slowly her eyes blinked open. "Will it always be like this? So intense?"

He smiled up at her. "Yes." He kissed her again, tasting her lips a final time. "It's like this with mates. Nothing can compare."

Avery wondered how much of the attraction was organic and how much of it was simply a spell woven into her blood by the gods. She didn't want to dissect that just yet. It was perfectly fine to be under a spell if it meant she and Ryse would have this magnetism forever.

But one thing did bug her. "Do you have to use the term mating? Every time you say it I think about those wildlife documentary shows I used to watch on television. They are usually talking about lions or warthogs or something equally barbaric."

Ryse's laughter filled the bathroom. It was such a lovely sound. "I can definitely be animalistic with you, my love."

Avery gave a nervous giggle. "Well there has to be about a hundred different terms for *mate*." She made air quotes. "Spouse, companion, better half, consort. Hell, I'd even answer to being your old lady. But mate rubs me wrong."

"What about lover?" Ryse touched her cheek. Avery hid her blushing face. The way he said the word turned her inside out. "Get dressed, my lover. Today you shall see what I do. We'll see what you think of me after that."

CHAPTER TWENTY-ONE

AVERY WAS READY QUICKLY. NIKKI HAD COME TO HELP HER GET dressed and braid her hair. Of course, with Nikki, nothing was simple. The braid on her head was intricate and beautiful and had a couple flowers laced through it. "What are we doing today?" she asked hesitantly.

"Today the Master intends on you getting acquainted with his Thracian side." Nikki's eyes did not meet hers in the mirror.

"Ah, hell." Avery fretted all the way to car. "Where are we going?"

"To the Thracian Training Center, my dear sister." Avery turned to see Prince Hayden walking out of the castle behind them. He was casually dressed in jeans and a hoodie, his shoulder length black hair blowing in the wind.

Sister. The thought made her stagger in her steps. Family. If she married Ryse, Avery would have a family. Hayden put his arm around her shoulders in an act of familiarity. "You don't have a weak constitution, do you?"

"What do you mean?" She slid in the car. He simply grinned. "Hayden?"

The car dropped them off in front of a collegiate brick building four stories tall. A dark-headed man as wide as a barn door guarded the front entrance. He wore the standard black of Thracian guards.

The only difference was above his left breast—the insignia of Ryse's men: the sword of Ares.

"I am Platon." He bowed deeply. "The Master requested you join the men in the contest pit at the rear of the campus," he bellowed in a baritone voice. "I will escort you through."

Hayden nodded and the three of them followed the guard. Avery questioned the need of an escort. She was quickly informed that most of these men were un-bound warriors in training. "Which means?"

"Which means they are all looking for a hot Deity chick to bind themselves to. And you fit the ticket, sister." Hayden put his arm protectively around her waist. Nikki walked closely behind them. "The Thracians come here to train. Upon graduation, they are assigned to the general armies since all the royal families have guardians. You, however, are fresh meat and of the finest cut, no less."

"If I may," Platon asked. Hayden nodded. "It is the highest honor to be selected by Master Ryse to stay here and work at the center in any capacity. To be bound to the Master's mate is of equal honor. There are over nine hundred men here right now that would fight for that position. Some would even beg." He turned and continued walking.

"Oh." Avery felt the need to crawl into a hole and hide. She looked at Nikki and whispered, "That minor detail wasn't in the book."

"Most Thracian Masters never take a mate, milady," Platon called over his shoulder. "Since Master Ryse is also a Deity, he did. You are the first. The men who serve you will go down in history." He walked them into the dormitories where the whispers and stares immediately began. Avery gazed around at the men who were doing anything from playing video games to writing and reading to talking and eating. It mirrored any all-male college campus in the human world. Except these males had very large muscles and intense eyes that followed her every movement as she walked through their common area. All of them were typical Thracians: taller than average, broad shouldered, and intimidating as hell.

The four of them exited the dorms to a training area. The expansive space contained a climbing wall, tires laid out in a grid on the ground, a muddy area covered with wires that the soldiers had to belly crawl under. There was an obstacle course and a rope climbing course the men were to climb. It was similar to the police training that Frank had mentioned to her years ago.

They entered another building that replicated the first. This one obviously housed the classes. Instead of food and video games, these men carried books and laptops.

Avery couldn't help but be aware of all the Thracian soldiers following in her wake. Men stopped what they were doing to join the procession. The term *circus freak* popped into her head and she cringed internally. Externally, she tried to remain as composed and confident as the Prince walking next to her. Even with Platon leading, Hayden holding on, and Nikki following, she felt exposed. The faces of the men were a blur. There wasn't enough time as they crossed the expanse of the common area to focus on anyone in particular—except for the one Thracian who was given as wide a berth as they were. Avery spared a glance in his direction before her feet were planted and Nikki nearly ran into her back.

The Thracian was standing away from those gathered to observe. He was only an inch taller than the others, but it was enough to make him stand out. He had blond hair past his shoulders, half of it tied back from his face. That face could have stopped traffic in the middle of NYC. It was flawless, so smooth it was unreal. With pouty lips and a boxed jaw, this man was worth a second look. As beautiful as his face was, it was his eyes that caught her attention. They were the color of a sandy beach—odd eyes that met hers for a short second before turning downward. He angled his face away as if hiding those unique eyes.

"What is it?" Hayden gently tugged her forward, but the instinct to go to this man, talk to him, was too great for Avery to ignore.

"I have to—hell, I don't know." She frowned at Hayden. "I need to talk to him." Avery pointed at the soldier and to her great astonishment his face went from tan to white to red.

Hayden gave her a confused glance before he nodded and waved the soldier over. Avery nearly laughed when he turned around trying to see who the Prince was summoning. Surprise lit his face when the crowd moved away as Avery approached. He bowed his head and went to one knee.

"Princess?" He swallowed hard.

"Stand up. Please." The soldier obeyed with haste. "I'm not comfortable with the kneeling thing yet. Heck, I'm not too comfortable with the Princess thing yet, but I'm workin' on it." She laughed nervously and the soldier smiled. He had a kind face that made her instantly comfortable in his presence. "You have really unique eyes."

He looked away again. "Yes, milady."

"Why do you hide them? Dyna has unique eyes and she doesn't hide her face."

The young soldier popped his gaze up, then down again.

Avery tried to hide her smile. "What's your name?"

"Dante, at your command, milady."

"I'm Avery." She stuck her hand out to shake. All the Thracians around them took in a collective breath as Dante slid his hand into hers. There was something that made his peers nervous—or jealous, if the stares and shocked expressions they received were any indication. Hayden had a single brow raised as he and Nikki watched the reactions of the Thracians.

Avery leaned in and whispered, "You draw as much attention as I do."

Dante chuckled with her. "You shouldn't be touching me," he whispered back in the same conspiratorial tone.

Avery rolled her eyes. She assumed Ryse had everyone afraid of offending her in the slightest. "Yes, I know. But where I come from it's just good manners to shake someone's hand upon introductions."

"As it is in my country."

"Where is that?"

"I grew up in a Haven South of Rome, milady." This didn't surprise Avery. Nikki had explained that all Olympians who didn't or couldn't assimilate into the human world remained in the Haven's. With his eyes and unearthly good looks, Dante would fit in perfectly with her at the freak show.

Hayden stepped up. "Not to interrupt, but we do have somewhere to be, sister."

Avery nodded, but kept her eyes on Dante. Her gut was telling her there was a reason those sandy eyes caught her attention. There was no rational explanation. She wasn't sexually attracted to him. Dante intrigued her in a new and unfamiliar way. It felt wrong to simply turn and walk off.

As if he saw the indecision in her face, Hayden made the verdict for her. "Dante, is it?"

"Yes, my Prince."

"Hand your things to someone who can put them safely away. You will come with us."

Dante's eyes touched on a few Thracians before he found a willing pair of hands. Avery noticed the fellow student took his books as if they carried a hex. Nonetheless, the soldier scurried off after Dante nodded in thanks.

"Okay then." Avery tried to break the awkward silence that followed. "Let's go see what's goin' on."

Hayden pulled Avery back to his side and Dante fell in step with Nikki. Platon gave the new member of their entourage a curt nod before leading on.

"Have a liking for the brute?" Hayden whispered, wiggling his brows.

Avery elbowed him. "I'm following a gut reaction. Ask me when I figure all this Olympian crap out."

Hayden laughed out loud and patted her arm. "Gut instincts are usually the gods' way of nudging you in the right direction."

When they exited the building, the sounds of many men gathered in one place filled the air. Even louder was the whistle their escort let out. It got all the attention of the men standing around. When they turned, the chatter stopped.

"Make way!" Platon yelled to the mob. The throng parted, letting their entourage pass by. Avery tried to remember that this was a much different world that the one she was used to. Here, she was a Princess, royalty. As she walked through the crowd and into a large circular area, she kept that in mind. There was an instant when she felt as though she had stepped back in time. "There is a Roman soldier at my back and I just stepped into the mini-Coliseum. This is kinda freaky," she whispered to Hayden.

Hayden laughed happily as he escorted her down the rows filled with Thracians. Whatever was going to happen in this place, she had a front row view. Down below in the sunken pit, there was a scene that gave her a sick feeling. Readying themselves for a fight were Ryse—and Brenden.

CHAPTER TWENTY-TWO

"HAYDEN, TELL ME WHAT'S GOING ON RIGHT *NOW*!"

Hayden's casual smile turned into a look of concern. "Avery, darling, you didn't think that Ryse was going to let Brenden be bound to you without putting him through hell first, did you?" She tried to answer, but couldn't speak. Hayden put his hand on the base of her neck. It was a very possessive gesture. Odd. "Brenden has to earn the right to be your personal guardian. No one can beat my brother, but that doesn't mean they do not have to try. If he is found fit, then Ryse will accept his request."

Ryse saw them sitting down and walked over. His shirtless body made Avery flush. Only the expression on his face could her snap out of the dirty thoughts starring this muscled god before her. Ryse was in full Thracian mode. The only protective gear he wore were two metal wristbands that stretched from his wrist to his elbows.

In contrast, Brenden was wearing a leather breastplate that wrapped around his back and protective leather padding on his legs. It still made Avery worry.

"Listen to me very carefully," Ryse said, bracing his arms on the half wall that separated the pit from the spectators. Avery instinctively leaned closer to him. "There is no one in this place more worried than you are and there is no one who needs to hide it more."

"Are you gonna hurt him?" she whispered, fearful and aware of the many sets of ears nearby.

"He has to prove himself and he has to be punished for going to you before he came to me."

"Ryse, please—"

"Avery!" he growled. It was a command for silence, one not to be disobeyed. "Do not question me on this. Sit here, watch, and remember that you have expectations to meet as my mat- con- sort." She almost didn't catch the slight twitch of his lips before he kissed her and walked away.

When she leaned back into the stadium-style seat, her back hit Hayden's arm. He gripped her shoulder and patted it comfortingly. They waited a few more moments and let the final men take their seats. Philippe, Cutter, Hammon, and Yankee—the Elites—came to sit directly behind her.

"You cook again today, Princess?" Cutter asked with a smile. "I dream of fried potatoes last night."

Today was full of surprises; Cutter actually spoke! "I suppose I could whip something up."

Cutter smiled and Philippe removed his cigarette to speak. "I eat anything you fix, *Principessa*." Even when he grinned, his eyes looked sad. It made her wonder what was behind them.

"Thanks, darlin'." Avery smiled. "Hammon, good to see you."

The charcoal-colored man nodded. "As always, milady, the pleasure is mine."

Avery's eyes fell on the last one to take a seat. Yankee appeared characteristically annoyed. She forced herself to address him. He was one of Ryse's trusted Elites, after all. "Hello, Yankee."

He turned his head, removed his sunglasses, then leaned over the back of her seat to talk to her. He pointed his sunglasses at Bren. "You really going to take little brother if Master Ryse doesn't kill him?" He sounded like the idea was completely preposterous.

Refusing to be needled, Avery joked, "What's the matter, Yankee, jealous?"

He looked at her with eyes that promised merciless death to those who cross him. "Not hardly. I think the two of you together might as well paint a big target across your chests."

"Excuse me?"

Yankee leaned down so close she knew his next sentence was for her only. "You are the first ever mate of a Thracian Master. Brenden, though he aggravates the piss out of me, is as famous. He's already had too many close calls in his young life, with people out to bag him for the prize that he is. Ryse might as well package the two of you up with a bow and set you on the curb." Yankee then sat back in his seat and slumped down.

Before Avery could reply or react, silence fell on the arena. General Falcon stepped out into the center. Ryse and Brenden came to stand on either side of him, two contenders ready to face off. Only one of them showed signs of worry.

Nikki reached over and slipped her hand into Avery's. Her delicate hand was shaking.

"Thracians!" Falcon's voice boomed like thunder around the arena. The one word brought all the men to attention. "Bow to your Master." Avery felt weird being one of the only three people in the arena not standing to bow. She, Nikki, and Hayden were not soldiers so Hayden told them to stay seated.

Falcon continued, "Thracians! Bow to your Prince." Hayden kicked back in his chair as hundreds of men bowed to him. Ryse gave him a cocky salute that he returned with a single finger. The exchange between brothers made Avery roll her eyes. Hayden laughed and clapped when Ryse flipped him off as well. "Thracians! Bow to your Princess and Master's Consort."

Oh, shit. Wanting desperately to sink into her seat, but knowing she couldn't show any signs of weakness, Avery kept her eyes on Ryse. The pride as he met her gaze was overwhelming. When he bent at his waist to honor her, she found herself smiling at her sexy warrior.

⸻

It was a smile that made Ryse's heart jump out of his chest. Without a doubt, he would take on the world for that woman.

Now that introductions were over, Ryse poised for—

"Thracians!" Falcon shot Ryse a wary glance. "Welcome honored guest, Princess Salina of Europe."

Shit.

Ryse looked up to see Salina and her entourage making their way down the stairs. Salina took a seat one row away from Avery and Hayden. The woman had evil written in her eyes. Ryse looked at Brenden. He didn't have to tell Brenden that this changed things. Brenden's gifts were rumored all over the world. The mysterious Elite had only revealed them completely to Ryse.

"Warriors," Falcon called their attention. "Shake hands."

Ryse and Brenden gripped forearms.

"You know I will not go easy on you," Ryse warned.

"And you know that I wish to keep my secrets."

"Then for both our sakes, I hope that you will be creative. I would hate for our audience to get bored."

Brenden smirked. "I gotta deep bag of tricks, old man."

Everyone in the arena knew that there was no possible way to beat Ryse. A warrior might be able to get in some good shots and Ryse relished the challenge that Bren presented. Some of that challenge would be trying not to kill this younger man. If Ryse put all his strength, all his powers into a fight, he could kill Brenden and every warrior in this arena in an instant with the flick of his wrist.

Brenden had to prove that he could be a challenge to someone as strong as Ryse. Only then would he be deemed fit to protect the one thing in this world Ryse cherished most. This meant that Ryse would have to let him get in some offensive strikes.

"Rules have been set prior to the match. Two tests will be given.

Round one is a natural fight. Neither opponent can use powers or weapons, only raw abilities. The second will include weapons, powers, or both. No one in the audience may interfere with these tests. Punishment for interference with the match will be implemented at the Master's discretion." Falcon held up his fist as Ryse and Brenden got into position.

"Begin!"

Ryse looked at Brenden. He was an Elite. He was special. But he had touched Avery. His arms had been on Ryse's woman, romantic or not, and now was his chance to take out the aggression he felt.

That thought was all it took before Ryse launched his body towards the boy.

CHAPTER TWENTY-THREE

AVERY DIDN'T BREATHE AS SHE WATCHED BRENDEN'S BODY FLY across the dirt floor of the arena. Ryse had tackled him with the skill of a professional football player. Brenden, half the size of Ryse, hit the ground and sent his attacker up over his head with his legs. Ryse did a quick flip and landed on his feet. Their next moves were made at lightning speed.

In typical crowd mentality, the Thracian spectators were cheering and making sound effects after every contact was made. As hard as it was to take her eyes off Ryse and Brenden, she couldn't help but look to see what everyone else was doing.

Nikki was sitting on the edge of her seat eyes focused, lips drawn. Hayden was entertained at the spectacle. He gently rubbed Avery's shoulders, and she wondered if he realized it. There was something twitchy about his movements. He was nervous and trying to hide it. Dante and Yankee, like most of the other men, were getting into the fight. Yankee enjoyed it a little too much.

Then she looked over at Salina. Bad idea.

The snake-witch was practically drooling. The lady sitting beside her leaned over, giggling with her like schoolgirls. Salina had one manicured finger pulling on the collar of her shirt, as of ready to rip it off.

"Don't look over there." Nikki nudged her. "That dreadful woman is practically undressing herself."

"She happens to be lusting over *my*—whatever he is." Avery turned back to watch Ryse. The first thing she noticed was the blood coming from his lip. But it was nothing compared to Brenden's swelling eye and busted nose. The blond boy was picking himself up off the ground after a kick to his chest. Compared to Ryse's large mass, Brenden appeared nothing more than a teenager. It seemed an extremely unfair match.

"I don't know if I can watch this." Avery made sure that her face gave away nothing. The comment was made for Hayden and Nikki only.

It was Hayden who leaned over to whisper in her ear. "Brenden isn't the only one with something to prove. If the men ever begin to doubt Ryse's strength, it opens him for attack. The same goes for you and me. So be strong."

His words made Avery turn. A moment's eye contact made her realize that Hayden was in the same boat. If he showed any fear or hesitation at what was going on before them, he would be viewed as the weaker brother. If he was viewed as weaker, he could be used as leverage against Ryse. Avery could be used for the same thing. So much for Hayden being the lighthearted little brother. This man had as many pressures as his sibling.

Hayden kicked back in his chair and propped his feet up on the railing in front of him. He could have been sitting in a recliner watching a WWE match on the television.

She sucked up her girly fears and turned to the match. The final move had been made. Rysc had flipped Brenden over onto his back and had him by the throat. Ryse was bleeding from both his lip and nose, and his chest was already bruising from Brenden's punches. Ryse released him with the roar of the crowd and stood over Brenden's submitted body. Then he held out his hand to offer his help.

"Stand. Nod in acceptance. Clap." Hayden pushed her shoulder so she would obey.

Avery complied. She stood and bowed her head slightly to accept the end of the match and applaud the two warriors.

"Test one completed. Master Ryse, pass or fail?" General Falcon asked as moderator for the match.

Avery's heart lodged in her throat as she watched Ryse take a moment to think. He nodded in acceptance. "Pass." Avery cheered in earnest.

Brenden walked up to Ryse and said something. Ryse nodded and walked away. Falcon announced a five-minute break before the final match.

⚊ ⚊ ⚬ ⚬ ⚊ ⚊

Ryse motioned for Hammon and Cutter to speak with him while he wiped the blood from his lips. Brenden had gotten in some very impressive shots. It was a nice challenge to meet someone so strong.

"We have a problem," he said to his two advisors. "Even in the middle of a fight, Brenden caught a scent."

"The boy is truly skilled." Hammon began scanning crowd. "What was it?"

"Someone here carries a scent he recognized from Avery's house."

"I do not see anyone that I wouldn't recognize." Cutter shook his head. "I've been watching students and staff. No one unfamiliar."

Ryse glanced up in the stands where Salina sat. Hammon caught the quick eye movement. "You think it is someone with her."

"Yes. You two to stay close to Avery and do *not* let her out of your sight."

He turned to look at his opponent standing across the arena, leaning casually against the wall. Brenden had hearing like none other. The entire exchange with Hammon and Cutter had not escaped him. He tilted his head to the side, towards Salina's entourage.

Ryse looked to his Elites. Yankee had seen the signal, too. He was heading up the stairs to the exit. Noting the subtle hints, Philippe followed.

Taking a chance, Ryse looked at Salina. The troll preened in her chair from his attention. There was no fooling him. As a Thracian Master, he had more of an insight to people's auras than the rest of his race. There was malevolence about her aura that he couldn't miss. He wondered how anyone else could.

"Warriors," Falcon called the arena to attention again. "For the next test, all Olympian and Thracian gifts will be permitted, including weapons. Since this is not a match to the death, Master Ryse will decide when the match is over."

He turned to the two men who'd joined him in the center of the circle. "Begin."

"Don't hold back," Ryse whispered to Brenden. "Show them what you are really made of."

"I can kill you," he warned.

"No, you can't. But if provocation is what you need to unleash your beasts, then I will be happy to give it to you."

Ryse knew that Brenden had more control over himself than all the Thracians in this place put together. To get him to submit to the animal inside would take even more control than leashing it.

When he found Brenden, nearly fifty years ago, he had found a monster. Hammon woke in the middle of the night sensing an Olympian power greater than anything the tracker had ever felt. Ryse and his Elites made their way to a town in Texas west of Dallas. What they had found was carnage.

Brenden was in animal form—a mixture of bear, cat, wolf and eagle—and scared out of his mind. It had been the first time he had ever changed. Beside him lay the body of young woman. Ryse immediately feared the worst. But the beast was protecting the body with a ferocity that did not make Ryse believe she was his prey. It had taken hours to convince the animal to calm down and let Hammon inspect the girl.

Only days later did they find out what really happened that night. Megan, Brenden's younger sister who he adored, had been on a date. Bren had received a frantic call made from a bathroom stall at a bar. Being only nineteen at the time, she wasn't supposed to be there in the first place. Meg pleaded for her brother to come get her. When Brenden had arrived at the bar, it was too late; the boyfriend had abducted her.

The frantic state he went into caused the first of his physical changes. Brenden had remembered being able to scent his sister's perfume among the smells of car exhaust. It was not something a human nose could have caught. He pursued the car on foot for nearly six miles, never getting tired. His ears picked up the sounds of struggle and the sounds of a woman's muffled cry for help.

Following the signs his body was giving him, Brenden ran from the road through the woods. What he found had caused him to growl, the wild animals restless beneath the surface.

His sister lay on the ground, naked and bloodied, a knife pressed to her throat. The anger boiled inside Brenden, forcing his body to change forms into the most ferocious of beasts. Brenden had killed the bastard, but not before he could lodge the knife into his sister's neck. The man's body would never be found.

Guilt over his sister's death was the one thing that always brought out his worst. As low and cheap as it was to use such a tragedy to provoke Brenden, it would work. Ryse needed the boy to show what a truly horrific beast he could be. He only prayed that Brenden would forgive his betrayal when the fight was over.

CHAPTER TWENTY-FOUR

B RENDEN KNEW THAT RYSE WOULD PUSH EVERY BUTTON HE COULD to make him fight. He didn't have to try to get upset. Ryse would piss him off. When he did change, he hoped Avery didn't get too freaked out. Glancing up at the gorgeous redhead beside the Princess, he prayed Nikki wouldn't get too freaked out, either. Whatever buds of affection they had blooming would die if she was terrified of him.

At this moment, he needed to focus on the killer in front of him. Ryse was pulling his power from his soul. His eyes were already beginning to glow.

Gods help him, this was about to get ugly.

It was time. Ryse felt the powers given to him from Ares begin to stir within his body. The microscopic particles of his physical being reacted to the mental command. With a light shining from the palm of his right hand, he thought about his sword: the weight, the coolness of the metal, the feel of the blade striking. It appeared. With the blade in hand, he stalked to his prey.

Brenden had his own weapons drawn—two six-inch blades. Since speed was one of his Olympian gifts, the knives were as deadly in his hands as the large sword. The boy held the knives and prepared to strike.

It was Ryse who began the dance. Brenden was still worried about letting go, so the Master flung his sword out with force that could have split a tree. Brenden dodged, getting only the very edge of the blade against his skin. Nothing more than a paper cut. Three more strikes were made, all offensive moves from Ryse.

"Fight me, boy!" Ryse commanded.

"I don't think this is a good idea, Master." Brenden circled him from a distance.

"If you want this position, you will fight, damn it!" Ryse twirled his sword quicker than a lightning bolt and felt the blade cut through the flesh of Brenden's leg.

The boy cried out and Ryse knew he was on the right track. "Who the hell are you to think you have the right?" Ryse danced around the boy until his blade struck him in the arm. "You are too weak to go against me. You are too weak to be Avery's guardian."

That hit the nerve Ryse was looking for. Brenden's knives came at him and sliced his chest. Ryse smirked at him.

"You can do better. Did you puss around like this with Meg's killer?"

"Do *not* go there, Ryse!"

Brenden's eyes began to change and Ryse pressed forward. Their blades engaged in a series of whips and lashes. Brenden tackled Ryse and they rolled on the ground for a moment before Ryse used his powers to push Brenden across the arena.

"More," he commanded. Bren was not giving his all yet.

"No."

"Would you not give more for Avery? Does she not deserve more than what you gave Meg?"

Bren went predator still. "You son of a bitch." The yellow demon eyes of his beast grew narrow.

"You were afraid then, and you are afraid now. Meg deserved better and so does Avery. You aren't even good enough to protect

Nikki." Bringing up Nikki was unnecessary, Ryse only wished to let him know he knew his secret. It was just another button.

And it worked. Screaming a line of profanities that would make a sailor cringe, the animals inside of Brenden took over. Ryse braced for battle. Now he would really have to defend himself.

⬤

"What is he saying to him?" Avery was unable to keep the fear from her voice. Ryse was glowing with a white light. Brenden was convulsing, his body contorting into something unknown.

"Whatever it was, it's making him change forms." Hayden pulled Avery into his shoulder protectively.

"No," Nikki whispered helplessly. "No, he can't." The panic and trepidation in Nikki's eyes was familiar. It conveyed the same fear Avery had for Ryse. Nikki cared for Brenden.

Avery took the other woman's hand. "It's okay. They won't really hurt each other. I hope."

The crowd hushed as Brenden's other form appeared. He was a beast as Avery had never seen. Brenden had not only changed into one animal; he had morphed into a combination. His body resembled a grizzly, broad and massive. Growls that came from his throat were from the muzzle of a wolf. Talons clawed at the earth beneath him. Brenden reared back on his hind legs and wailed out to the sky. The sound pierced Avery to her core and pain and anger in that animal's cry was heartbreaking.

CHAPTER TWENTY-FIVE

How could Ryse push him to do this? How could he be so cruel and heartless? I can't be with a man that would torture another living creature.

The gargantuan creature charged at Ryse and went straight for his jugular. She cringed as Ryse threw down his sword and crouched to receive the frontal attack.

Monsters, all of them. Monsters. I have to get out of here. I have to get away from these barbarians. I'm not like them; they'll kill me. I have to get out of here.

Avery tried to leave but a firm hand caught her. Hayden pulled her closer to his side. "Calm down, sister."

"Something is wrong, Hayden." She tried to shake the terror in her mind. But it was spouting up from a place she didn't recognize.

"It's alright. Ryse is in control."

"It's not Ryse that I'm worried about." Head in her hands, she watched the men battle. Brenden was raw power and brute strength. But Ryse was grace and agility with a lethal edge. The fight below was bloody.

This is too gruesome. I can't watch. How could they want me to witness this? I have to get away from these people. Even Hayden. He's forcing me to endure this. I have to go. I have to go.

"I have to go. I can't watch this." Her body shook.

Hayden bent his head to her ear. "Brenden is winding down, Avery. It's a show, probably so Salina can see Bren's strength. Trust me, okay?"

She took a deep breath and nodded. She had to get a handle on herself. Ryse was only testing Brenden, not hurting him. It was a show. Hayden moved his arms and cheered on his brother.

For Salina! It was all for Salina. Ryse had wanted her to see his strength. He still wants her and nothing I do can change that.

Avery shook her head. This was not right. These thoughts were not her own.

I'm going crazy. It's too much.

Avery looked over at Salina watching Ryse as a cat watches fish in a bowl.

I can't compete with her. She's beautiful, powerful and she's already been with Ryse once. How do I know that he wouldn't go back to her? And what am I compared to her? I'm nothing. I'm not Deity material. I'm just a farm girl. I'm unclean and he will never be physically satisfied with me like he was with her. I'm not good enough to be his mate. He will never love me and I'll never be safe away from here. I'd be better off dead—

The thoughts stopped as soon as a heavy hand rested on her shoulder. Avery turned to see Dante crouched behind her, his face contorted into an expression of confusion. His sand colored eyes had no pupils.

"What are you doing?" Avery asked.

"Prince Hayden." He ignored Avery's question. Hayden turned to look at the Thracian soldier who had his hand on the Princess. His eyes zeroed in on the touch and a familiar possessiveness glinted in them. "May I have your permission to move next to the Princess? She is in need of my assistance."

Hayden narrowed his eyes at Dante for only a second. "You have amazing intuition, sister. Nikki, let Dante take your seat. Come sit by me."

Avery watched, clueless, as the move happened. Nikki didn't question her orders. They were both lost when Dante took his seat and put his hand on Avery's forearm. He looked at her with those incredible eyes. "If you have any more thoughts that are not your own, let me know. But you should not."

"I'm sorry?"

Hayden put his arm back around Avery's shoulder. "It seems that of all the Thracians in the center, you picked the one you would need today. Dante has a defensive power."

Thoughts that were not her own, defensive powers, all those things flowing through her mind that she would never usually feel.

"Salina," Avery growled. Salina was a telepath, able to infect people with her thoughts.

"Smart girl," Hayden smiled. "You keep Dante nearby and she can't reach you."

She whipped her head around to look at Dante. His lips barely showed a smile before he returned his attention to the pit.

Ryse was fighting off the beast without breaking a sweat. Brenden had gotten in some good blows. The blood on his arm and chest were seeping proof. But Brenden was worse off. Even with his beastly fur, Avery could see him bleeding heavily and panting with exhaustion. It didn't slow him down. Bren was gnashing his teeth, sinking them into Ryse's body. Quick movements from Ryse had the teeth out of his flesh and Bren's head flying backwards. It was a close fight.

Her heart nearly burst from her chest when she saw Ryse levitate in the arena to dodge an attack. He stretched out his arms to the sky and his body lifted from the ground. A white light glowed in his eyes and it scared the hell out of her. With a loud clap, a wave of sound spread from his hands. It hit Brenden and he went down. The shock wave burst out and hit everyone in the arena. It knocked the crowd back to their chairs. Avery was glad she had been sitting. If she had been on her feet, like the rest of the spectators, she, too, would have been pushed over.

When the crowd gained their bearings, Ryse was the only one left standing, Brenden's unmoving body at his feet.

"BREN!" Nikki screamed and covered her mouth.

CHAPTER TWENTY-SIX

"I THOUGHT YOU'D KILLED HIM!" AVERY EXCLAIMED AS THEY SAT IN the medical center patching up the guys.

Ryse smiled and pulled Avery to his chest, "I'm sorry, my love. Now that the beast is out of the bag, people should begin to hear about the monster that is guarding my woman." He hadn't wanted to use Ares' gifts to end the match. But he could sense Nikki's worry and Hayden's frustration about something. It had been time to prove his point and Brenden had done well.

"Speaking of, brother," Hayden interjected. "It seems that the Princess has already begun choosing guardians. The warrior-in-training, Dante, waits in the hall."

Ryse nodded. "Come, Avery. Let's give Brenden a minute to rest. Nikki, keep cleaning his wounds." He ushered Avery out the door, but not before she turned and ran to hug Brenden. The boy chuckled and returned the hug, assuring her he was fine.

Out in the hall, Dante was standing at attention his eyes straight ahead. When Ryse and Hayden came out of the room with Avery in tow, he went to one knee.

"Rise," Ryse commanded. "I want all of us to convene in the secure conference room at the Palace in one hour." He looked at Hammon. "Do we know where Yankee and Philippe went?"

"No, Master."

Ryse nodded and clenched his jaw. "Find out." Once more he turned to Dante. "You are about to complete your final stage of training, are you not?"

"Yes, Master. I have a couple weeks left."

"Go to your dorm. Get your belongings. I'll have someone prepare you a suite close to the Princess. Be in the conference room in an hour."

Dante bowed and left quickly. Ryse looked at Avery, who was still pale. "Come. You and I need to talk."

Avery slouched. "I hate it when you say that."

⚊⚊· ᵒ°ₒ ·⚊⚊

Nikki bandaged the wounds on Brenden's arm. She remained quiet. Her head was full of thoughts she wished would go away. Ryse had used his powers to stop Brenden; the whole audience felt it. All she could think about was the picture of Ryse kneeling over Brenden's body, still and broken. The blast of power had knocked him unconscious.

One of the first ones to her feet, Nikki hadn't been able to breathe. Terror gripped her. Only when she saw Ryse pull Brenden up from the ground did she take in air again.

"Your hands are shaking," Brenden whispered as she tended to his arm.

"They are not. You be still," she barked out, trying to cover the way his sweet honeyed voice caressed her ears. The feelings had never been spoken, the thoughts never voiced. What she and Brenden had was nothing more than glances that lasted a little too long or smiles that seemed too intimate in otherwise casual settings. Yesterday at dinner he had touched her elbow to ask for a refill of his glass then she had winked at him after a clever joke he made. Such minute things. Such great things.

Nikki finished up with his arm and moved to the two gashes across his chest and abdomen. "Stand," she demanded.

"Yes, ma'am." He stood up and let her clean him. Her shaking hands gripped a wet cloth that she slowly wiped his skin.

"Nikki," Brenden stopped her hand. "Please."

She lost it. "What were you thinking? Do you realize what could have—" Her words froze on her tongue when his knuckles caressed her cheek.

He smiled that boyish grin and rubbed her face. "You're so pretty, Nikki." Brenden reached up and tugged at her ponytail. "Real pretty."

"And you're an idiot, Bren." Tears fell down her cheeks. She wiped them away. "Curse you, making me cry."

Brenden couldn't help but smile as she gained her composure. "You weren't worried about lil' ol' me, were you?"

Nikki put one hand on her hip and jabbed the wet cloth at his torn torso with the other. He yelped with pain. "Yes, you fool. I was worried about you. I can't for the life of me justify the emotion."

She wiped him down and covered him in a healing cream. The caress of her hands made him suck in a sharp breath. The fuming façade dropped and she looked at him with worry. "Did I hurt you?" Brenden's lazy smile spread his lips wide and Nikki realized she had been played. "You're a scamp."

"And you're an angel."

"Don't say things like that." She took a large role of gauze in her hand.

"Why not?"

She looked at him as if he were dense in the head. He shrugged at the implications of her look. "Brenden, you are now the head guardian of Avery. Your sole focus has to be on her. I'm her Shadow Lady. Don't you think that's a conflict of interest?"

"Do you think I can't multitask?"

Wrapping his wounds, she circled him with her arms, taking care to make sure they were not too tight to be uncomfortable.

When she passed around to his front again, he bent down and tried to kiss her.

"Stop," she said, turning her cheek.

"Why not? You know there's something here, Nikki."

His back seemed to be a safer place so she brought the gauze around. "You're a Thracian and I'm a servant. There are lines, barriers. And if we do…then we can't…and I…well, I don't want to start what was never meant to be finished. Things will get complicated and we both have duties we must fulfill. If it goes badly and I have to look at you everyday—"

"Ryse knows."

"What?" Her fingers fumbled in their task of cutting gauze and she nearly dropped the scissors.

"He knows that I have feelings for you. It was what set me off today. Ryse said that you and Avery and…and Meg deserved better."

Nikki went completely still. It was no secret that Meg was not to be mentioned. Slowly, carefully, Nikki stepped to look him in the eye. "You know he did *not* mean that. He was only fingering a wound so that you could change forms."

"Yeah, I know." But it still hurt him deeply and that emotion was written like a book all over his sweet face.

Nikki took a gamble with her own control and palmed his cheek. "If it were true, he would never allow you to be Avery's guardian, especially if he knows I might be a distraction. The Master trusts you. I know Avery holds you highly."

"And you?"

Nikki paused, searching for any sign of hesitation in her heart, but none existed. Instead of doing the proper thing, Nikki was honest. "I can barely remember how to breathe when you are near. And I fear it will only get worse as the days go by."

Never in a million lifetimes would she have guessed that her first kiss would be in a clinic room surrounded by sterile furniture and bloodied rags. And never in a million lifetimes would she have guessed that it would have been so perfect.

—⋅—⋅ ⚬ ⋅—⋅—

The minute they got into their room and the door was closed, Avery turned to face Ryse, but no words came to her. She sat down in one of the chairs and put her head in her hands.

"Brenden did very well today. He earned the right to be your guardian. Dante also proved to have potential for a position with you as well."

"Ryse. Shut up." Avery rubbed her temple. "Please," she added.

He came to stand in front of her. "You're upset."

"Very good observation, Captain Obvious." She looked up just in time to see his lip twitch as he controlled the urge to smile. "Will I ever get used to this?"

"Yes, my love." He took her cheek into his palm. "You have been here for only days. Don't expect to it to be a quick adjustment. You are still young to this life."

"Ryse, how old *are* you?" she said, tilting her head to the side. "I'm supposed to be your consort and I don't even know how old you are. I know not to believe my eyes around here. Especially after today."

He moved his shoulders in a flippant manner. "I am somewhere around two hundred and seventy-five. I lost count."

Her jaw dropped to the floor and her eyes popped out of her head. "Jeez, you're old!"

The rumble of his laughter filled the room. Avery loved that laughter. It was his light, happy laugh. She had the feeling not many people heard it. "And you are but a babe!" He chuckled.

"Here I was, thinking we were gonna have an uneventful day." She smirked.

The light coming in from the wall of windows was shining on his black silky hair. Ryse had cleaned up after his match and the black shirt he wore did wonderful things to his coloring. His eyes made

Avery think of melted chocolate—melted chocolate that she would love to pour all over just to feel his tongue lick—

"Avery!" he exclaimed with a devilish curve to his lips. "What were you thinking just now?"

Dang, how did he know? "Nothing."

"I'm serious, Avery. I could almost read your thoughts." His face was puzzled and delighted at once. Avery was embarrassed and tingling inside from the nature of her thoughts. "What were you thinking?"

Avery bent her blushing face down and spoke to her lap. "I was thinking about the color of your eyes."

Ryse picked her up out of the chair with so little effort and held her. "And?"

"You're a very good lookin' man." She pet his chest. Those eyes held such delight that she smiled. "Can I tell you something?"

"Anything," he said, running his hand through her hair.

"This morning, when you told me that the gods made us for each other, I didn't believe that. Mostly 'cause I have no idea what kind of guy I prefer personality-wise. But I will say that if old Zeus and I sat around making men the way I like 'em, you'd be the end result." She rubbed his chest and his round muscular shoulders. "I could look at you all day long and never quit feeling like the luckiest woman alive."

Ryse sat there quietly. So quietly that it made her blush. "Say something," she whispered.

Ryse's face gave away nothing. It made her wonder if he was feeling anything at all. What she said wasn't exactly the most poetic of compliments, but she hoped that's how he would take it. Maybe he was perturbed that she focused on his appearance not his abilities, especially after the morning they'd had.

"Ryse?"

"No one…" He let out a ragged breath, cleared his throat and started again. "No one has ever paid me such a compliment. Not anyone who mattered anyway."

"I have a real hard time believing that you don't have women falling at your feet." She buried her face into the curve of his neck.

"Other women's words have been nothing but noise in my head. It's different coming from your lips." He squeezed her tighter. "Your opinion means the world to me."

"When I was sitting in the arena, and Salina was putting all those thoughts into my head about you being a monster, I knew something was wrong. I'd never look at you that way."

Every muscle in his body went rigid. Ryse pulled her face up to meet his. The kind and loving Ryse was gone and the gladiator from the arena took his place. "The bitch did *what?*"

CHAPTER TWENTY-SEVEN

THE TENSION IN THE ROOM WAS THICK. TROY SPOKE FROM THE HEAD of the table and all attention went to him. "First of all, I would like to congratulate Brenden for his valiant match this morning. My son tells me that you put up an honorable fight and earned your wounds well. Praises to you on your new position."

Troy began pumping his fist on the table. All the men in the room joined him. All the Elites and heads of security were there. It was a thousand wonders that the table held up. Avery took her cue from Dyna and clapped. Brenden took the praise and with humility and honor. He bowed his head to his king.

Troy continued, "Next I would like to express gratitude to our young soldier, Dante. I believe Dynasty should inform you of why his presence was so pivotal this morning."

Dyna stood regally, her chin high and her eyes landing on each person in the room. "Yesterday evening I was given a vision of to-day's events. In my vision, Dante was not present. There was no one to stop the onslaught of negative thoughts streaming into Avery's mind. I blame this partially on the fact that her aura is still unre-leased and therefore she is completely unshielded from such mental attacks. This is a problem I plan to remedy myself today. The prop-ositions placed in Avery's conscious had one goal in mind: to make her leave. Salina preyed on her own internal fears and indecisions. Had her games worked, Avery would have tried to run, or worse."

Avery felt the need to slump in her chair and bury her heated face. Would anyone notice if she slipped out of the room? What Dyna was saying insinuated that she was weak, frail and disloyal to Ryse. The many eyes that looked at her now were full of everything from pity to shame.

"Make no mistake, gentleman," Dyna said taking the attention off Avery. "Our little Grace would not make such a decision on her own. I've seen her heart and there is no question in my mind where her loyalties lie."

Ryse took Avery's hand and pressed it to his mouth. "Nor mine." His words were for her, but he said them loud enough so that the entire room heard.

"This only goes to show how vindictive the thoughts were," Yankee said, balling up his fist in front of his mouth. Heads nodded in agreement.

"May I speak, Majesty?" Dante said from his corner of the room.

"Yes, warrior. I am anxious to hear your thoughts," Troy answered.

Dante stepped up to address the table. "My gift often allows me to absorb some of the powers being thrown at the charge I am shielding. It's often a negative thing, but today it allowed me to see what the European Princess was depositing into her mind." He lowered his head. He only spoke again when he could unclench his jaw and steady his shaking hands. "She was not only trying to get the Grace to leave. Salina was trying to convince Avery that she would be harmed. She painted the picture of Master Ryse being a monster and Prince Hayden being a threat. Other things, which I will not say in respect for my Princess, were much worse."

Dyna peered at the young warrior and cleared her throat to hush the irate men in the room. The woman possessed such grace and poise to make her equally as powerful as the men. "Dante, my vision ended with her trying to commit suicide. Is it your opinion that Salina was attempting to put that notion into her mind?"

"What?" Ryse stood so quickly that his chair flew out from behind him. Troy held up a hand to calm his son.

Dante didn't flinch like Avery did when Ryse exploded. He kept his stoic demeanor and answered the question. "Yes, my Queen. I heard it myself before I decided to step in." Then he turned his head to Avery. "Please forgive me for not intervening sooner. But I did not know how such physical contact would be taken."

"It's not your fault, Dante," Avery said, trying to comfort his obvious guilt. "I'm glad you were there."

"I believe we can all say the same." Troy gave his eldest son a piercing look. Ryse nodded in agreement, but he did not take his seat when Hammon righted his chair. He paced behind Avery.

"Doesn't this constitute as an attack on a Deity?" Ryse barked out.

The General and the Prince exchanged glances. As unofficial Historian, Hayden knew the laws of their people well. Avery could read his face, though she had only known him for a day.

"I'm not a Deity," Avery sighed. "I'm just a farm girl with freak abilities." Unable to make eye contact, Avery looked down. Ryse touched her nape.

"Since the Princess has not been marked or bound in any official way," Falcon began, "she is not technically a Deity. We all know she has the anointment of the gods for the potential of mating with a Deity. As of now, she is not blood bound to the protections of our Deity laws."

"That's bullshit!" Brenden and Yankee said in unison. For two men that disliked each other, they sure did think a lot alike.

"I have to agree," Troy said under his breath.

A debate of how to handle the problematic snake-witch Princess proceeded. Mixed in the conversation was the disappearing scent Brenden had caught during their match. Philippe had searched but found no one unauthorized. Yankee pestered Brenden about it being a distraction so that they didn't see him get his ass kicked.

That brought up the question of Salina's involvement in the attack at Avery's home. How else would a person with that scent show up there and in the arena with today?

The questions and scenarios were tossed about for nearly two hours. No longer were they all sitting at the table, but up talking, pacing, and thinking. Dyna had motioned for Avery to join her in the far corner of the room. Hanna, Dyna's Shadow Lady, had joined Nikki in bringing refreshments. Both ladies stayed with their mistresses in their corner.

"Is your room to your liking?" Dyna asked conversationally.

"Yes, it's great. Thank you."

"Good. I want you to be comfortable. This is your home, my darling." Her obvious affection was heartening.

"I guess it's time to work on that aura-shielding-thingy, huh?"

The fairy goddess laughed, the sound like church bells ringing. "Yes, my darling. We shall work on the aura *thingy.*"

Avery's face fell at the way Dyna emphasized the last word. "I'm sorry. I should clean up my vocab."

"Not at all. Your southern heritage is part of your charm. I know Ryse loves it. Never change who you are."

"Everything about who I am is changed."

"And you feel like you've lost a great deal?" Dyna took her hand as she nodded. "You can have such a life here, my darling, doing all the things you love."

Avery thought about all the things she loved about home. Couldn't she have that here? And more? Instead of serving her town's people at the café, didn't she serve a group of soldiers yesterday? The Palace was located in the hills of Tennessee, which was plenty of wide open space. Shopping with Nikki's unlimited pocketbook sounded fantastic. How could Avery ever doubt that she would make new friends? Already she had Hayden, Brenden, and Nikki. Wasn't that the most important thing anyway? She could still be Avery, just with a new group of friends—and family.

Avery could really have a family again. The thought was nourishing to her soul. In the years since her parents' death, she had longed for a mother's embrace, a father's firm but loving influence. Would Ryse's family fill this void in her life?

"Yes, Avery. You would be a beautiful addition to our family. I would so enjoy a daughter." Dyna smiled and the tears in her eyes nearly spilled over. "But I don't want to pressure you, my darling. If this is not what you want—"

"I do. I do want this." She looked over at the man who was to be her husband. "I want him."

Right on cue, Ryse glanced up and caught her gaze. He excused himself from the conversation he was having with Brenden and Cutter to make his way to her. As proof that she really did want to be with him, her heart fluttered and the warmth of him spread over her body, soothing her.

"Are you alright, baby?" He touched her cheek and the skin beneath his fingertips tingled. She nodded, unsure if she could trust her voice not to betray the unsteady rhythm of her breath. Peering into her eyes, he touched her chin. "Strong and stubborn. Why don't you go rest? We can finish up here without Brenden and Dante. I want to keep them both near you at all times, okay?"

"I don't want to rest." She shook her head. "I need to think."

"Kitchen?" He smiled.

Holy *crap* his smile was angelic. Yes, she could live a million lifetimes and never take that smile for granted. "Um, I'd like to *do* something. I haven't had any real exercise in over a week. Can I do that?" And she would like to work off some of her sexual tension. But he didn't need to know that.

"That's a great idea, my love." He turned to Nikki. "Show her to the pool or the ladies' gym. I will go get Brenden and let him know. Don't leave without him." With a sweet kiss, he left to round up her entourage.

"Clear your mind, Avery. It's a good thing to fully consider all options before making rash decisions." Dyna played with one of her curls.

A knock on the door jolted everyone out of their conversations. Gabrele, Troy's guardian, opened the door to reveal an unfamiliar man.

"I have a message for General Falcon," said the newcomer with a bass voice.

Falcon walked to the door and took the white letter size envelope. Taking out the papers he cursed under his breath. Then he looked at Ryse. "This is a formal petition for Dante to be assigned to the European Guard immediately, signed by Princess Salina."

"What the fuck?"

"Are you kidding me?"

"Such a joke."

"Bullshit."

"He's not even done with training."

"He belongs to Avery."

It was the last statement from Hayden that hushed everyone. He held up his hands. "I know, I know, she's not technically a Deity yet and therefore she could not have a claim on any one warrior." He flopped down in a chair. "But I have no doubt that her singling out Dante among a crowded hall of Thracian warriors was no coincidence. The gods ordained that, I'm sure."

"The only reason Salina wants him is because she doesn't want Avery to have him, or anyone else for that matter. A man of his talents is a prized gift." Hammon, who had been nearly silent this whole time, spoke up. "However, the Princess couldn't know what his specialty is."

Yankee waved off the letter and said, "All she's trying to do is piss someone off. It's stupid."

It was General Falcon who put the ball in the right court. "Dante, I know that when we questioned you last year about where you wish to be assigned, you said that you would like to be with your family in your home country."

Dante nodded, his brows crinkled in thought. "With all due respect, Master Ryse's mate wasn't an option then or a conceivable possibility, for that matter. No offense."

For some reason, his comment seemed to entertain his senior officers in the room. Even in the middle of everyone being pissed about this petition, they laughed. Ryse cracked a minute smile and nodded in agreement.

"Nice rebuttal," Yankee said, patting the brother soldier on the back. "But there won't be that option if you use the word 'mate' around our Southern Belle Princess."

"Why?" Dante asked.

Avery's head fell backwards. "Cause it reminds me of a couple warthogs goin' at it in the bush. And I would like to think a little higher of the institution of marriage."

It seemed to tickle Troy, whose face was bright red with laughter. "Such a firecracker," Troy chuckled, but gained his composure to close out the meeting. "All right, let's be done with this. My final decisions are as follows. One, this form," he pointed to the petition from Salina, "will have to be filed and signed by both Dante and Falcon, if accepted. Until then, it means nothing. Two, keep Salina away from Avery and on a leash. Her father will be none too pleased with the activities of his daughter. I say we let him handle the brat. I suggest everyone be on high alert, but we will not let this woman know she has caused anything more than a headache. Is that clear? I do not want her disrupting my household again. Keep an eye out on all her movements. If she uses the wrong lavatory, I want to know about it. Ryse, Avery, do something about this bonding issue. I will not lose a daughter to a technicality."

CHAPTER
TWENTY-EIGHT

DYNA KNEW THAT SOMETHING HAD TO BE SAID TO THE YOUNG warrior who was to either be the salvation or death of her new daughter. In many circumstances, her visions from the gods were usually warnings or preparations. Every vision she had of Avery was like watching two movies projected onto one screen. One vision was determined by Dante's presence, one without. His own inner conflicts determined how the two visions ended.

She found the soldier already guarding his post as Avery went for a private swim in the poolroom. Samuel, who her son affectionately called Yankee, was there, having joined him after the meeting adjourned. The two were casually talking when she walked up. Samuel and Dante both stood straight then bowed to her.

"Gentleman," she acknowledged. "I wish a word with you, Dante."

"Yes, my Queen." He stepped forward.

"You will be fine for a moment alone, Samuel?"

"Of course." There was a confidence in him that Dyna respected. He had a long and trying life. His skills had been put to shameful uses before Ryse found him and beat him into shape—sometimes literally. Now, many decades later, he was a different man. Samuel had honor, pride. Except for a mouth that made her want to grab for the soap, he was one of her favorites.

Dyna walked into the game room. Closing the doors behind them and leaving her own Shadow Lady, Hanna, in the hall, she stood alone with Dante.

"You are Xavier's son, correct?" The way he moved slightly away from her was not unnoticed.

"I am." A short prick of an answer; he was not proud of this.

Dyna tilted her head slightly. "Do you know your father's political views, Dante?"

He went completely motionless. "I do."

"I want you to know that no one will force you into a position serving Avery."

"With all due respect, milady, no matter the position the gods choose to place me, my heart and hands are in their service alone."

Dyna smiled at the boy, so young and yet so wise an answer. "Do you seek service with my new daughter?"

"If she would see me fit and my Master approves, yes."

"I'm going to tell you something that the gods have shared with me, Dante." Dyna clasped her hands in front of her and paced while she spoke. "Many prophecies have been foretold to me of late. I usually see things that will certainly come to pass, things that the decisions of other's will make happen. A long time ago I learned that it was not the gods' intentions that I try to change the futures, but prepare for them. I will, however, inform you that my visions of Avery are often double-sided."

"What do you suppose that means?"

Dyna stopped her pacing and made eye contact. "I believe that your decisions affect their outcome. Much like today, in one vision, you chose not to intervene with the messages being sent to Avery. In the other you did."

"Do you question my motives, my Queen?" He furrowed his brow, breaking his soldierly stone face.

"I do not."

"What do you ask of me, then?"

Dyna came to face to face with him. The tall woman she was,

she looked this brute in the eyes evenly. "I ask that you meditate on your own convictions. Then make the decision given to you based on where your heart will serve best. This choice will have consequences either way, Dante. You know of what I speak. When you make up your mind, be certain that your resolve is unwavering. A path taken with ambiguous steps will lead to sorrowful ends."

CHAPTER TWENTY-NINE

R*YSE, AVERY. DO SOMETHING ABOUT THIS BONDING ISSUE.*

Better stated: hurry up and get married already. It was so simple in Troy's eyes. Either she was Ryse's wife, or she wasn't. As her daddy would say, it was time to shit or get off the pot. Maybe it was that simple. Ryse said they had decades to get to know each other, but their time was cut short by necessity.

It's an oath. Nothing else. That's what she kept telling herself. For her own safety, she could do this. Yes, that she could handle if it saved her life. All she had to do was promise Ryse eternity.

She swam until her body ached, then sat wrapped up in one of the fluffy towels in a chair by the pool. Dyna had suggested that she be physically and mentally tired when they released her aura so that it wouldn't be as potent. After the last couple hours of physical activity in the pool, that condition was met. She had asked to be alone to clear her mind. Brenden and Philippe guarded one door, Yankee and Dante at another. Ryse had taken the time to talk to his father. Even Nikki had let her be alone for a few minutes conveniently staying outside where Brenden stood.

After living alone for so many years, the sudden constant presence of people was daunting. The quiet of this room was peaceful. The only sound was the water being churned by the filtering system and pushed back out through a fountain in the corner. The mosaic murals depicted great oceanic creatures swimming with the gods of the waters. The muted colors made it calming and inviting while still being a grandiose work of art. Columns lining the pool were wrapped in vines and stretched to the arched ceiling, giving the whole room an underwater garden effect. She slowly walked around the pool, taking in the different materials in the wall that created the scene. Her hands skimmed over the rough surface touching glass, pottery, tiles, and hundreds of other elements.

"Might I have an audience, Princess?"

She spun around. "Dante. I didn't hear you come in."

"I apologize." He stood at a respectable distance.

"Stop apologizing to me. You saved my life today." She walked over to him and motioned for him to sit. "Pretty sure I should be thanking you or baking you a cake or something."

"Samuel, uh, Yankee was right. Your accent is charming." Dante averted his eyes. It was amazing that a hulking man of Dante's size could blush after paying a lady a compliment.

It was also hard for her to believe that Yankee would say such a thing. "*Yankee* said my accent was *charming*?" Dante opened his mouth and then shut, thinking twice about what he wanted to say. Avery shook her head and sighed. "What did he really say?"

"He said your accent was *hot*."

Avery laughed out loud at the adjective that was much more like Yankee. "Yeah, that sounds 'bout right."

"You don't mind that he speaks of you with such familiarity? So intimately?" Dante questioned.

"I grew up in a small town. I'm pretty used to people being too familiar with me." She smiled at the seemingly shy Thracian. She shrugged. "Besides, I trust the Elites. No hesitation." It was a borderline lie; they scared her shitless. But Avery knew in a life or death situation any of them would give their lives for her.

"I saw Brenden hug you today. Is that normal?"

Avery shrugged her shoulders. "Probably not. I don't know all the stinkin' rules. Ryse is weird about things. Hayden is the only person he doesn't scowl at when he hugs me. But Brenden is special to me and he—well, we have a common pain."

"I see." Dante twisted his hands around each other.

"What's up, Dante?" Avery put her hand on top of the knot of his fingers. "You can speak openly to me. Don't be worried about the rules 'cause I don't know most of them."

Her light laugh seemed to relax him and he looked up at her, eye to eye, for the first time. "I wish to be one of your guardians. But you should know some things first." She nodded expectantly. "You know that I haven't finished the program yet. But also," he said, dropping his eyes, "my father is in the service of Prince Ashton."

"Um…I'm lost."

His head popped up, shock on his face. "Prince Ashton is against Master Ryse exercising his rights as a Deity." He continued to stare at her with chagrin. She continued to stare at him like a deer in the headlights. "He believes that Ryse being a Thracian is a sign of Queen Dyna's infidelity, that Prince Hayden is the true heir and Ryse is not a Deity of pure blood. Therefore, he will not recognize you as anything more than the mate of a Thracian soldier. My father is Ashton's faithful follower."

She understood now. "Ah. And what do you think, Dante?"

"I believe in the Master's joint heritage with my very soul. He is honorable and following the path of the gods. While I cannot pretend to know the gods' plans for Prince Hayden, I do not question his legitimacy or that he too shall be a reigning Deity somehow."

"And what about me?"

Dante looked at her for a long second. He took a deep breath. "I believe you are a Grace. Even with your aura bound, I can feel it with my abilities. Master Ryse is a one of a kind Deity; of course he would be gifted with a one of a kind Grace. Anyone can see the growing bond between you. That is truly divine, given his nature."

Avery huffed. "He's not always easy to deal with." They shared a smile and she noticed his dimples. "Will your father be angry with you?"

"Yes," he said, losing the dimples. That pained Avery. There was sweetness to this warrior. The gentle giant touched her heart.

"I don't want to cause you family problems." She put her hand on top of his knee. "My parents were taken from me and I would never wish that separation on anyone. I think having you as a guard would be sweet as honey. I hope you know that no matter what, I'll always have a place for you in my heart because of what you've done for me."

His light sandy eyes found hers for another long moment. Avery wondered what he saw that made him look at her with such concentration. "And that, my Princess, is why I choose to devote myself to you and the god's will for your life." Dante took her hand and kissed the back of it. "You honor me."

"Right back atcha." She smiled. "I have a sneaking feeling you'll be needed."

Dante stood and headed to the door. "Princess," he said, looking back. "Those things that Salina was trying to make you believe, none of them are true."

"I know." Avery tried to brush it off, shrugging and waving it away, forcing a smile.

"And I know that she used fears that already existed in your mind and twisted them."

It was Avery's turn to bury her head in shame, except she didn't. It was one thing to have fears and a whole other thing to let the fears rule you. "That she did."

"If I may say so, though my Master may have my head for it later, you are more naturally beautiful, inside and out, than she could ever be with all the makeup and magic in the world. The Master adores you. It's written all over his face every time he looks at you."

Dante left her sitting there, wrapped in a towel and completely dumbfounded.

CHAPTER THIRTY

EVERY NERVE IN RYSE'S BODY WAS LIKE A LIVE WIRE. NEVER IN HIS long life had he been so nervous. His father had talked to him about what would happen if Avery agreed to do a blood oath. It would be different than a physical union but just as legal.

Troy made a declaration, "We will have a morning gathering, tomorrow in the grand dining hall." He spoke to one of the servants that attended him. "Every guest of this house will be in attendance, including Princess Salina. Send her a personal invitation on my behalf." Troy turned to him. "Let Salina see the way the gods favor your mate." They both hesitated and smiled.

Ryse had no doubt that Troy was thinking about Avery's sentiments on the word as he used. Mate. It was comical the way she shied from it. His delightful little farm girl, who had her own interesting southern vernacular, still judged his. "Your union will put aside all questions. When your mother and I first joined together it was also in a blood bond. Your mother's blood mixed with mine was a potent combination. Everyone in the room was wrapped in the magic it created. I have no doubt that it will be the same with you and Avery."

So now Ryse was on his way to their shared suite and make this proposal to his woman. Their option of taking it slow was now off the table.

"Brother!" Hayden ran up to him with a file in his hands and a crazy look upon his face. "You need to see this."

Ryse took the pages and began reading. "What exactly am I looking at? You know I'm not made for science."

"These are Avery's test results."

"These checked boxes are confirmed?" Ryse said, his eyes bouncing between the file and Hayden's face.

"They are all the powers she could have."

"Could?"

"Avery's base Olympian gift is fire. You've seen that. But there is so much more. Ryse, she has the power to absorb others' gifts through blood." Hayden was practically dancing.

"That's impossible."

"So was a Deity-Thracian until you. Pot. Kettle. Now listen." Hayden explained how he and another scientist began breaking down her blood, testing against control samples of Olympians with various gifts. Ryse's head was already spinning and Hayden's scientific babble was flying right over him.

"Christophe accidently mixed a drop of Avery's blood with a control on a slide. There was a spark and when he examined it, Avery's blood was different. It was a mixture—even the DNA had shifted and changed patterns. It's incredible! We've been playing with her blood all morning."

"That sounds terribly disturbing." Ryse scowled. "Are you telling me that Avery could have anyone's powers or she could have none at all?"

"I am telling you that your sassy Texan could have any power she can use that sexy little accent to get. I don't know how long she keeps those powers. They might wear off over time, but I'm pretty sure one blood exchange will do it."

Ryse had to take a seat. "Do you know what this means?"

"It means my sister-in-law is one badass mother fu—"

"Watch it. That's my woman you are talking about," Ryse

snapped before he smirked. Hayden could always lighten his moods. Gods, but he loved that boy.

Hayden's grin widened. "It's no surprise that she gravitated to Dante. Their powers are similar. The gods bless her yet again."

There were two very different possibilities that were going through his mind. One, Avery would never have a real power of her own besides fire and that gift terrified her. Two, those big green eyes could convince every race of Olympian to donate blood and she'd be the most dangerous woman on this planet. It would be an endless consumption of powers.

And what would happen when they took their blood oath as a mated pair?

"Have you showed this to anyone?" Ryse snapped into action.

"Only I and Christophe, the genealogist, have seen it. When I realized what it was, I made him swear on his life that he would take it to his grave unless you instructed him otherwise. He took a blood oath." The magic of such an oath guaranteed his silence.

"Show this only to mother and father, privately. Have mother put these results in the vault." Ryse was on his feet and moving.

"Ryse, you have to tell her. This could be dangerous." Hayden grabbed him, his voice dropping to a whisper. "Think about what will happen when she is blood bound to you, and what about *Brenden*." Hayden looked straight into Ryse's eyes.

Taking Hayden's shoulder in his hand he said, "I will not let anything hurt her. Not even her own blood."

Ryse told Hayden his plan and asked him to do some things while he went for reinforcements.

Before he turned to leave Hayden snagged his shirt. "Hey, can I ask you a question?" Ryse nodded. "Before you met Avery, did you, ah, have dreams about her? Intimate dreams?"

Ryse blanched. "Hayden, you are my brother and I love you. But I'm not going to talk about your erotic dreams right now."

Hayden blushed and chuckled. "No jackass, not those kind of

dreams. What I mean is, did you feel like she was trying to make contact with you through your dreams."

Ryse rocked back on his heels and studied his little brother. No one knew why the gods had given their parents two sons, but Ryse has always suspected Hayden had a grand destiny ahead of him. Now he was dreaming about a woman? "I'm afraid I never had the pleasure. The first time I walked into Avery's café was the first time I'd had any clue as to who she was. Why do you ask?"

Hayden took a deep breath and sat back down on a bench. Ryse joined him. These dreams were disturbing his brother. "For the last few months I've dreamed of this woman." Hayden looked around to ensure their conversation wouldn't be overheard. "They feel so real, Ryse. When I touch her, I can feel the textures of her skin, the softness of her hair. Her lips." He grinned. "She's out there. I can feel it in my soul. But it's as if the gods keep her hidden. I've tried to ask her questions. Where are you? What's your name? How can I find you?" He shook his head, his face pinched together. "She says she can't answer. Not that she doesn't want to, but that she physically cannot form the words to give me clues."

"But you speak of other things?" Ryse assumed.

"Yes. She has a sister. They move a lot. She constantly feels in danger." Hayden met his brother's eyes. "She needs me, Ryse and I have no way to help her." He ran his hands through his long black hair. "Hell, I don't even know if she's real." He let out a breath and laughed bitterly. "Probably just me being a horny bastard, huh?"

Ryse smiled, knowing the frustration Hayden felt. "I wouldn't put it past you." He teased. "But I suggest you pray. Listen vigilantly to the gods and see if it is their will that you and your Lady be united. If it is your purpose to find her, the gods will make a way. They will guide you to her as they guided me to my Avery." Ryse slapped his back in camaraderie.

"Thank you, brother." Hayden grinned. "Don't worry with me any longer. Go to your Grace."

Outside Avery's suite, Brenden stood a vigilant guard with his new sidekick, Dante. They seemed to be getting along fabulously. But that meant that he was going to have to deal with Brenden and the things he had said to him this morning. Some of them had been below the belt.

When he walked up they both nodded. Brenden, always able to read the physical responses of people with those highly trained senses, eyed him suspiciously.

"Dante, I have spoken to General Falcon and a couple of your instructors. We all agree that should you choose to stay in the service of my Princess, you will go straight into the internship of the Elites. We will train you from now on. You will not return to the general population of Thracian students."

The boy, with only decades of life compared to Ryse's centuries, smiled. "Then I am most pleased that the Princess has accepted me on board. I filed the proper paperwork with General Falcon already. All we are waiting for is—things will be finalized soon, I am sure."

"Yes." Ryse let out a breath hoping the warrior was correct. "Good."

"Hey, Dante," Bren said, putting a hand on his shoulder. "Will you go track down Avery's dogs? You might check with the stable master to see where his little boys are playing. I have a feeling they will be with them."

"Yes, sir."

Once Dante was out of sight, Brenden squinted at his Master. "What's up? I can smell sweat on your palms." Brenden crossed his arms over his chest.

"My father has decided that I should convince Avery to bond to me tonight."

"It would be best." Brenden nodded.

Ryse straightened his shoulders and lifted his chin to deliver his apology with honor and respect. If there is one thing his kingly father taught him, it's that admittance to fault is a part of being a good leader. "I shouldn't have brought up Meg. I apologize."

Brenden raised a brow and pursed his lips. "Guess I'm sorry

for all the names I called you, too." He held out his hand and Ryse grabbed his forearm in a Thracian-style shake.

"I wasn't going to mention that. But damn, son, do you kiss Nikki with that potty mouth?" Ryse grinned, knowing all was forgiven with him and his Elite.

"Watch it, brother. I will fight for the honor of your woman and mine." Brenden threw a couple fast play punches to his stomach, making sure to not actually touch him.

"Yeah, yeah, yeah." Ryse got down to business. "Right now you and Hayden must help me do something I have no creative capacity for." Ryse took a deep breath and Brenden made a face of inquiry. "You have to help me propose the bond to Avery *romantically.*"

Brenden's eyes went round as saucers. "Oh damn. Master Prince Ryse Castille, the romantic." His laughter both warmed Ryse's heart and aggravated him. Brenden looked at his watch. "Well, it's almost lunch time; Avery wants to go piss Valarie off in the kitchen again. Then she's off to meet with the Queen. I guess that should give us time to work something up."

"Any ideas?" Ryse said. The two men, both bred for fighting and death, stared at each other with blank looks on their faces.

"We need Nikki," they said in unison.

CHAPTER
THIRTY-ONE

THE PHONE CALL CAME IN ON SALINA'S PRIVATE LINE. HER BROTHER'S voice was harsh and unyielding on the other end. "Have you lost your goddamned mind, Salina? Using your powers on her—in *public*?"

"Nothing happened, Ashton. I don't believe she even knew what was going on. She is a half-breed after all. Her humanly ignorance is making her weak. No one will know that I slipped her a couple harmless thoughts," Salina lied easily. Ashton might be her accomplice in all this, but he was still out for himself, as was she. Quite proud of her brilliance, she smirked to herself and checked her lip-gloss in the mirror.

"Listen to me you stupid, vain little girl," her brother started, his harsh words slapping the confidence right out of her. "You are going to drive her straight into his arms. Is that what you want?"

"No! I want him!" she whined.

Ashton yelled, "They are not foolish, Salina! I have no doubt they have already figured out your game and are two steps ahead of you." He blew out a breath and took a moment to gather his thoughts. "Get out."

"What? Why? You said I could have my shot at Ryse again." Her stubbornness returned along with her will to get what she had already claimed as hers.

"And now you have blown it. Get out of there. Make something up. You're a talented liar."

Salina set her jaw. "I can't. The King is holding a brunch and I've been asked to attend."

"Then you had best not fuck this up. I will not continue to clean up your messes just because you have this mindless obsession with the bastard Prince."

"I know what I'm doing." Ashton would eat his words. She had a plan and it would get rid of that pathetic farm girl one way or another.

CHAPTER THIRTY-TWO

"OKAY, MY DARLING. I WANT YOU TO FOCUS ON SOMETHING that makes you very happy."

Dyna's words made Avery picture her childhood home: the cozy house, the wraparound porch where she would sit in the cool morning air, the feel of Ryse's lips on her neck, acres of rolling hills and forestlands, kissing Ryse, the open Texas skies, waking up to see Ryse—

"Avery." Dyna stared at her with a raised brow and her lips tugging up at the corners. "Pick one."

"That's easier said than done." Avery blushed. "There are a lot of things that made me happy at one time, but it seems all of them are eclipsed by what I feel for Ryse."

A very understanding Grace laid her hands on Avery's shoulder. "That makes his mother very pleased. But you need to focus on one thing, and not Ryse. We don't need your aura that wild. There is a reason for the isolation."

Dyna had ordered everyone away from the area around the tower they were in, except for Dante. He would act as a guide for when Dyna began teaching Avery to shield herself.

"Let's try again, my darling. Think of something that makes you happy." Avery centered her thoughts this time on cooking. It was safe. She thought of different foods and how to prepare them, and the joy it brought her to see other's appreciating her talent. "Good. I can feel you focusing."

Dyna instructed her to think of this while she placed her hand on Avery's forehead. "You are going to feel my presence in your mind. It may be a slight pressure. Don't fight it."

Even as she spoke, Avery could feel something building inside of her head. There was a tugging at the base of her neck. It felt like someone was running their fingers under her skin along her scalp, reaching for her eyes. At first the sensation was soothing like a massage. When Dyna began chanting under her breath, the massaging fingers turned into a vice.

"Almost there Avery, please keep focusing on your happy things. It will ease the pain."

Avery closed her eyes and took a deep breath. She tried her hardest to focus on cooking. Ingredients for rosemary braised lamb shanks and the process of preparing it played out in her mind. The lamb shanks browned in a pan of oil while she sautéed onions, carrots, and garlic in another pan. Then she mixed in—

"Ah!" Avery screamed at the spike of pain behind her eyes. They clenched, her world dark.

"Think of the lamb, Avery. You are doing well." She muttered something to Dante who was now at Avery's side.

Avery could feel Dyna digging around the areas of her conscious, searching for the locks her parents had put into place years ago. One by one, Dyna broke them. It felt like the equivalent of someone breaking a pad lock with a sledgehammer.

Avery became dizzy and nauseous. "I'm going to be sick," she whispered weakly.

"No. No, you're not. Talk to me." Dante's voice was at her ear, calming and soft. "Are you thinking about cooking?"

"Yes." Avery could feel the tears on her cheek. Dante wiped them away.

"What do you do after you sauté the onions and carrots and

garlic? Speak it out loud if you have to," Dyna said, prodding her mind in another direction and trying to take her focus off the pain.

"I, um, I mix in wine and tomatoes, chicken and beef broth, then rosemary and thyme."

Snap. Another lock broken. More agony. Some of the pressure released in that area, but it didn't dull the pain.

"What's the next step?" Dante asked.

Through clenched teeth, she finished telling him how long the lamb sits in the boiling sauce before letting it simmer. When Avery thought her brain was about boil and simmer, Dyna removed her hand. Avery's eyes flew open in shock as she felt the same burst of energy erupt from her as it had from Ryse that morning in the arena. Dyna was ready for it. Avery and Dante were not.

Avery flew backwards and landed hard against her chair. The world was a kaleidoscope of colors and emotions of the auras of everyone within the Palace. To her eyes, Dyna was surrounded with a strong steady cloud of lights that glowed like an angelic rainbow. Dante was surrounded by a different color of light, his surprise and worry creating ripples and waves in his aura.

"Dante!" Dyna commanded. The sentinel put his hand on Avery's shoulder and everything went quiet. Her breath was ragged and shallow at first but then steadied as Dante neutralized the power.

—·—   ⚬   ·—►

On the other side of the Palace, Troy and his two sons felt the blast of godly energy. The eruption, as quick as it was violent, brought Ryse to his knees.

The three men had been looking at Avery's genetic results and discussing how it could be a curse as much as a blessing. Ryse worried that she would be powerless if not surrounded by other people with powers for her to draw from.

"Holy Zeus!" Troy exclaimed. "Such a mighty aura!" He took

a seat, his own knees giving out. "I bet there is not a person in this Palace or at the Thracian center left standing."

"You alright, brother?" Hayden said, helping Ryse back to his feet.

"Yes, I'm fine. That was…unexpected."

"That," Troy took a heavy breath, "that was a sign that our Avery is anything but powerless."

"Can you open your eyes, my darling?"

Avery slowly blinked her eyes into focus.

Dyna wiped her tears and smiled like a mother reassuring her injured child. "How do you feel?"

Assessing herself physically, Avery felt fine. But her head was dizzy and she had a major ache behind her eyes. "I could use an aspirin."

Dyna smiled and glanced at Dante. "Are you alright, son?"

When Avery followed her line of sight, she saw Dante, kneeling beside her, his face practically glowing with the heat of a blush. "Dante?" she said, taking his hand from her shoulder and holding it firmly with both of hers.

"I'm fine, Princess," he said, but his voice was shaking. "Your aura is vast and a little hard to contain."

She looked at Dyna, frantic. "It's hurting him? I'm hurting him, aren't I?"

"Not pain, Princess." Dante eyed her with a wild and carnal look. Once again his sandy eyes had no pupils. When Ryse had opened his aura only slightly to her, the energy and passionate heat of him consumed her with desire. That had only been a taste of his aura. Now here sat Dante, taking on the full brunt of hers.

"Oh! Oh my," Dyna said, blushing. She pressed her hand to her chest. "I'm so sorry; I forgot how strong the mating instinct is in the first century. Do you need to leave Dante? I could contain her until I teach her the rudimentary shields."

"I'm fine, my Queen." He turned his gaze to Avery for only a second of eye contact before he looked away. "Forgive me, Princess."

Avery knew that for the comfort and protection of her soldier, she needed to learn about shields quickly.

CHAPTER THIRTY-THREE

RYSE HAD HIS PLANS MADE. THE EVENING WAS SET. FIRST, THEY would be dining al fresco in the gardens. Valarie had been asked to prepare a full meal of Avery's favorite food. After dinner, arrangements had been made for an outdoor movie.

Ryse stood with one of his father's personal tailors looking at three different shirts. The lady smiled up at him, awaiting his choice. They all looked the same. All of them were midnight blue with subtle differences that meant nothing to his eyes.

He turned to his modern and savvy little brother with a helpless look. Hayden and Hammon were aiding him this evening. Both men laughed.

"What the hell is the difference?" Ryse snipped. "They are all blue."

"The one with pin stripes is nice," Hammon said, taking the shirt in hand.

"It's also made out of a thinner material so you won't sweat, not that you aren't going to do that anyway." Hayden grinned.

Ryse narrowed his eyes at his little brother. Hayden was finding this process all too hysterical. His enjoyment was getting on Ryse's nerves. "Fine, that one will do." He took the shirt and put it on. "Has she received the invitation?"

Hayden handed him a bottle of cologne. "Yes. Here."

Ryse looked at the bottle and sniffed it. "What is this?"

"Cologne. Very expensive cologne from my personal stash." Hayden wiggled his brows.

"Breathe, my old friend," Hammon said, standing behind him in the mirror. "Remember that this is still Avery you are going to see. Only the setting has changed."

Ryse nodded, knowing Hammon was right. Avery was the same woman he had woken up with this morning. But he was going into a situation completely unprepared. This was not a military operation. Though, that is exactly what he had turned it into in his mind. This operation had many variables at this point. Her aura had been released from the locking spells. Now she would be able to sense him the same way he could sense her. Every heartbeat, every breath, every ripple of emotion in his aura would be open to her if he dropped his mental shields for her, which he would as a sign of trust.

Gods help him, he'd never been so nervous.

Avery stared at the embossed invitation as she sat in front of her vanity mirror. The words made her heart skip a beat in anticipation. Ryse had invited her on a date—a real, human style date. The single blue rose that accompanied the invitation sat in a vase in front of her. Nikki had informed her that blue roses meant love at first sight, or attaining the impossible. It made the rare flower even more beautiful in her eyes. She read the note once more.

My dearest Avery,
Please do me the greatest honor of gifting me
with your presence this evening.
Join me for dinner and a film in the gardens.
Until then, know you inhabit all my thoughts.
With deepest affection,
Ryse

A chill went down her spine. Such a two-sided coin, her Ryse. Part warrior, part Prince, and both aspects were as attractive and strong as the other. Learning about him had become the center of her universe. She hadn't had time to think about much else besides Ryse and this clandestine world she was now a part of.

She sat at the vanity while Nikki fixed her long auburn hair. Avery looked at a reflection she couldn't believe was her own. Nikki had done up her face to look like a runway model. It wasn't too much, but her eyes were smoky shadowed and her lips a luscious deep red, blush accented her cheeks.

The déjà vu made her heart hurt and she felt tears sting her eyes. It seemed like only yesterday that she was sitting in this same exact situation with Izzy at her back.

"Avery, if you cry and mess up that makeup I'm going to curse you," Nikki said, grabbing a tissue.

"I'm sorry." Avery carefully blotted the tears out of the corners of her eyes. "Last time I was getting ready for a date with Ryse, Izzy was doing my hair."

Nikki's hands stopped working and she smiled sympathetically at her in the mirror. "Sorry. I know I'm no Izzy."

"No, but Izzy was no Nikki, either." Avery smiled at her new friend. For only being in her life a couple days, Nikki had somehow become just as vital to her survival as Ryse, and Ryse was her oxygen.

"Tell me about her. Happy things only." Nikki smiled. The next few minutes Avery talked about her oldest and dearest friend. Proms, dances, boyfriends, graduation, and funny things that happened in the café were but a few of the things that Avery thought of when she relived her days with Izzy.

"When Brenden came to town, she about had a heart attack," Avery remembered fondly. Izzy was a flirt and Bren had been undercover. Avery looked up to see Nikki biting her bottom lip. "Not that anything came of it. He didn't pay her much attention."

"You make it sound like I have a premise to be jealous." Nikki smiled at her. "Why would I be worried about Brenden or who he flirts with?"

"How about cause you are completely and totally crazy over him?" Avery said, angling her head accusingly at her hairdresser.

Nikki's lips fought to hide the silly grin that threatened to spread across her rosy cheeks. "He kissed me!" she blurted out, then clamped her hands over her mouth.

"Was that your first kiss?"

Nikki nodded and did a crazy little dance behind her while she laughed. The girls gushed about men for the next twenty minutes until Nikki realized that their time was running out.

"Okay! Hair is done. Time for your dress!" Her excitement was infectious and Avery smiled as she followed her into the closet. Nikki walked over to the drawers and pulled out some delicates. "Here. Put these on."

Avery took them and walked behind the changing screen, shedding the robe she had put on after her shower. Nikki handed over a dark bluish-purple dress. The silky stretch of the material slid over her skin like a glove. "Nikki, are you sure this is my size? It's very tight, especially on my rear end."

"That's the point," Nikki said.

Fidgeting with the dress, Avery stepped out from behind the screen. "I don't know. I feel like a hundred pounds of potatoes stuffed in an eighty-pound sack. Does it look okay?"

Nikki's eyes got big as saucers. "Oh yes!" She covered her mouth as she smiled.

With a little adjusting and some last minute curls to her hair, Avery was ready for her date. She took a few minutes to breathe before Hayden arrived to take her to meet Ryse. Her heart nearly jumped from her chest when there was a knock on the door. Nikki opened it. "You're not who I expected. But it's a great surprise," Avery said as Dyna pulled her into a mother's embrace.

"You don't think I could let you go off on a date with my son and not visit you first?" Those otherworldly lavender eyes smiled at her. "And I come bearing gifts." Hanna, quiet and always there, stepped up with a white leather jewelry box. With a shy smile, she handed the box to her mistress. "Thank you, Hanna." Dyna took the box and opened it for Avery to see.

"Oh my god!"

Sitting on the black interior was a stunning heart-shaped diamond necklace. Framing the quarter-size blue diamond were smaller white diamonds. Dyna picked up the silver chain and unhooked it. Stepping behind Avery, she latched the necklace. Speechless, Avery walked over to the mirror on the wall and touched the pendant with one shaking hand. The weight of it lay against her chest. The diamond was staggeringly gorgeous.

"This was my mother's," Dyna said, putting her hands on Avery's shoulders. "She gave it to me on my fiftieth birthday." Avery gave her a questioning look. "We are immortal, my darling. Fifty is considered young for our race. It was a gift for my first outing with Troy."

"Dyna, it's so beautiful. I can't possibly—"

"The gods only gifted me with two sons, my darling. In tradition, I have to pass it down to my daughter. That is you, isn't it?" Avery turned to face this woman that would have her as family. A simple nod was her answer. There was eye makeup that could not be ruined, after all. "I wish you a very pleasant evening. Worry for nothing, and enjoy all the treasures of the night."

Avery hugged Dyna tightly before she left. Then she stared in the mirror at the diamond hanging from her neck. Again, the sound of a knock at the door made her jump. "God!" she said, letting Dante in. "I'm as jumpy as a stray cat in the junk yard."

"Sorry mis—" he paused, halfway in the door, holding the leashes of her two dogs. He stared at her, awe-struck, accidently dropping the dog's restraints. They came to Avery and she pet them before remembering that she was in a nice dress. "Apologies. Let me get them." He yanked their collars and pulled them back. The dogs went to their beds and sank down.

"Thanks, Dante."

Nikki conjured a lint roller and whisked the dog hair off the skirt of the dress. "Good as new."

Avery tugged at her dress under Dante's gaze.

"Don't worry, you look…" he searched for the word, "…beautiful." Avery figured his choice of safe adjectives was for the best.

"Thanks."

"Prince Hayden approaches," he said, heading to the door. How did he know that? Avery could sense auras now, but she didn't know Hayden was near until he was knocking. Dante winked at her and opened the door for his Master's brother.

"Damn." Hayden said, rushing in to look at her. He motioned for her to spin so she gave him her best runway turn. Hayden came up to her and put his hands on her hips. "Okay, forget Ryse, I'm kidnapping you for myself." He pulled her close to him and began showering her with kisses on her face. She giggled and swiped at him playfully.

"Hayden, you dog!"

"It's not fair!" he said, spinning her in one hand. "Some bastards have all the luck." He let out a dramatic sigh and shook his head. Wiggling his brows he teased, "You sure you don't want to give the younger brother a try first?"

Avery laughed and kissed his cheek. "One of these days you're gonna sweep a very lucky, very *patient* woman off her feet."

"Alright, fine." He took her around the waist. "Come on, let's go so my lucky brother can sweep you off yours." He looked at Dante as they exited. "Keep an eye on the room. You will be called before the Princess returns."

Dante nodded and winked to Avery. "Have a lovely night, milady," he said, shutting the door behind them.

They passed Brenden in the hall and he let out a whistle. "Since you will be with the Master all night, I've been given time off."

Avery hugged him and whispered in is ear. "A certain redhead would love to see you for a while." The deep blush on Bren's face made Avery smile.

CHAPTER THIRTY-FOUR

RYSE WAITED IN THE GARDENS. HE FIDGETED NERVOUSLY WITH HIS shirt tucked into his black slacks. Slacks. What kind of damn Thracian wore *slacks*? He looked like some sort of modern day businessman. Hell, he looked like his father.

He heard the sound of the car coming down the road and his stomach turned over. He had picked a secluded area on the grounds far from the Palace and training center. The only people allowed within a thousand yards were Hammon and Philippe. The tracker and Elementalist were providing guitar and violin services. Philippe was also on standby if the weather didn't hold out. Rain would be no problem when one could control the elements like Philippe.

His heart rate spiked when the black SUV came to a stop.

All thoughts were gone as one sleek black high heel slipped out of the door. His eyes trailed up the leg, joined by the other, as they slid from the car. Those legs, those sexy firm legs were deliciously bare above the knee. Avery closed the car door and it pulled away slowly. Standing there, she looked like his personal angel. The fabric of her tight dress shaped her plentiful hips and was loose again at her waist. On one shoulder was an elbow length flowing sleeve. The neckline of the dress plunged from the right shoulder down under her left arm, revealing the upper curve of her left breast. The naked shoulder was tempting him—fresh, cool water in a desert drought.

Her gorgeous curls spilled over her right shoulder and arm. It offered her neck as a gift, one he would gladly take. Around her neck was a jewel he knew well. It made his heart kick into another gear.

Remember why you are doing this.

Only after going over her tantalizing body once more did he seem to remember how to move. Slowly, as not to wake from the fantastic dream, he walked to her and gazed into those emerald eyes. They seemed deeper, more mystical. The black fan of her lashes fluttered.

"Hey there, good-lookin'." The sweet satin of her voice, low and seductive, licked over him. She smiled and his heart became enslaved. Somehow he still couldn't speak. Her beauty was staggering. "You sure clean up nice, baby." Her hand reached for the collar of his shirt. He didn't miss the fact that she was shaking.

"Ryse?" Her eyes went down nervously and she bit on her bottom lip. Gently, he cupped her chin and lifted it so she could look into his eyes.

Heartbreakingly beautiful.

"The gods should be jealous of you tonight." His words a bare whisper against her lips before he kissed her. The magic of her overtook him, feeding him until he felt more acutely aware of her than ever before. He knew what was refining his senses. "I see that mother helped you release your aura successfully." He traced her jaw line as she nodded. "I can feel you now."

Avery looked up at him with a hint of hesitancy. "That's good, right?"

"Yes, my love." He smiled, amazed at how such a woman could ever have the self-confidence issues that she possessed. If she only knew. "Can you sense anything about me?"

The gleam in her eyes was priceless. She nodded and pushed up on her toes to kiss him on the cheek. "You're as nervous as I am." Then she smiled and once again, he was lost to her enchantment.

"Did Nikki let you look in a mirror before leaving? How could a man not be nervous around such a goddess?"

A mischievous glint in her eyes formed as she teased him. "Hayden wasn't nervous at all. He nearly molested me when the door opened."

"Did he now?" Ryse realized his little brother now had a co-conspirator. *Great.* "I guess I should find him and teach him what happens when he molests my Lady." Ryse pulled her body close to his, noticing that her heels gave just enough extra height to put her lips closer. He decided that high heels were damn good things.

"He kissed me—a lot." She wiggled her brows.

"Did he kiss you like this?" He pecked her on the cheek. She giggled and nodded. "How about this?" He delivered one kiss on her lips. Again, she smiled and nodded. "On the lips? Really?" He made his worst attempt at being playfully angry. "Humph, I have some real competition here." The happy smiles being given to him were like patches to the broken pieces of his soul. "Fine, but did he kiss you like this?" Threading his hands through her hair gently, he pulled back her head, exposing her neck as a sacrifice. He placed a series of slow kisses from the base of her neck all the way up to her ears. Smiling to himself when he felt her hands clench his shirt, he nibbled at her ear. There was no need to read her aura to see that she enjoyed it. Even so, it was shining with ripples of her delight. Avery had closed her eyes and bitten down on her lip.

"Did he kiss you like that, baby?" Ryse whispered against her skin. Avery shook her head, letting out the breath of air she had taken in many seconds ago. How in gods' name could any one woman be so innocently attractive? "Well, that's good," Ryse smiled triumphantly. "Because if any other man kisses you like that, I'll kill him."

"If another man kissed me like that you wouldn't have to," Avery whispered. Ryse tilted his head and squinted his eyes at her. "I'd kill him before you had the chance." She grinned again.

"That's my girl." He kissed her forehead before taking her hand and leading her across the gentle arch of a bridge to their destination for the evening. Seating her like a true gentleman, Ryse then sat across the table from her and let her have a moment to take it all in.

Avery scanned everything. The candles danced in her reflection and there was no mistaking the surprise and happiness upon her face. "This is *so* beautiful, Ryse." Then he could see her ears perking up. "Do I hear music?"

"Provided by Hammon and Philippe."

"Hammon and Philippe?" She searched for the two men.

"You won't see them. They're giving us music, rain protection, and privacy. Wine?" He took the bottle from the cradle of ice and poured two glasses. "It's from a family vineyard in Spain."

"Family vineyard?" she asked, taking a taste of the light wine.

"We have quite a bit of family in Spain still. A distant cousin on my father's side owns a vineyard and is gracious enough to keep us stocked up. He and his wife are both Gaians so their vineyard is one of the most successful in the world."

"People of the earth." Avery nodded. "That explains why this is the best wine I've ever tasted." She looked over at the cart that carried many silver covered dishes.

"Tonight, Madame," Ryse said, rising to his feet and throwing a napkin over his arm. "You will be treated to a three course meal. First up is a grilled shrimp salad in a vinaigrette." She smiled and made an oohing sound. "The main course will be lobster and steamed vegetables and the third course is a surprise. Would you like to begin?"

"Please. I'm starving."

Ryse licked his lips. He was starving as well, but the food was the last thing on his mind.

He served them their first course and couldn't help but revel in how she seemed to eat differently than anyone he had ever seen. It made him think of the most erotic things. How was he supposed to eat and not choke on his food watching those lips?

"What?" she asked, finishing her salad. "Why do you keep looking at me like that?"

"Can you tell by my aura? Try?"

It was entertaining as hell when she squinted her eyes and looked at him like he was a dissected frog. "It changed."

"I imagine it did. That's because I went from thinking how much I love your mouth to how adorable you look when you focus on something."

As if she couldn't get any more damned cute, she blushed and tilted her head down before peeking up at him shyly. "I guess I have a lot to learn about auras, huh?"

Taking some time in between the first and second course, he told her what the different colors meant, what the variations in ripples could mean. Avery listened and they devoured their lobster.

The conversation never seemed to have a stopping point. Avery had so many questions about everything from auras to magic to history of Thracians to how they train. She was a captive audience, listening to him like there would be a test afterward. The plate in front of her had been pushed aside so she could fold her arms on the table and listen.

Figuring now was as good a time as any, he decided she should know about her amazing blood. "I bet Hayden is having a field day doing research right now," he said after gliding genetic research into the stream of conversation. "He came to me, very excitedly, this morning and told me about the results of your blood scans."

First, he told her how the blood was tested and matched to figure out what skills an Olympian had. The explanation he gave her was a lot less scientific than the one Hayden had given him; she seemed to understand better than he did. "So he began placing a drop of your blood in with blood donated from our controls."

"People who have very specific and specialized gifts?"

"Exactly. When your blood was introduced to theirs, it absorbed that particular gift."

"Is that normal?" she asked. Her posture changed, and she leaned back in her chair and folded her arms protectively across her chest. Defensive. Scared. Worried. Her aura was a neon sign above her head.

"Hayden's never seen it. He would know. It's very rare that an Olympian is able to absorb the powers of another into their blood."

"So what does this mean? What am I?"

"There isn't a classification for you." Her face dropped, her brows furrowed. "What this means is that you can harness the powers of those around you. You can take them in, use them, make them your own. It's nearly the same thing I can do with all the Thracians who have bound themselves to me, only on a much more physical level. We will have to do some testing and see. I imagine that we will all be pleasantly surprised. Think what you could do," he said, getting up to stand beside her. He lifted her into his embrace and looked at her. "You could have the powers of everyone around you. It's amazing."

"What if no one wants me to share their gifts?" She touched his cheek and he leaned his face in to her palm. "I guess that is why my powers never tried to rear their ugly head all these years, huh? 'Cause I don't have any."

"You have one for sure. I've seen you manifest fire with my own eyes." They watched each other for a moment while.

"I don't think that's a gift." She lowered her face. "I felt like I had lava running through my veins. Then I turned into a campfire. It was painful."

There was no way he was going to let her fears take over. "Avery, baby, we are going to test you and find out what exactly you can do. I will keep a hundred guards with every talent known to the Olympian world around you to make sure you are never caught powerless."

"I know you would."

"Come, sit with me." He guided her onto the comfy large couch and they leaned back against a wall of pillows. He held her close and he could smell the fragrances of the shampoo in her hair, feel the softness of her skin and the warmth her aura was emitting. "You know I would do anything to make you happy and keep you safe," he whispered against her skin.

CHAPTER THIRTY-FIVE

Yes, Avery knew without a doubt that Ryse Castille would do anything in his powers to keep her safe and happy from now until eternity's end. Tonight had been one little glimpse of the life she was ready to sign up for. But how to tell him? Blurt it out? Be subtle? Give him hints until he figured it out on his own?

"I wish a thousand times over that things had been different from the moment we met," he said, cutting into her thoughts. "Everything would be easier. We would have all the time in the world to grow together and learn each other."

"We still can," Avery said, propping herself up to look at his face.

"Don't you feel rushed, overwhelmed?" he said, shaking his head slightly.

Avery took a long breath and thought about it. Everything had been rushed, yes. It seemed like since the time he stepped foot in her café, things had been put into fast forward. The events all happened so fast that she didn't have time to really process what was playing out. "I'm not sorry, though." She finished her thought out loud. "Ryse, you have been the center of this crazy world of mine for the last week and a half. It's been the Texas Giant of roller coasters, only this one has been all emotional, I admit. And somehow, it all fits—you, me, your family, my place in this world. It fits."

"I've caused you a lot of unnecessary pain." He looked into the sky, avoiding her gaze. She pulled his face down to meet her eyes.

"You have also been the glue that keeps me from falling apart. Perhaps I'm mimicking your strength already."

He pressed his lips to hers, gently teasing her bottom lip with his teeth, "My beloved."

"I need you, Ryse. I've never needed anyone. But I need you."

"Do you *want* me, Avery? Do you think you could learn to love me even if we have to do things backwards?"

He didn't have to explain. First they needed to get married, then they could worry about dating. There was no need to worry about it in her mind. She had made her decision. The details could be worked out later. "I already love you, Ryse." She smiled at him.

The enormity of those words was written all over his face. Two deep, warm eyes stared at her for the longest moments before she noticed the slow ring of moisture that was building at their rims. His hand moved and he took a small black velvet box from his pants pocket. He held it up in front of her and grinned. "You'll want this then?" he teased her, holding up the box.

Obliging him to play his cute games, Avery tapped her lips, pretending it required deep thought. "What strings come attached?"

Ryse laughed, the sound like a warm fire at home on a winter day. So soothing and so rich, it made her toes curl in delight. "Plenty, more than you can imagine and more than I can explain in one night. But part of that is my undying love and devotion, everything I have and everything I can be."

He smiled when he said those words, but they did not diminish what they really meant. Their relationship wasn't solely about the bonds Avery would vow to him, but those he would vow to her as well. It would not be a one-sided agreement. Deep down inside of this gloriously beautiful man, there was enough love and passion to last her a thousand lifetimes. She saw it every time he looked at her. Every kiss was one small ember escaping from the fires that burned within him.

"Promise me something first."

"Anything," He ran his free hand through her hair.

She took a deep breath. "Don't hide things from me. Please. There's nothin' in this world that I can't handle as long as you're honest and up front. I'm tired of not understanding things because someone else decided to protect me from the truth. I'm not weak."

"Oh my sweet, sweet, Avery. You are nothing close to weak. I see strength in you so deep it moves me. After everything you have been through, there is no one who could ever mistake you as weak." He took a deep breath and his face changed a little. "It is in my blood to protect you. On that issue I will not budge. Every power, every gift I have was placed in me to protect those under my charge. If you are in danger, I will do whatever it takes to keep you safe."

"Accepted."

"Then I promise to always be honest with you." He sealed that vow with a kiss. "Will you promise me something in return?"

"Anything."

"No matter what happens, no matter what you might have to witness me do," he paused and pinched his lips together, "never fear me."

The request took Avery by surprise. She looked at Ryse, touched his face. "I could never—"

"Avery." He gripped her hand tightly. "My job, my calling is dealing out justice. I am often the assassin and punisher of the gods. Sometimes that means being a monster. There have been people close to me that I've had to punish. For that reason, everyone avoids me. My own father once confessed that he feared the obligations given by my station."

Avery whispered his name, feeling the pain in his eyes. This man before her was so open, so vulnerable to her now. How could she ever betray him when he bared his soul to her and none other? "I know what you are. It scares me," she said honestly. "But I couldn't fear you. I know you'd never hurt me. And when the time comes that you have to do something hard, I'll be here for you to fall back on. I promise you that."

"In that case, my love." He opened the small black box and her eyes nearly popped out of their sockets. "I believe this belongs to you."

So much for smearing the makeup. Avery clasped her mouth closed with her hand when she realized she was hanging it open. Ryse pointed out the features of the ring to her. The thin band was white gold. Resting on top was a heart full of tiny sparkling white diamonds in a carat that only an Olympian could harvest. Intertwined vertically through the middle of the heart were a strand of emeralds and a strand of black diamonds. He took the ring from the velvet bed and held her left hand.

"I thought the emeralds looked like your eyes," he said, sliding it on her finger. It fit perfectly. "Even the black diamonds are fitting, don't you think?"

"They are very much like you," she said, wiping her tears. "Made stronger under pressure, unique, dark and beautiful." Avery held up her hand and looked at the ring glistening in the candlelight. "It's so amazing."

"It's only the beginning of the pleasures I plan to give you." As if her heart couldn't beat any faster, he gave her the kind of kiss that made her skin tingle in exhilaration. "I love you, Avery."

"And I love you." She smiled and wiped her face. "Didn't that invitation say something about a film?" It was an effort to get the attention off her blubbering, but thankfully he obliged.

"Yes, milady." With nothing more than the flick of his powerful wrist, a theater size screen appeared over the water. "I thought you would like this one."

The screen came to life and the familiar title of her favorite musical danced on the screen.

"Aw, Ryse!" She laughed. "This is perfect!"

CHAPTER THIRTY-SIX

"MISTRESS," THE HANDMAID SAID, LEANING OVER THE CHAIR Salina was sitting in. "I have news that the man you wanted to talk to is currently in the sauna in the first basement level."

Salina slapped her book shut. "Perfect. I will be headed there. Please make sure that there is no one else around." Salina walked down to the first sub level of the castle in nothing but her bathrobe. She had one objective tonight and clothing was not needed to achieve it.

After a lengthy conversation with her brother, he informed her that one of the first things they would do with Avery was test her blood to see what powers she possessed. Salina and Ashton needed this information. There was one man who could get it for her. This man happened to be sitting in a sauna.

Opening the door to the steamed room, Salina pretended that she didn't see the man sitting there in his towel. With her back turned to him, she dropped the robe before the scientist had the chance to object. When he cleared his throat, she turned, wrapping the robe around herself like she had been caught unaware.

"Oh, I'm so sorry! I didn't see you there," she laughed nervously.

"My apologies, milady. I will leave so that you may have your privacy. I was done anyhow." The man stood and headed to the door. A slight push of telepathy hit him as she spoke.

"I don't want to make you leave. Please sit. I would enjoy some company. What's your name?"

He turned to her, trepidation on his face, and stood still. He was not in the best shape, but like all Olympian males, he had a fairly nice physique. His eyes were soft and innocent looking, a pretty shade of blue. He was nothing that Salina would call special and he certainly didn't compare to Ryse. But he would do.

"Christophe, Princess. I really should go."

"No." More power hit him. "You should stay, Christophe."

"It is inappropriate for me to remain here with you only clad in a towel, Princess. It disrespects you and puts me in a compromising position. I am a married man."

Ooh! Even better! This couldn't get any easier. "Christophe, do you know that when a member of the royal family demands you to sit, to refuse is a personal insult? You don't want to offend a Princess, do you?"

Christophe swallowed hard. She had him. "No. I do not."

"Then sit," Salina demanded. By now she was streaming things into his mind. It was only a matter of keeping him slightly distracted by conversation so that he wouldn't notice. "Tell me about your wife? Do you have children?"

As Christophe spoke of his wife and three children, Salina began to mentally seduce him. Images of her naked body flashed into his brain. The man deserved some credit, he was quickly making the images disappear, feeling complete guilt that he even allowed himself to think that way. It would make her victory even sweeter.

"And why is such an attractive man like you at the Palace at this hour, not home with your wife?"

"I was working. Decided to take a break."

"What are you working on?" She picked up her long mane, pulled it off her shoulders and sent him an image of kissing her neck.

"It's confidential," he spit out. "I should get back to work. Good night." He rose again and Salina panicked. She couldn't lose him. Pushing a level of telepathy and mind control at him that had put many men at her feet, she controlled his strings like a master puppeteer.

She stood in front of him, smiling. Using her powers to make others bend to her will was a sort of seduction for her. But when it came down to it, once she blocked Christophe's inhibitions and conscience, he was a man. There wasn't a man on earth who could resist a naked goddess in front of them. Dropping the robe, she soaked in how he looked at her body. Salina was every man's dream and she knew it. Her bountiful chest alone could drive a man insane. And she used it unashamedly.

Remove your towel, she commanded him mentally. Christophe removed his towel, revealing a hearty erection. *Grab me. Bring me to your waist. Take control.*

Obeying her commands, he pulled her onto his lap with his strength. This was definitely a perk of the job and now she owned his soul. Not caring about the wife or the kids who would cry about him being unfaithful, Salina took him. The moment he released his seed into her, she dropped all the magic, letting the reality of what had happened hit the mild mannered scientist like a ton of bricks. He panted, groaning as he held the woman in his arms close.

"Theresa," he said his wife's name with ecstasy.

"Not even close," she sneered.

Yanking her back by her hair, Christophe looked up at her with confused, fear-filled eyes. "What in the name of the gods happened?" He surveyed his surroundings like he had awoken from a nightmare. Salina straddled him, his body still connected with hers in the most intimate of ways. "What have you done?" He pushed her off him onto the floor.

"What have I done? What have *you* done?" Salina put on her bathrobe and sneered at him. "I wonder what Theresa would think if she knew that you defiled a Princess?"

"You can't do this!" he said, standing and covering himself. The shame and terror of his expression was fuel to her sadistic fire.

"Now, Christophe, if I begin to cry and scream that you over-powered me, would they believe you? Especially seeing as how your seed is now inside of me? That's rather incriminating evidence, don't you think?"

"What do you want?" he asked. "You must have a motive for your actions."

"I want information. Unless you want to face rape charges from a Princess, you will give it to me." Knowing she had her prey backed into the corner, she went in for the kill. "Tell me about Avery's tests."

CHAPTER THIRTY-SEVEN

SOMEWHERE BETWEEN DON LOCKWOOD SINGING IN THE RAIN AND Kathy Selden doing voiceovers for Lina Lamont, Avery was feeling mighty fine. She lay in front of Ryse, spooned with him curled close behind her. One naked shoulder shuddered under his lips, his hand rubbing up and down her arm. If he had kissed her once, he had kissed her a thousand times up and down the length of her shoulder and neck.

"You're not even watching the movie," she whispered as she angled her neck for better access. Feeling his smile made her skin tingle.

"Sorry, you are very distracting." Nudging her ear with his nose, he moved even closer. The ring on her left hand shined brightly as he raised it into the moonlight. "I think I like my ring on you."

"So possessive," she giggled.

"Very. I'd like to see other markers of mine on you."

She rolled back so she could look up at him. "You mean your brand?"

"I know that some women don't care for tattoos. Where I want to put it, it's not exactly a place where you could hide it from yourself. You would have to look at it every day."

With a smirk on her face, she put her right arm behind her head. "It will look like yours, right?" He nodded once. "Above my heart?" Another nod. "And I can wear clothes like this to show it off?" A grin and a nod. "I don't see the negative side of this unless it's gonna be excruciatingly painful."

He wiped a strand of wild hair from her cheek. "It's going to hurt, love. Unlike a human tattoo, this one will only sting for a moment then the pain is gone."

"Needles?"

"No needles. All it takes is this." He held up his hand. She looked at him incredulously. "Are you ready for that?"

It was a question that she had already answered, but there was this ping of uncertainty that came out of nowhere. How could she fear this? Ryse had promised her forever for heaven's sake. "I wear your ring, might as well." She had a thought. "Can I wear your brand if I am not blood bound to you?"

"Well, the ring is more to please the human side of you, my love. Taking my mark begins the process. It's usually the first step. Making love to you completes it."

...Making love to you...

Those words, those sweet words. Amazing how shadowed fear of the past is scattered in the light of his promises and commitment. "Do it."

Ryse placed his hand, palm down, above the curve of her left breast. Avery couldn't help but wonder if Nikki had picked this dress because of its lack of material right in this location.

"Though I give you this mark, and you give me your loyalty, it is the gods that you are truly bound to. You are promising to uphold their will by joining in a lifelong union with me as my wife. In return, I also vow the same loyalty and commitment to you. Do you swear?"

She looked up into his eyes and knew with every fiber of her being this was the right thing to do. "I swear."

"So shall it be." Under his hand, her skin tingled. The tingle soon turned into a burning sensation. As hard as she tried not to think of the cattle they used to brand back in Texas, there were such similarities she couldn't help but wonder if this was how it felt. Ryse's eyes glowed with the light she had seen emanate from him that morning in the arena. It was the power of the gods using him as a vessel for their works. His hand glowed with the same light and the burning became nearly unbearable. She turned her head and bit down into her fist to keep from crying out. Every Thracian who served Ryse directly had to be marked like this, she knew. Avery wasn't the first, nor was she the last person to have to deal with this kind of pain. But dang, it hurt! And it didn't damage her pride not one bit to admit it.

It only took a minute for the brand to be tattooed in her. It was the longest minute of her life as the fire snaked around her skin to create the design. Only when she felt Ryse's hand begin to cool did she dare look at him. The holy glow of his eyes faded leaving him blinking and finally the sweet chocolate she loved so much was staring at her.

"Are you okay, baby?" he asked, wiping the tears she hadn't even realized had come.

Nodding her head in an outright lie, she allowed Ryse to pull her into a sitting position. For a second, she saw stars and thought she might be sick. The haze quickly cleared and she shook it off. Ryse offered her another glass of wine. "Does it still burn?" he asked, touching the skin around the brand.

"Only a little." The look in his eyes made her come to a halt. "What is it?"

He was studying the tattoo that seemed to still be forming on her breast. When she looked down, she could see what confused him. The tattoo was much like Ryse's. An ornate sword decorated with swirls and curves that was both elegant and mighty.

That's where the similarities ended. Growing out of the sword was some sort of new design. "What is it?" she asked.

"I'm not certain yet. Often it takes up to an hour for the forms to solidify." He looked up at her and drew breath. "We shall wait and see, my love."

Avery took in the features of his face. They never failed to stun her. The feel of his skin, a bronze that glowed with healthy vitality, was smooth and silky under her fingertips.

"Have I told you how very handsome you look this evening?" One side of his lips pulled back, but he said nothing. "I didn't think it was possible for you to look any better, and yet you surprise me all the time."

"I could say the same." He arched his knee on the back of the sofa, the other leg hanging down to the patio. Avery found herself positioned between his legs, and moving closer, she leaned to press her lips to his. Gripping a hand full of her hair, Ryse held her tight, consuming her mouth. He reclined back into the pillows and brought her on top of him.

If there was one thing Avery could do every minute of every day for the rest of eternity, it was kiss Ryse. The smell of him alone was beyond satisfying, and his taste was downright euphoric. She licked out her tongue along his neck and reveled in the taste of his skin. The low growl that came from his throat let her know that she had done something right. Two hands gripped her shoulders. Pulling back, she looked down into his eyes. "What's wrong?"

"If you keep this up," he said, his voice dropped low and raspy. "I'll not be able to stop. You have no idea how badly I want you right now."

Avery moved her hips, slightly rubbing against the rigid form that pressed against her stomach. "Oh, I have a pretty good idea."

Ryse took in a hiss of breath between his teeth. "Avery," he moaned. "You shouldn't tease the animals."

"Will they bite?"

In one quick motion, Ryse had her naked neck bared and his mouth to her pulse. His teeth grazed her skin and it sent a quiver of electricity straight to the flesh under her panties. He pulled her left leg up, and a warm, large hand slid under the stretchy blue fabric of her dress to grip her thigh.

No more fears. No more nightmares about being taken advantage of or hurt. Ryse would never hurt her, never push her too far, and never try to quiet her if she told him no. Even now, in this passionate momentum they had started, she could throw on the brakes and he would respect her wishes.

There was no stopping tonight. Avery wanted to feel him, all of him. She wanted to experience the warmth of his skin naked and moving against her own. Now that she could sense his aura, his desires were amplified in her mind. He wanted her desperately. The need to show her the depth of his love was an overpowering wave of seduction.

"Last chance to stop." Hot, heavy breath against her skin.

"No stopping." Words said in between nibbling on his ear. "I love you. I'm yours. In every way."

He stopped to grip the sides of her face and make her look him in the eyes. "We don't have to rush *this*. Are you sure?" Now his aura conveyed his own insecurities.

"Don't you want me?" Avery asked, reading into the ripples of hesitancy.

"Gods yes!" He nearly laughed at the absurdity of the question. "But I don't want you to look back and think you didn't have a choice or it was too fast or—"

"Ryse," she said, pressing one finger to his mouth. "No fears. No regrets. *My* decision is yes." Taking his mouth again, she relaxed and let the sexually deprived woman inside of her take over. That woman wanted Ryse out of his shirt. Now.

CHAPTER THIRTY-EIGHT

NIKKI STUDIED HER HAND OF CARDS. HORRIBLE. KNOCKING FROM under the table added to her irritation. "DANTE, IF YOU don't quit tapping your foot on the leg of the table, I'm going to slap you." She picking up a card and making it the one she needed with her magic.

"Sorry. I'm just on edge." He laid down a card.

"What's up?" Brenden tried to sneak a peek at Nikki's cards. She thumped him on his forehead. He rubbed it and scowled at her.

"Something isn't right."

When Dante said those words, Brenden was on his feet in a millisecond and Nikki's heart froze.

"Tell me," Brenden demanded.

"I don't know. But my premonitions are rarely wrong."

CHAPTER THIRTY-NINE

NEVER IN ALL HIS YEARS HAD RYSE WANTED SOMETHING OR someone so desperately. Avery's arousal was sweet perfume to his senses. He wanted to show her what sex could be, what lovemaking was supposed to feel like.

His strong-willed woman said that she was ready for this. The brain between his legs wanted to take that word at face value until she lay limp in his arms, ruined for any other man and begging for mercy. Thoughts of passion swam inside his mind.

The brain sitting on his shoulders still remembered the broken woman he had bathed in the safe house. He remembered the way she stared into the air, looking at nothing. Her mind had been in such shock, so ripped apart that she hadn't even fought him when he tended to her. Never again did he want to see her in that condition. Walking around with a raging case of sexual frustration was a small price to pay to make sure that nothing broke her again.

Instead of diving in head first, he took it slow, and let her lead. Right then, she was leading him to be shirtless. He held his breath as two luscious lips explored his bare chest. When she pushed the shirt back, he sat up and let her guide it down his arms and off. She sat back and her eyes perused over the expanse of naked flesh. The swear word that she muttered under her breath was in obvious appreciation. Even the least vain man in the world would have taken that to heart, letting it fuel his ego for all eternity. Until this tiny Texas girl came into his life, he wouldn't have given a second thought to his own physique. But now he would do anything to keep that hunger in her eyes.

"My turn." He slipped one finger in the curved neckline of her dress and ran his finger over her new tattoo. When Ryse put his lips on her, she thrust her hands into his hair. Avery was a delicious treat to his palate.

In his haze of sensations, he nearly missed the sound of a vehicle speeding down the road.

Nearly.

A SUV he recognized as one of his own came to a skidding halt. He and Avery were hidden in the canvas tent over the couch, but he still whispered for her to adjust her clothing.

"This better be a goddamned emergency," she said, fixing her dress. Ryse slipped on his shirt and stood to adjust himself. Deep breaths of cool night air filled his lungs as he tried to reign in the aroused man and let the pissed Thracian take over.

"They wouldn't be here if it wasn't. I gave very strict orders," he growled. If those orders were disobeyed for anything less than a catastrophic event, there would be hell to pay, and it would be paid in blood. He asked Avery to wait under the tent while he walked out to meet the unwelcome party.

Yankee rattled off apologies. "Get to it!" Ryse yelled, his mood taking a serious dive south.

"There's a situation."

They drove up to the Palace in record time; Ryse burst out of the car and made his way to Avery's suite. Whatever had happened, Yankee didn't want to talk about it in front of her. But his Princess was hot on his heels as they sprinted down the corridor.

"Move!" he yelled at the people who had gathered in front of the large wooden doors leading to their suite. They parted and ducked out of his path. Cutter was standing guard by the door and spoke in his native tongue so Avery wouldn't understand.

"She shouldn't see this."

Ryse nodded then turned to Avery. "Stay here with Cutter until I know what has happened."

The scene inside was pure chaos. General Falcon had a team of techs checking over every inch for evidence of the intruder. Philippe was crouched over something on the floor along with Hayden and a man in a lab coat. Across the room Hammon, Brenden and Nikki were talking. When Ryse walked in, they came to him.

"What happened?" he asked his right hand man.

"Someone has poisoned the dogs. Dante is out right now with a team rounding up everyone who has had access to them in the last forty-eight hours."

"Dante sensed it." Brenden took over the recollection. "We were playing cards downstairs; there was one guard in the suite with the dogs. When we arrived here, we found…"

Hammon finished for him, "Master, this poison has made the animals…odious. The Lady does not need to witness this."

Odious? Ryse approached the two German shepherds and found out exactly what he meant. Both the animals had gaping holes in their chests where their tissue had been eaten away. Their other organs and bones were all exposed. Their life's blood spilled onto the floor. The gruesome scene was all too familiar to Ryse. He'd seen this kind of damage before when Andreas, his first Elite, had been murdered. A cold chill went up his spine. No, Avery did not need to see this.

Philippe rose to his feet, holding a vial. He handed it to Hayden and then spoke to his Master in Italian. "We have isolated some of the poison from the blood of the canines. Christophe is going to analyze it to see where it might have come from. I concluded it was ingested in their food. Their stomach seems to be the source of the spreading."

He was interrupted by a commotion at the door. Avery had gotten past the threshold and Cutter was trying to restrain her. "Please, milady. You should wait for Master!"

But it was too late; she'd seen the carnage. Ryse felt her emotions rip loose in a tidal wave of anguish, knocking the wind out of his lungs.

⚬

"Nooo!" Avery screamed before running to her beloved pets. Her body hit a wall of warmth as Brenden intercepted her and wrapped her in his arms. "Let me go! My boys! Let me go, damn it!"

"Get her out of here!" she heard Ryse growl. "Her aura is wide open! Where is Dante?"

Brenden pushed a struggling Avery out the doors. His body was a vice around her. It took little effort for him to pick her up and take her down the hall. He barricaded them in another suite; Cutter followed, acting as a guard outside the door.

"What happened? Who did this?" Avery cried once Brenden released her. Nikki took her, wrapped her in a blanket, and sat her on the bed.

"Someone tell me what happened. Now!" she screamed, pushing power out of her aura. Brenden fell to his knees in front of her. Nikki slid off the bed, kneeling. "What are you doing?"

Nikki's voice was strained and forced through vocal cords that did not want to work. "Your aura, Avery."

Dante came through the door and ran to her. The moment his hand touched her cheek, a calm feeling came over the room. Avery took in a battered breath, realizing the strain her aura had put on everyone, herself included.

"Better?" he asked. Anxious eyes peered down at her. She nodded and felt her body collapse under the fatigue of her exertion. "Whoa!" Dante caught her against his chest as he sat next to her on the edge of the bed. "I have you, Princess."

Nikki, recovered from the blast of power, remained kneeling in front of Avery. "Avery, you need to bring your barriers back up so that Dante doesn't have to absorb your aura." She spoke softly and slowly.

Avery nodded, closing her eyes to concentrate. She envisioned the thick walls slowly rising in her mind. The barrier, impenetrable

198

and strong, boxed up the mental image of her aura. Her breathing regulated and she felt Dante relax beside her.

"There you go. Good girl." Nikki touched her cheek, comforting her friend as best she could.

Avery continued to rest against Dante. Her eyes flickered to Brenden, who paced the floor. "Please, please tell me what is going on. What happened to my dogs?"

Slumping on the bed, Brenden took her free hand. His eyes looked up at her with both pain and rage. "They were poisoned. It was in their food. Philippe was able to take some of the blood and extract the poison."

"They suffered, didn't they?"

Brenden clenched his jaw and gave one solemn nod. He released her and began pacing again. She buried her face into Dante's chest and cried. Hesitantly, he put his arms around her shoulders. Dante held her as she grieved over the loss. Castor and Pollux had been the last pieces of home, pieces of Frank that carried over into this world. They had been her companions for many years and it broke her heart to think of life without them.

Every tie to her former life was gone. She didn't know if the gods allowed this to happen, if it was part of some pre-destined plan or if her pain was even a concern of theirs. But one day, she would have revenge on the person who killed her boys.

―⋅― ⸙ ⋅―▸

Hours later, Ryse stood in the shadows of a block-walled room. His own rage was a beast inside of him waiting to feast on blood. Servants had been questioned. Alibis had been checked. It all came down to one Thracian soldier and a butler who was sweating bullets.

Yankee and Brenden detained the men in a cell. When Ryse walked in, they were questioning them.

"Did anyone enter or exit the room while you were on guard?" Yankee asked as he leaned back on a table.

"Not that I saw."

Brenden paced behind the suspects. Ryse watched him analyze the soldier. He looked to Yankee and signaled he didn't believe him. The answer was not a lie, nor was it the whole truth, either.

"What do you mean, not that you saw?" Yankee asked.

"While I was standing there, no one came in or out." The soldier was sweating, his hands shook even as he held them tightly in his lap. His pupils, though focused on Yankee, were dilated.

Brenden crossed his arms over his chest. After a moment, he narrowed his eyes and shook his head. Not a lie. Not the truth. Yankee casually leaned over the table, his gaze piercing the fellow Thracian. "Soldier, were you standing by the door for the entire length of time the Lady was gone?"

"No." Truth.

"Why not?" Ryse hissed from his shadowed corner. Confrontation with the Master made the soldier twitch.

"I'd be very careful to tell the *whole* truth, soldier. The Master is a bit unpredictable right now," Yankee said.

Through more direct and some obviously embarrassing questions, they found out that the soldier left his post for half an hour while he and his girlfriend, one of the maids, had sex in a closet by the pool room.

"You abandoned your post?" Ryse screamed in the man's face. "Have you not been taught better? Answer me."

"The Princess wasn't there." The soldier broke. "They were just *dogs*. I didn't think it would be a big deal. They were both sleeping when I checked on them after I got back, they were the same as when I left them. They're just *dogs!*"

Ryse backhanded the man and knocked him out of his chair. Using a gift he rarely accessed, Ryse threw out his hand and seized control of the soldier's physical form. The man levitated from the ground and Ryse slammed him against the wall. Magic pinned the man to the blocks and lifted him higher until his feet dangled in the air.

Ryse was barely in control. Ares had descended and was as

much a part of his being as he was. His eyes glowing as Ares passed judgment on this Thracian son. *Guilty.* The one word gave Ryse the power to take the man's life. "Guilty," Ryse repeated as the spirit left his body.

"Wait! Wait! I have information!" the soldier squirmed. "I saw the Princess, the British one and her maid, I think."

"You have two seconds," Ryse snarled.

"She was looking for him," he pointed to the butler. The butler had been so silent Ryse had nearly forgotten him.

Ryse turned his attention back to the soldier. "Your information has been noted." His eyes glowed again as he petitioned Ares in case there was a change in his adjudication.

His unworthy heart is that of a coward. Verify his information, then rid my bloodline of his impurity.

Ryse released the soldier from his magical grip and pulled the patch off his uniform. "Ares finds you unworthy of the Thracian blood. You will be detained until your testimony is proven, then you are to be stripped."

"Stripped?" the soldier argued. "You can't strip me of my… my…*blood!*"

"Your blood is mine." As if to prove his point Ryse held out his hand and called forth the life-giving flow. He could feel the stream moving to meet him. The soldier's face pooled with blood as he screamed. Ryse's anger was so deep, so volatile, that all he wanted to do was murder the man, no matter what Ares commanded. Blood seeped from the soldier's nose.

Ryse dropped his hand and stumbled back. "Yankee, you finish," he said before leaving the room. Falcon met him in the hall. "I'm fine!" he barked before his General could even speak.

"Master." Falcon bowed deeper than usual. He knew better than to question Ryse at this moment. A glowing light still ringed his feral eyes.

CHAPTER FORTY

RYSE FOUND AVERY IN ONE OF THE SUITES, CURLED UP ON THE BED under her quilt, fast asleep. Nothing but a lamp gave the room light. She had changed into cotton pajamas. Dante slept in a chair by the bed, his hand secured to Avery's by a piece of ribbon so that even in sleep he was protecting her. No magic could disturb her sleep as long as Dante held her hand. A vicious ping of jealousy flamed inside his soul, still raw from Ares possession.

On the other side of the bed, Nikki looked up at him. She had one hand petting Avery's shoulder. "She's worn out, Master. So is he. She had some trouble containing her aura and Dante bore the brunt of it," she whispered, her ivory skin seeming more pale than usual. "She passed out right in the middle of crying." Nikki looked down, gave Avery one last affectionate caress, and then moved off the bed.

"I want to rest with her awhile. When he is done with the interrogations, take Brenden and make him sleep. Tell Hammon and Cutter to set up watch. I want you and Brenden fresh for her tomorrow." He dismissed Nikki and began taking off his boots. Dante stirred and was surprised to see Ryse. He looked down at the hand tied to his and then back up at Ryse again.

"Is her aura under control?" Ryse asked, unable to sense her through the shield of Dante.

"Now that she sleeps." He gingerly untied the ribbon and peeled her fingers from his hand, smiling at the tight grip. Ryse noticed the affectionate way he smiled. Dante stood and walked to the door to leave.

"Dante," Ryse said, bringing him to a halt.

"Master?"

"Man to man, what do you see when you look at her? Speak truthfully, free from consequence."

Dante took a deep breath, thinking for a moment before the words came out his mouth. Ryse appreciated that about the boy. Too many of the young Thracians would spit out words that were unfiltered and rash. Dante seemed to meditate over every word that crossed his lips. It was a sign of wisdom and maturity beyond his years.

"I see a beautiful woman with a beautiful heart." His eyes lingered on Avery's sleeping form. Again the affection was noted. "No one has ever looked at me the way she does. I've never stood out among my peers, and I've been overlooked because my gift is not an offensive one. Yet, Avery picked me out of a crowded hall of Thracians." Dante looked Ryse in the eye. "I never thought of my ability as a gift until she made it one. She has given me more encouragement and purpose in the last few hours than anyone else in my entire life. Even after Avery knew of my father's convictions, her view of me never changed." He glanced away. "As it does with so many."

"You speak as though you have deeper feelings for her," Ryse smiled and Dante began to stutter.

"Well, no Master. I, she only…"

Holding up a quieting hand, Ryse said, "I understand, Dante. She is easy to love. That doesn't mean I'm not going to keep my eye on you." Ryse smirked, delivering both a tease and a threat in one.

"Master," Dante said as he opened the door. "I know the questions will arise, so I would prefer to answer them now." Ryse nodded. "I did not harm the Lady's animals and would give my own life's blood to bring them back if it gave her happiness. And no, I do not agree with my father's political views. There is more honor in this family than in all the other Deities combined."

"I have no doubt of your devotion, son," Ryse forced a tight smile.

As soon as the boy left, he lay with his wife. As bulky as he was, it was hard not to move the bed as he crawled in beside Avery. She mumbled his name in her sleep and he pulled her close. Having her smell, feeling her warmth, sensing the calming slumber in her aura, tasting her skin as he kissed her—all of this let him relax. *She lives. They didn't hurt her. Avery is alive in my arms.*

He repeated this mantra over and over in his head, trying to make his brain believe it. The greatest fear in his soul was losing her. Life would end for him if she were killed. Thracian Master or not, Deity or not, without his partner, his wife, he would be forfeit. Taking one deep inhale of her scent, he closed his eyes and forced himself to go to sleep. The protection ward he placed on the room would keep everyone out and them safely in.

During the quiet of the night, he felt hands on his body. Fingertips grazed the naked flesh of his chest. Sweet lips caressed his neck and he prayed he wasn't dreaming. When he blinked his eyes open, two emeralds gazed back at him. Neither of them spoke in the darkness. The small lamp in the corner of the room cast only enough light to make out the features of her face. He touched her cheek and she pressed her face to his palm. Moving her legs around his body, she inched closer to him and took in his lips. Her kiss was demanding and powerful.

She needed him. And tonight he would give her whatever she needed, no questions asked.

It wasn't what most couples experienced on their wedding night. There were no candles, no flowers, no fancy meals or private patios with romantic ambiance. There were no overused lines or poetic words. There was only the mutual understanding of two people who needed to feel the other alive. Too much death and pain had been thrown at them in such a short period of time. Now, in this moment, it was about life and about being together no matter what bullets were shot from the guns of the world.

In the back of his mind, he kept looking for any sign of irres-olution. He found none. This woman, *his* woman until the end of time, had no fear as she sat on top of him and removed her shirt. Elegant curls of her auburn hair fell over the tempting curves of her breast. When she bent down to kiss him again, her hair curtained his face. Avery always smelled sweet, like a warm spring day sprinkled with sugar. He took in her scent and let it feed him. The hunger he had for her was all that burned inside now. The rest of the world be damned. Tonight he was going to live for Avery.

Using colossal effort, he restrained himself, letting Avery set the pace. Not once did he try to assert the dominance that was bred into him. She needed to be in control and not to feel pressured or forced. He would not let any thoughts of her past creep into these precious moments because he felt the need to be dominant. He used all his self-control not to go insane from the feel of her touch. The way she bit her lip and the innocence of her movements as she removed her remaining clothing was a reminder that she had never seduced a man before. He was her first. That precious knowledge touched his heart like nothing else.

Every care was taken not to push her too fast but desire drove him insane and ran through him like wild fire. He cupped her breast and her breaths quickened. She gasped when he took her into his mouth and her hands tunneled into his hair. Avery rolled them over so he was on top. Gently, he used his fingers to ready her, and that alone made her arch her back off the bed. When they finally con-nected, only a whimper crossed her lips. Ripples of fear and love mingled in her aura, the power aroused him to a near painful state. But he did not miss how that whimper shook, how her eyes widened and moisture pooled in their corners. He kissed her tears away then coaxed her into a deep, sensual kiss while their bodies adjusted to each other. Fingers dug into his shoulders and sides as they moved together. Each rocking movement made him dizzy, made his muscles coil tighter and tighter until all the world faded away, everything but his sweet Avery. Her moans were music to his ears. The salt of her skin and the perfume of her sex triggered an animal slumbering beneath his own skin. He picked up the pace, urged on by Avery's hands clawing at his back. It wasn't going to take much more to send both of them over the edge. He wanted her on top when they did. The magic of their bond would consume her and he wanted her to experience it. Ryse rolled and sat her atop him, loving the way she gasped at the new position.

His father had warned him of the effects of the bond. The two of them, intimately together, hitting the pinnacle as one, sent an atomic shock wave of magic bouncing off the walls of the room. Light bulbs exploded, the furniture shook and some of the wood splintered as the wave of their mating bond solidified into a swirl of blue, white and green stars that danced around them on the bed. After a moment of shock, Avery put her hands in the air and her head fell back as she received the divine gifts. Now she was linked to the gods for all eternity. They would speak to her as a Deity and reveal themselves to her.

Tears of joy showered her cheeks and a smile of pure delight spread wide across her face. In that moment, he could feel her thoughts. She was free. The tainted views of intimacy and intercourse were gone, erased with the loving visions of her husband.

She was glorious. It made his heart burst with pride. Seeing her like this, naked and open, arms spread to the heavens, her hair gently waving in the magical whirlwind about her, a smile that could light the world, crying in release of the fears that chained her for so long—she was a goddess. The image of her burned into his brain until he could close his eyes and still recall every detail. Then, as she wrapped herself tighter around him, he lost all thoughts. The only thing that mattered was showing her the depths of his love and devotion.

CHAPTER
FORTY-ONE

INSTEAD OF THE SUNSHINE WAKING HER UP AS IT HAD THE LAST TWO mornings, it was the feel of fingers tracing circles on her back. Avery was lying on her stomach across Ryse's chest. The only thing she wore was his ring. That was enough.

This morning, Ryse's steady strong heartbeat was quite different from the snare drum she had collapsed against last night after their lovemaking. Her own body was a mystery of sensations.

"Good morning, my love." Ryse kissed the top of her head. "How do you feel?"

"Like a coon dog sprawled out in the sun."

Ryse chuckled and it made her whole body move. "I'm guessing that is a Southern way of saying 'well'." Raising her head to look at him, she smiled and nodded. "You were very upset last night. No regrets?" he asked, running a hand through her hair.

Avery recoiled. "No." Oh god! Was he having regrets? He had been the one so adamant about not rushing things. Did he just sleep with her for the hell of it? "Do you—"

"No," he stated, touching her cheek. "By the gods, I swear to you that last night was the most…" He blew out a breath and his eyebrows rose. "Well, shit, there are no words."

Avery smiled. "I love you."

"My goddess, my beautiful wife, I love you, too." He pulled her mouth to his and she felt the passion behind his words. "As much as I wish we could hide in this room all day, we have a killer to catch and my father's brunch in the middle of all of it." He was quiet for a moment, tracing the lines of her face. "I'm so sorry about Castor and Pollux, my love. I will do anything to make this easier for you."

Avery closed her eyes and rubbed the bridge of her nose. "They were all I had left of my old life, you know, the last living pieces of Frank and our friendship. For many years they were the only companions I had at home." Empathy was evident upon her lover's face. She touched his furrowed brows. "Now I have you."

"I would get you more pets if you desire."

"No." she said, touching his lips. "No replacements. I have a feeling they would only be another way for someone to upset me and I don't want that. I loved my boys, but I don't need that companionship now. I have you." Kissing Ryse only solidified that thought in her heart. "Besides, if I ever feel the need to curl up with an animal, I could always get Bren to shift into that—that *thing* he is." The disgusted look on Ryse's face made her laugh.

"That is very wrong in many ways," he said sarcastically. Something about seeing Ryse this loose erased any sorrows she might have felt. That's not to say she didn't want the blood of whoever killed her precious boys. Justice would be served.

But maybe after one more tumble with Ryse. Besides, this room was going to have to have some major repairs after what happened last night. Might as well finish the demolition.

After they both collapsed, once again panting and sated, Avery asked, "Do I get to show off my brand today?"

Ryse's smile melted her into the sheets. "You know, you are quite a contradiction of yourself. You don't like the term 'mated,' but you are one hell of an animal in bed. So which is it, baby?" he said, running his fingers over her breast. His eyes followed the curves and stopped when he saw the mark. With the wave of his hand the room was illuminated and he was staring at her tattoo. His jaw was clenched.

The look on his face scared her. "What? Ryse, what is it?"
"Get dressed."

Ryse burst into his parent's private sitting room without so much as a knock, pulling Avery by the hand. Avery remembered the roses and cream room well. Standing, looking into the lit fire was Troy. The masculine man was highly out of place in the feminine room. General Falcon was standing close to him talking. Dyna sat in a wingback chair and was in deep conversation with Hayden. All eyes turned to Ryse.

Troy addressed him immediately. "General Falcon has been informing me of all the events that went on under my roof last night while I lay unaware, sleeping in my bed. Would my eldest son like to tell me *why* I was not alerted?" Troy's acidic voice carried a resonance in it that made Avery feel like a grade school child getting scolded by the principal.

"The situation was being handled," Ryse barked back.

Troy looked at his son with nothing less than the sheer power that made him King of all the Deities. "Oh, I see very well how this situation was being handled. General Falcon was just informing me that our only witness has gone mad after having his blood sucked to his skull and the person he tried to incriminate killed himself by the same poison he used to kill the dogs."

"Good!" Ryse said, letting Avery's hand go. Would anyone notice if she tucked tail and ran?

She slowly slumped away from the two male lions locked in a dominance battle. She stood behind Dyna and Hayden, safely hidden. Hayden hugged her to his side and took the hand she had placed on his chest. It shone with Ryse's ring. "Congratulations, sis," he whispered in her ear before kissing her cheek.

"And what is so goddamned good about it?" Troy screamed, commanding their attention. "The informant never spoke of who gave him the poison in the first place!"

"Father, I think you know *exactly* who gave him that shit!" Ryse met his challenge with his own raised voice.

Troy grabbed his son by the nape of the neck the way a lion would grip a cub and looked him in the eye. Taking a voice so low and threatening it made Avery want to run from the room again, he leaned close to Ryse. "You watch your tone with me, son. Not even *you* will disrespect me in my own home. And if *Ares* has a problem with it, then he can take it up with *Zeus!*" Everyone in the room shriveled against his aura. Ryse slumped under the staggering power of his father. Troy's words were accented by thunder. As if nature itself cowered to his rage. "Now you will calm yourself and speak to me the way you were raised to speak to your elders." He pushed his hand off Ryse, making his son take an involuntary step backwards.

Dyna and Hayden stayed out of it, keeping their eyes down. Avery took her cue from them even though a feral instinct to protect her husband radiated from her skin.

Ryse closed his eyes and took a deep breath, bowing his head. "Forgive me, Father."

"Ryse, I understand that you have been under a lot of strain. But I expect you of all people to keep your head on your shoulders." Troy placed his hand on the wall of the room. He was putting up a protection ward. Ryse had explained them this morning. An invisible ripple went through the walls. "Everyone in this room knows that Salina had something to do with this. We all know it, but we have no evidence. To charge a Princess, especially the daughter of such close friends, would be a disaster if she proves innocent."

"I cannot hurt Filene like that," Dyna spoke up.

"If the girl did this, Filene will be hurt no matter what. Right now, she is being careful and leaving no loose ends," Troy said to his wife.

"The one lead we have in her direction is the butler who spoke to Salina's Shadow Lady. Without a formal petition, she is protected under confidentiality laws," General Falcon informed them.

If a formal petition were made, Salina would know they were

on to her and she would go home before being proven of anything. Once in her home country, she would be under the control of her parents, and they were her jury.

"I'm not meaning to diminish the situation," Ryse said. "But I have something that I believe needs to be discussed. Falcon, my family and I need to talk privately."

Ryse was sending Falcon away? Dang. What was so wrong with her brand that the General couldn't see it? She unconsciously pulled her shirt tighter against her neck.

The General nodded and left the room. Once he was gone, everyone looked expectantly at Ryse. He turned to Avery and his family followed his lead. Hanging her head, her eyes went to the floor and felt her cheeks turn an unhealthy color of red. Dyna was the first to gasp, recognizing something that Hayden and Troy only noticed a moment later.

"Oh!" Dyna stood, eyes watering and hand dramatically over her chest. "You've mated!"

Oh god! How embarrassing! The mother-in-law could see sex written all over her face. This was beyond mortifying.

"Yes! Her aura is completely different." Dyna exclaimed as she touched Avery's cheeks. "The gods have descended their blessings upon you, my darling. You glow of their radiance."

Hayden huffed and slapped Avery on the butt. "I don't think it's divine radiance that is making her glow," he muttered under his breath.

"Hayden!" Dyna scolded. She then grinned at Avery slyly and whispered, "Physical bonds do make the aura the brightest." Dyna winked and hugged Avery close. "My heart overflows with happiness."

The mood in the room seemed to lighten as everyone congratulated Ryse and Avery on their impromptu marriage. Even Troy managed a hearty handshake for his son and a kiss on Avery's cheek. Hayden went on a tirade making insinuating comments while Avery showed off her wedding ring. It was silly when she thought about it, wedding rings were a human tradition, not Olympian.

"While we both greatly appreciate your affections," Ryse said, pulling Avery against his side, "there is something that you all need to see. I gave Avery my mark last night. But hers is a variation that I've never seen before. Between the four of us, I was hoping we could figure out what it means."

He looked down at Avery, who was not exactly comfortable with what he was silently asking her to do. He furrowed his brow and touched her chin. "What's wrong? This morning you were asking if you could show it off," he said quietly.

"That's before you started acting like I had a scarlet letter across my chest," Avery said, wishing she could bury her head deep in the sand.

"There's nothing *wrong* with it, love. I've just never seen anything like it." He kissed her. Hayden said something about getting a room and Ryse glared at him. "Come on, love, show them."

Avery unbuttoned the first few buttons of her shirt and pulled the left collar down over her shoulder. Troy, Hayden and Dyna gathered around her like a circus show and looked at the tattoo.

"It's a lion."

"Why a lion head over the sword?"

"There is only one goddess who used lions in her marks."

CHAPTER FORTY-TWO

ALL EYES TURNED TO HAYDEN. HE CONTINUED TO EXPLAIN. "RHEA, the mother of Zeus, Poseidon & Hades—her chariots were pulled by two lions. Throughout our history, only a chosen few have been marked with lions."

"The mother goddess?" Troy asked incredulously, his voice barely an awed whisper. "How is that possible? Avery took the mark of her mate. Why would she also be marked of Rhea?"

"I'll have to study the history again." Hayden brushed his hands through his hair, clearly not liking that he didn't know exactly what the symbol meant. "She still has Ryse's sword, but the lion's head is on top of the sword." He went to touch the tattoo, but Avery swiped at his hand.

"Back, mister," she said, pointing a threatening finger at him. "No touching."

"I second that motion," Ryse sneered at Hayden.

Hayden chuckled and shook his head. "What a pair." He grinned at Avery. "I thought you were on my side?"

"I'm a married woman now, sorry sugar." Avery leaned into Ryse and was comforted by the strength at her side.

Breaking into a side conversation, the men huddled together and began debating. "This has to be related to her blood results…"

Avery covered herself and met Dyna's eyes. The amazing lavender color framed in black lashes was such a striking blend. It was like she could see exactly what had happened in that bedroom since last night. Awkward.

A light giggle crossed the woman's lips. "Are you ashamed that you lay with your husband?" Dyna asked as she pulled Avery into a separate part of the suite.

"Well, I, we…" Blowing out a deep breath, Avery tried to speak with the composure of an adult. "I know that technically Ryse and I are bound as an Olympian couple. But I wasn't raised as an Olympian."

Understanding lit up in Dyna's face and she put reassuring hands on her new daughter's shoulders. "You still feel as though there should be a formal wedding to make it official."

It wasn't a question, but Avery answered anyway. "Yeah. Is that crazy? I feel like I ran off to Vegas and got married by Elvis. I mean, I'm wearing his mark, his ring, but it still seems very fragile and possibly breakable."

Taking her hand, Dyna moved for her to sit down in a chair. She rubbed Avery's arm while she talked. "I promise you there is nothing breakable or fragile about this union. A mating is very permanent, especially when done with a branding. At this point, the blood bond is nothing more than a bow tied on the package." Dyna tilted her head as if reading into Avery's silence. "You aren't afraid of your feelings changing, are you?"

"No, I love Ryse more every day." That wasn't the problem at all. Every time she looked at him, heard his voice, felt his aura, or took a breath of his scent, her affections for him grew. It was rooted deep despite the short time frame of their relationship.

"You fear *his* feelings will change?" The way Dyna said it, it sounded like the most incredulous and unthinkable concept. Avery felt stupid for worrying. But it was her fear.

"Oh, my darling!" Dyna pulled her into an embrace. "Think about how much you love my son, then think about having to wait a century to attain that love. Trust me, I don't believe the gods themselves could pry that man away from you." She kissed the top of Avery's head. "Have confidence in your bond. You must be a united front, being as one. Our people will look to you for their security and safety. But they will also analyze your relationships, your marriage and friendships. As their future Queen, you have a responsibility to be the kind of woman, friend, mother, and Olympian you would want your populace to be."

Avery listened closely. Dyna was in full mentor mode now. Words of wisdom and advice flowed freely.

The brunch was set for ten that morning. Even with everything that had happened the night before, Troy still wanted to host the sit down meal in attempt to look like no one suspected Salina. Avery had less than half an hour before she had to face the snake-witch and not nearly enough sleep. Nikki had promised to have an assortment of stylish one-shouldered outfits to choose from.

Avery, Nikki, Brenden and Dante were heading up to one of the guest apartments to get ready. Her suite was still being quarantined until they knew the source of the poison. Ahead of Avery and Dante, Brenden and Nikki were walking rather close and whispering to each other. Looping an arm around Dante's elbow, Avery leaned over and whispered, "What's with those two?"

"Lover's quarrel." He smirked. "Bren was rather agitated when he was done with the interviews last night. I think he was snippy to her."

Nikki stopped dead in her tracks, turned to Brenden and smacked him with all the force her tiny redheaded body could muster. She grunted, and without so much as a look behind her, went into the guest apartment. Brenden, holding his cheek, looked at Avery and Dante with wide eyes.

Avery tilted her head and smiled innocently and in her thickest southern accent asked, "You gonna tell me why she did that, darlin'?"

Bren's eyes thinned into tiny slits and his nostrils flared. "You women are so damned crazy."

"True," Avery conceded. "But Nikki is one of the sweetest people I know, so what did you do to set her off?"

Brenden's mouth hung open. "Me? Why do you assume it was me?" The look that both Dante and Avery gave him was the equivalent of both of them saying "*Duh*" in unison.

"You don't have time for this," Brenden said, ushering Avery into the room. "Just get dressed in here, we'll be next door." He pushed until he could close the door behind her. She was left facing Nikki.

"I don't want to talk about it." She looked pained and twitchy. "Please pick a shirt."

Avery pulled Nikki into a hug and let her friend sniffle on her shoulder. Nikki was stiff and unyielding. "You sure you don't want to talk about it?"

"Please stop. We don't have time, really." Nikki let her go and insisted on getting dressed in silence.

Before joining the guys in the hall, Avery took Nikki by the shoulders and looked her straight in the eye. "I hate this, Nikki. I hate us not talking like friends. Whatever is wrong, you can tell me."

"Avery, let's face the facts. You are a *Deity* now," she said the word with such distance that Avery didn't even recognize her. "I am a Shadow Lady. I am your servant. We need to make that line very clear." Avery started to speak, Nikki cut her off. "No, Avery. We don't get to be friends, or pals, or bosom buddies. Please let me do my job like I have been trained for." There was no room for questioning her. Her stern face said it all. Nikki held open the door for Avery then looked at the floor while she walked through.

What had happened? Just the night before they had sat there like best friends, Avery crying on her shoulder and Nikki comforting her like the loving dear that she was. What had changed? What had Avery done to deserve such a breakup from her only friend?

Standing in the hall and wearing their standard black were Brenden and Dante. Both men looked very professional. Black slacks, black shirts and black ties. Dante had his sandy blond hair pulled back or...*wait a minute.*

"You cut your hair!" Avery said, shocked at how it had happened in the last twenty minutes. "How?"

Dante's eyes squinted like the answer was obvious. "With scissors, a comb, and mechanical clippers."

Avery put her hands on her hips while Brenden laughed. "I meant how'd you do it so fast? And why?" She motioned for him to turn around so she could see. The back of his neck was cleanly shaven and short. The soft blond hair was longer on top, parted to one side and swooped down long on the other side. Avery reached up on either side of his face, petting at his newly uncovered neck.

"It's a family tradition to cut one's hair when they are bound to their Deity. One of Master Ryse's people did it. Is it not to your liking?" Again, he looked at Avery with big puppy eyes seeking her approval.

"It looks fine! I was shocked that you could cut it in such short time."

"Ain't he pretty?" Brenden teased, rubbing Dante's head and laughing.

"Bren!" Avery scolded. "You messed it up!" Avery stretched up on her toes to comb her fingers through Dante's hair. "There."

"That was so motherly, it was disturbing." An upstate accent was a dead giveaway to the new person in the conversation. Something about Yankee both intrigued and scared the living daylights out of her.

CHAPTER FORTY-THREE

"Hello, yankee." Avery greeted him, remembering his "hot" comment. It made her grin, which clearly made him uncomfortable. His eyes skated around, finding something besides her to look at. "Master asked me to bring little brother this patch. Said something about substituting for a blood bond. He could have found someone better to deliver it. I think this is punishment."

"Yeah, for me," Brenden said, taking the green and gold armband from Yankee. On the hunter green background in gold thread was an embroidered lion's head with a tall winged sword behind, identical to her tattoo. She couldn't help but notice Dante eyeing it covetously.

"Soon enough, darlin,'" she said to her shy warrior. He let one corner of his mouth turn up.

"Well, come on," Yankee said, watching as Avery slid the band to Brenden's bicep and straightening it. "Don't want to be late to the party. Bring your My Size Ken doll, too." His comment was directed at Dante. The clear lack of enthusiasm was not making Avery feel comfortable about the event. Neither was the fact that Nikki stayed silent behind her the entire walk.

Brunch took place in the opulent grand dining hall on the top story of the Palace. The long slender room was decorated in Castille colors. Hunter green and gold linens dressed the table. Avery felt tiny in the massive space. Especially when all the people filling it kept glancing at her.

Taking in a deep breath and squaring her shoulders, Avery lifted her chin and remembered that she was no longer a small town café owner. Now she was the wife of one of the most powerful and influential men on this planet. She was a legitimate Deity and a Divine Grace. She bore a mark that no one could ever question.

"You look fine," Brenden, her escort, whispered in her ear as he held her arm like a gentleman. Nikki had conjured a one shouldered, strawberry red silk top and white jeans. The red high heels nearly made Avery eye level with Brenden.

"Thanks. Hey, we need to talk about…" She motioned her eyes over to Nikki.

Brenden gave an exasperated sign but nodded in agreement. "She's been acting weird since this morning. She went to the kitchen to get breakfast and came back crazy." He sighed. "Females."

"Later, me and you. We'll go for a walk or something." Avery smiled and scanned the room. There was only one set of eyes she wanted to find.

And there they were.

The way Ryse looked at her would never get old. From his place by one of the three fireplaces, he smiled at her. If she had not been so chilled with nerves, she would have melted into a puddle. His black shirt stretched across his muscular chest and arms. He looked casual, as did most of the people in the room. He excused himself from General Falcon and a woman to make his way over.

Thank the gods he belonged to her.

A blonde in a pink halter-top suddenly blocked the view of him. Avery nearly choked when Salina smiled at her.

"Avery," she purred. "I don't believe we have been formally introduced." She stuck out her hand cordially. "Princess Salina Avondale of the European Clan." The accent made her almost sound polite.

"I know who you are," Avery said with her brightest fake smile. She did not move to shake Salina's hand.

"No need to be crass. I'm merely making introduction."

"You'll have to excuse me if I don't feel the need to reciprocate."

Her eyes lingered a moment too long on Avery's brand before she gave a stuck-up huff, smiled and walked over to Dante. The hairs on the back of Avery's neck bristled. Salina could mess with Avery all she wanted, but making a move on her men was another insult completely.

"Oh, you are very nice looking indeed." Salina's accent made everything she said sound so proper even if her actions were not. She touched his chest with manicured nails. Dante stood rigid and never took his eyes off Avery. "I believe you will make a great addition to my *personal* guard."

"He's spoken for." Yankee came out of nowhere. "The Master is taking the Ken doll, here, under his wing as an Elite Apprentice. So very sorry, Princess."

"He's not marked," Salina spit out in a loss of her self-control. Yankee apparently had the same weird effect on her as he did everyone else.

"He will be this morning. Especially since the Lady Avery is now fully bonded to the Master. It makes things so much more... permanent. Our Master's consort now has the Elites to back her." Yankee accented the last sentence as a warning. Avery caught it. Salina did, too.

"Lucky you," she sneered to Avery.

"You have no idea," Avery said calmly.

Salina took her leave and Yankee made a slight nod to Bren. "I'm sticking close, little brother."

Brenden rolled his eyes. "I don't need your supervision."

"It's not for you." Yankee flashed his eyes to Dante, then to Avery. What did that mean?

Ryse walked up before Avery could ask. "What did *she* want?"

Brenden released Avery's arms and moved back with Nikki and Dante.

"At first, it was an attempt to play nice. But she's already burnt that bridge and swept up the ashes."

"Give her some of that Southern charm, huh?" He smirked as he kissed her cheek and whispered, "You look delicious." He nipped at her ear and she tried hard not to melt. Taking in a deep pull of his scent didn't help matters. Instead, it nearly made her eyes roll back in her head.

"You can have a taste later," she promised.

"I will take you up on that." He gave her a dirty smirk that sent a shot of pure joy between her thighs. Even thinking about it was making her blush. Oh, the joys of the newly married!

Sitting down to the meal was awkward. Ryse was on one side of her and as much as she wanted Nikki to take her other side, her Shadow Lady stood back behind her with all the other servants in the room. This broke Avery's heart. Didn't Nikki know she was more than some *maid*?

Hayden sat down beside her and put his arm around the back of her chair. Everything about him was so confident and carefree. Avery knew that behind the illusion of a pretty face was an extremely brilliant mind. That pretty face looked so much like his older brother, she couldn't help but love it.

"So, you and Ryse." He wiggled his brows provocatively.

So much for that previous thought.

"How is that any of your business? You must be nutty if you think you and I are having this conversation," she laughed.

Hayden chuckled. "I'm not trying to be a perv, Avery. I simply inquire because your bonding makes certain gifts achievable for you. I'm curious as to what abilities you have gained from being with my brother. Call it scientific curiosity." He waved his hand with aristocratic flair.

"Haven't you ever heard the phrase 'curiosity killed the cat'?"

"Doesn't it finish with 'satisfaction brought him back'?" Hayden looked smug as he took a drink of his juice.

"Yes, but then I beat the shit outta the cat and he died after all."

Hayden nearly spit out his drink before throwing his head back in laughter. At least one person found her antics humorous. "Oh, Avery! How I have missed you being in my life all these years! You make things so much more exciting." He leaned over and kissed her cheek, sending her into a full-blown blush. The red of her shirt paled in comparison. Ryse leaned behind her, making a threat about public displays of affection with his *wife*.

When Troy and Dynasty took their seats in front of the three of them, Avery noticed that Dyna's eyes looked bloodshot, like she had been crying.

"Dyna?" Avery whispered across the table. With a ghost of a smile, the angelic Queen bowed her head slightly in acknowledgement. "You've had a vision?" Avery asked. Dyna nodded again. "Can you tell me?" Avery pleaded.

"I cannot change the things I see. And I will not burden you with my knowledge. It is the will of the gods that such things should come to pass. It is my duty to accept their will and not interfere."

"Maybe you don't have to interfere. Let me do it for you?" Avery attempted a joke but failed in the eyes of her mother-in-law.

Dyna reached out and touched Avery's hand on the table. "We all have our responsibilities, my darling. There are roles we all must play. You will play your part soon enough."

CHAPTER FORTY-FOUR

AVERY'S STOMACH KNOTTED AS SHE LEANED BACK IN HER CHAIR. Dyna's eyes cleared and no one else noticed their exchange. The staff began putting food in front of them and everyone ate. But Avery had lost her appetite.

"Eat, my darling," Dyna said with her serene smile. "You will need your strength."

Avery didn't like the sound of that, but it did prompt her to finish her meal. It also made her follow Dyna's eyes everywhere she looked. The wise old angel gave away nothing. The brunch was eaten without incidence, yet Avery wasn't able to get comfortable.

Ryse leaned over and threaded his fingers through hers. "You are on edge, my love. What's the matter? Is it Salina?"

"I'm fine."

"Right." He kissed her cheek. The fact that he seemed so openly affectionate to her in this public setting made her feel good. Some part of her feared that Ryse would try and keep his stone façade, not allowing people see the kind and gentle side of him.

Once finished with their meals, Troy stood and tapped his glass to get everyone's attention. As always, Troy was the perfect balance of regal and lethal, handsome and wise.

"I have invited you all here this morning to celebrate an era of new beginnings for our family and for our empire. Today we will recognize the unity of my eldest son, Prince Ryse Castille and his Grace, Avery McClain." Applause rose from the table and Avery leaned over to accept the kiss that Ryse offered. "It's been a long road for my son and his Lady, one that has been littered with tears and joys. One that is not over—indeed, it is just beginning.

"On this day, Lady Dynasty and I ask that you all join us in the blood bonding ceremony to complete their pairing in the eyes of the gods." He motioned for one of the servants to come forward. The man held a silver tray with a goblet and ornate carved knife. Troy motioned for Ryse and Avery to stand. The server set the goblet down in the middle of the table and took the blade in his hand.

"The exchange of blood is the symbol and physical representation of the commitment that one makes to their mate." Ryse grinned as Avery cringed at the term. Troy suppressed a smile, then continued. "The partnership between a man and his *wife* is the most sacred of bonds in our world. It is not to be taken lightly. This bond is not about emotions or feelings that you have for each other. It is about the choice two people make to love one another every day, no matter what this world throws at your feet. Emotions are fleeting. Feelings are ever changing. But you can choose to love and to fight for that love. You choose to be the anchor for each other, to support and encourage, to challenge and grow together from this point forward as one."

Troy took the knife from the servant and presented it to Ryse over the table. Making a thin line down the middle of his palm, Ryse let his blood drip into the goblet. He then handed the knife to Avery. She copied his actions, trying not to wince at the sting of the knife splitting her skin. When their blood droplets mixed in the chalice, it magically filled with red liquid. "The gods fill the chalice!" Troy exclaimed joyously. "The union is blessed!"

Ryse picked up the drink and put it to his lips, but he was distracted by Hayden's loud cheer.

"Let us toast the new couple! Bring champagne!" The hall was filled with applause and chatter as flutes of champagne were dispersed.

Ryse leaned over and whispered, "I love you." But Avery was watching Dyna. Her smile was flat, her expression was blank. If ever a person was on autopilot, it was her.

Nikki came over with a serving tray and handed Ryse, Hayden, and Avery their flutes. Avery smiled at her, but Nikki looked pained and stressed, like she was on the verge of a nervous breakdown right there in the middle of everyone. Leaning across the table, Nikki handed Dyna and Troy champagne.

That was an odd thing to do. Hanna was right behind them with a tray.

Avery examined Nikki closely. She was sweating, one eye kept twitching and she kept glancing at something behind Avery. Following her line of sight, she noticed that Salina was watching carefully.

As Ryse and his family lifted their drinks, Salina smirked. Turning her eyes to Nikki, she caught her gaze shortly and then Nikki closed her eyes and turned away.

"…so let us toast, to my son and his new wife! To Ryse and Avery!" Troy said, signaling for everyone to drink.

Panicked, Avery looked at Dyna as she watched Troy take a sip of the champagne. The expression on her face said it all. It was the look of a woman saying goodbye to her husband. This was it; this was the vision that had her so upset. Something was in the champagne.

And Nikki knew it.

"No!" Avery screamed. Dropping her own flute, she knocked Ryse's out of his hand. Then turned to Hayden who had barely taken a sip. Then, with a strength she could only hope was the gods working in her, she leapt across the table and swiped Troy's flute to the floor. He had finished his drink. Whatever was in the champagne was now in his system.

Shock rang out throughout the room. People gasped and champagne flutes were thrown down.

"What in the name of Zeus is going on?" Troy demanded, gawking at Avery as if she had lost her mind. Gabrele, the King's guardian, pulled Avery off. For all anyone knew, she was attacking the Deity.

Avery looked for Nikki. The redheaded woman was crouching by the wall, head in her hands. She pulled at her hair like a mad woman. "Nikki! What have you done?" she screamed. Shaking her head, Nikki spared Salina another glance before running out of the dining hall. "Dante! Get her, now!"

"I've got her." Avery watched Ryse extend his hand, palm out, towards Nikki's fleeing body. She came to a halt as if she'd run head first into a brick wall. With the flick of his wrist, Nikki's body fell to the floor where Dante pinned her down.

Avery had never seen Ryse do this before. She knew he had more powers, but she didn't know he could control people like that. It was a terrifying thought, one that she would have to explore later.

The king was holding his chest and coughing. His wild, unfocused eyes looked around at Avery, Dyna, and the people gathered around him. Hayden had followed Avery over the table and was looking at the champagne spilled on the floor.

It was smoking on the tiles.

"Oh, gods no!" Hayden said, taking his father's head in his hands. "Father! Father!"

Ryse stood, horrified, on the other side of the table. "Avery, what is going on?"

"Nikki knew something was in the glass. Your mother had a vision. I just put the pieces together."

Ryse climbed the table to be with his father. Troy was on the floor, blood coming from his mouth. "What? How?"

"Be still, Father," Ryse said, moving to his side. Dyna had propped him up on her knees and held his head. Tears streamed down her face. Ryse looked up at her. "You saw this? You knew and did nothing! How could you, Mother?"

"I only saw him dying. I did not see how or when," Dyna pleaded through guilt stricken tears. She stroked his head.

People emptied the dining hall, fearful of the poison that was killing their King. The Elites were in action, gathering the flutes Nikki had passed out and clearing out the spectators. Bren was vigilant at Avery's side, making sure she hadn't had anything to drink.

"I'm fine!" she said, brushing him off as she watched Ryse, Hayden, and Dyna hover over Troy. The Paeans had been called in, and the healers worked to try and extract the poison with their magic. It didn't seem to be working. Troy was spitting up blood and his body shook in agony. He screamed out and Dyna went hysterical. Hayden pulled his mother into her arms and forced her move away so the healers could work. Ryse stayed, holding Troy's hand whispering to him. He stroked his father's face.

"Get back!" one of the Paeans yelled as Troy's chest began to boil. Yankee jumped in, pulling his Master from the contamination. Ryse fought him, trying to reach for Troy. Philippe used his magic to freeze the area of Troy's chest but the poison was too powerful.

"Let me go, damn it! Let me go!" Ryse screamed at Yankee. The other man was almost as strong as Ryse, but not nearly strong enough. Philippe aided his fellow Thracian to contain their Master. Avery tried to get to him, but Brenden held her back.

They watched, helpless and terrified as the body of their King was eaten from the inside out by the poison. Troy's screams and Dyna's cries echoed across the hall, her body limp in Hayden's arms. Titus, her Guardian, ushered them as far away as possible, yelling out orders to her personal guard. Between her men and Hayden's, Thracians walled them up.

There was nothing to be done. The poison had done its job and soon Troy's corpse lay still and lifeless.

Avery buried her head in Brenden's shoulder and cried. He ushered her away, Hayden and Dyna behind them. But Avery didn't want to leave Ryse. He was on his knees, looking at what was left of Troy's body. Anger and pain radiated off him like a toxic fume. Avery broke free from Brenden and ran to him. She dropped to her knees in front of him and wrapped her arms around his neck. Ryse crushed her in his arms and stared in shock.

"You have to move, baby," she tried to convince him. "There is poison all over this room, please, Ryse. Please move, baby. For me." She looked over his shoulder at Yankee and Philippe. They nodded and both took one of Ryse's shoulders. He allowed them to pull him to his feet but brushed them off as he backed away.

"Father," he whispered as Paeans in white suits commence in cleaning up the scene.

Everything had happened so quickly. One minute Troy was toasting, the next his body was being eaten, dissolved from the inside out. Nothing could prepare someone for this. There was nothing that could make a person process this catastrophe.

The royal family was taken to a private room, barricaded by layers of guards. Avery watched as they sat, motionless. None of them spoke, none of them moved. They were in shock. Even Ryse was unanimated. It didn't last long. His body suddenly in motion, he left the room, Elites in tow. Avery followed. Damned if she would sit on the sidelines.

"Tell me exactly what happened," Ryse said to her. Avery gave him a quick version of everything. The moment Salina was mentioned power surged off him. "She will die for this if it's the last thing I do."

CHAPTER FORTY-FIVE

RYSE KICKED IN THE DOOR TO SALINA'S SUITE. TWO THRACIAN guards were ready to attack before they realized who had entered. Even then he could see the battle in their eyes.

"Stand down or die," Ryse threatened.

"What is the meaning of this?" Salina sauntered out of the bedroom, her Shadow Lady pulling her baggage behind her. Her snakelike grin spread across her face, "Ryse, darling, you should be with your mother at a time—"

"Do you realize what you have done, Salina?"

"Pardon me! I know you are terribly distraught over King Troy's death, but really, accusing *me*?" She touched her chest, innocent and insulted.

Brenden, who was like a wall in front of Avery, took a good whiff of the room. "Master, she reeks of lies."

"Shut your snout, mutt," Salina hissed. "How dare you even address me, you abomination!"

"Silence!" Ryse shouted, his voice full of Ares' power, shaking the walls. "Salina, you will come with me, and you will be questioned along with all your men and ladies. By the gods, I swear if you have had a hand in this, your blood will stain my blade."

"Sorry, Ryse, I can't do that," Salina took a small remote from her pocket. Her face hardened as she looked over at Avery. "You've pissed off some very important people, bitch. Your death certificate has been signed."

Avery gritted her teeth and stepped forward; she was no coward. "Don't think I'm afraid of you."

"Whatever helps you sleep, farm girl. Time for me to go." Salina held up the remote and pressed the button.

"Restrain her!" Ryse commanded just as the Teleporter appeared beside Salina. Avery knew him immediately. He looked around, took in the company, and his face burned in anger. The Elites were fighting Salina's guards to get to her.

"You brought me into the lion's den!" The Teleporter said before trying to step away from her.

"You will not leave me here!" she screamed, lunging for him. Before she could make contact, Avery tackled her.

"Don't let him get away," Avery commanded. As she fought with Salina, Dante wrapped his arms around the Teleporter's neck and blocked off his abilities. As long as Dante touched him, he wasn't going anywhere.

"You little whore." Salina slammed her fist into Avery's face, taking her by surprise. "Enough of you." From under her belt, Salina took a six-inch blade and raised it above her head. "See you in Hades."

Avery remembered how Jerry's blade went through her body when she was on fire. She tried to call up the power. But she didn't know how to activate the flames. By the time she felt the lava bubbling up in her veins, it was too late.

Her world stopped as Salina plunged the knife into her chest repeatedly. Even with the Helioan power flowing through her veins, it was too late. The first strike hit her heart, and she could feel it rupture. The pain exploded across her chest like the burst of a balloon. The fierce pang, the agony seized her, spreading out to consume her entire being. These were her last moments on this earth and all she wanted was Ryse. Brenden made a flying leap, his body already shifted into the beast. He knocked Salina off and had her by the throat. Avery hoped to hell he killed her.

"Avery!" Ryse was by her side, towels in his hands, pressing them in her wounds as she coughed up her life's blood. "No! No, no, no! Find a healer!" He called out, "Philippe, use the water in her blood. Stop the flow." Ryse met her eyes, desperation and frantic terror in his. "Fight it, hold on. I'm going to heal you. You'll be okay. I swear. I promise you, Avery. I won't let you die."

The last thing Avery felt as Philippe tried to freeze her body was a deep regret that she didn't get enough time with Ryse. By the gods, how she loved him. And now that she had finally found the missing piece of her soul, she was dying. With the last bit of strength she had, she reached up and touched his face. "Love...you...forever."

"Avery!" Ryse's cries were muffled in a haze of white noise. She felt her spirit rise and float away. Seeing those below her made her ache. The room was littered with Thracian soldiers, good men who were caught in Salina's spell. Yankee stood guard over the ones still living even as he stared down at Avery's dead body. She would miss him and prayed this didn't make him even colder than he was. Hammon and Philippe worked over her body with Ryse. Those two men would keep Ryse going. She knew their love and devotion to their Master would never cease.

But it was too late for their magic. She was gone. Avery thought about Cutter, her silent but smiling friend, who was guarding Nikki far off in the Palace. How she would miss them both. Whatever part Nikki had played in this day Avery knew there had to be a reason. Nikki was too kind to kill.

She saw Dante backing away from the smoking body of the Teleporter. A syringe of poison protruded from his chest, his own hand wrapped around it. Dante turned to kneel by Avery, tears freely flowing from his eyes. Brenden had rendered Salina unconscious and was lifting his head in a sorrowful howl. Even in beast form he mourned.

Avery knew her life on earth was no more. The last image she saw was of Ryse bending over her body and stroking her hair, sobbing, begging her to hold on. She didn't want to leave him. But she was already gone. Everything went black.

CHAPTER FORTY-SIX

RYSE KNELT IN FRONT OF THE SHROUD OF HIS BELOVED AVERY. How was it that she was dead? He'd gone over the situation a million times in his head. How had he missed her slipping past him, tackling Salina? How had Brenden missed it, too? In his mind, he replayed Salina stab Avery. He could recall every slice, every deep gash in her chest. The crazed look in Salina's eyes and the way she screamed in victory with each blow was burned into his brain. Such anger, such malicious evil unleashed. Six times Salina had plunged the knife into Avery's heart. She might as well have been stabbing him. Ryse felt nothing besides the pain of Avery's death. Each time he closed his eyes he saw the shock on her face, he heard the gurgling as she choked on her own blood.

She didn't deserve this. Her short life had been full of heartache and disasters. Now to have found happiness and to have it taken from her seemed unfair. How could this be the will of the gods? How could they dare to assume he would ever live again after taking Avery from him? For two centuries he'd been true to his faith. He prayed, he worshipped, he did their will and acted in their name as their hands. And this is the reward for his service?

Damn them! Damn the gods and their will! Damn them for letting him taste of love, and then seal his lips forever. His fist came down on the marble coffer that held Avery's body up. The sound resonated in the empty temple.

Here he mourned alone for his soul mate while in the next temple room his mother did the same. Two bodies, two souls, two servants of the gods gone from this world. Fucking Salina! He longed for the day he would split her head from her shoulders with his sword. And if the gods thought they would take that revenge away from him, they had another thing coming. He would kill her. He would enjoy it and he would do it where every person in the Haven could see it. Salina would be the example for everyone who dared to strike at his family again.

"Master?" Hammon came to kneel beside him. His truest friend placed a comforting hand on his shoulder. "I beseech you to come and eat or allow me to bring you provisions."

"No. I cannot eat while she lies here like this. I fast." Ryse looked up at the cream colored lace that covered Avery's body. He could see her hair, her closed eyes and lips, hands folded in death over her chest. His ring, the symbol of their new union, on her finger. "How is my mother?" he asked, trying to think of anything else than the scene in front of him.

"She is in mourning, praying over the King's tomb as you do now. Her ladies and guards are with her as well as Prince Hayden. Samuel attends to her also."

"The others?"

"Philippe, Brenden, and Dante are in meditation right outside the door. Cutter remains with Nikki. She collapsed upon hearing news of Avery and the healers had to be called in. She gave full testimony to General Falcon. The moment she said Salina's name, she seized. Her mind had been programmed not to reveal that information. She is currently under healer and Thracian supervision, still unconscious."

"Will she live?"

"Her body functions; her mind is a different matter. We have called in your cousin Evander to look at her. She is our best witness as of yet. Salina's Shadow Lady hung herself in her cell with her shirt. The gods shall be her judges."

"Damn it!" Ryse said in frustration. "And Salina?"

"We are keeping her sedated in a coma."

"Good. I want the pleasure of ending her life myself."

Hammon sighed and helped Ryse to his feet. He'd knelt so long his legs were numb. They sat on one of the many pews in the temple.

Ryse knew the man beside him had witnessed something similar. The two had never spoken about what drove Hammon to the Thracian center so many decades ago. But today, Ryse needed comfort.

"Was it thus for you Hammon? When your Grace was murdered?"

Hammon blew out a deep breath. "Yes, my friend. When my Grace was taken from this world, I thought my life would end." He looked at Ryse with eyes of obsidian. "It seemed unfair that I drew breath and such a pure spirit didn't. My heart breaks all over again for you, Ryse. No Deity should have to bury their Grace like I have. I was lucky to have an heir to take over my station." After the death of his mate, Hammon had passed his crown to his son and taken a position as a teacher at the Thracian center. When Ryse came of age and gathered the team of Elites, Hammon had been his second choice as a member. The ex-Deity swore his life to Ryse and had been by his side since.

Ryse thought about the fact he and Avery would never have a child together. Tears rolled down his cheeks.

Hammon scrubbed a hand over his face. "You should eat, sire. You will need your strength to lead your people."

Ryse narrowed his eyes and looked at the altar. "You think I would lead anyone anymore? My very reason for living has been taken from me and I feel nothing but hatred to the gods."

"You do not mean that, Ryse," Hammon whispered. "You are the blooded son of Ares and Zeus. You do not mean those words."

"Didn't you? Didn't you curse the gods when they allowed your Grace to die?"

"I was not the man you are, Ryse. You have a destiny greater than all of us."

"I am clearly not as necessary to their plans as I thought. Two hundred years I searched for her!" He rose and pointed at Avery, his voice bellowing in the temple. "Two hundred years of waiting, hoping, praying! I've done everything they commanded! And why? What was the purpose? I've had her for less than a month! My soul has never had peace until she gave it to me. And now they take her? They allow Salina, a treacherous evil snake to poison my father and defile the body of my soul mate. What was the point of it all? Why do they punish me?" He was screaming now. Hammon lowered his head. Ryse knew the man had no answers.

He turned his body to face the marble statue of Zeus. The god stood tall, arms open as if to receive the soul of the person on the altar below. Ryse shouted to the statue, "Hear me, oh gods of the heavens! Damn you all! Curse you for this!" Ryse knew the moment the air stirred that Hammon had retreated out of the temple. He was not one to stay and bear the god's wrath. Ryse didn't blame him. Hammon had had his fair share of confrontation with the gods. Ryse, on the other hand, awaited it. Welcomed it. The air in the temple turned into a torrent of wind, whipping his mourning robes around his body. "I don't fear you! Every gift you have given me has been for naught! I could not save her. I could not save my father. What good are your *divine gifts*," he sneered the words, "if I am unable to save those I love? Take it back, you fools! Take it all back. I don't want this life if I cannot live it with her."

"You have the temerity to throw away the gifts of the gods?"

Ryse stumbled back when he realized the voice of Zeus was not in his head, but coming from the lips of the man standing before him. Zeus and Ares, gods clad in power and washed in light, stood proud on the other side of Avery's body. Zeus was a golden god, his face beautiful in its fierceness. Ares was draped in silver, looking as though he was made of steel. Their auras were overbearing in their anger, but Ryse stood tall. He would not back down, not even to the ones who created him.

"Answer me, my son," Zeus commanded calmly. "If you have the audacity to call upon us, then at least answer when we speak."

Ryse stared at them for a moment more before he said the words that might damn his eternal soul. "You bastards."

Taken aback, the gods exchanged a look, then focused their eyes on him. Ares only held up a hand, but it was enough to push Ryse to his knees. Magic attacked his body. "You have forgotten your place."

"And you have forgotten your promise!" Ryse spoke even as his vocal cords felt cinched. "You—you promised me a mate, an heir. You promised that I would have the power to defeat my enemies and fight for the things of light in this world. You lied!" He coughed and wretched until Zeus put a calming hand on Ares.

"We did not foresee the depth of Salina Avondale's depravity. These events are just as much of a shock to us as they are to you. Such is the consequence of free will." Zeus remained contained and spoke with an even tone. "I am distraught of the passing of your father and your mate. But it changes nothing of your destiny. You have a mission, a predestined—"

"No!" Ryse rose to his feet. "No longer. You can ask nothing else of me. I've devoted two and a half centuries on this earth to pleasing the both of you and all I have ever received in return is death. I've had to take the lives of people close to me. I've had to watch one of my closest friends and Elites die in my arms. I've searched for Avery most of my life only to find her life, too, has been hell. Now she lie cold before me and my mother weeps in the next room for my father. You can take your destiny and predestined bullshit and give it to someone else."

"Do you think we cannot do so?" Ares boomed.

"I welcome it! I would happily die right here, right now to be with her again." Ryse pulled back the lace and touched Avery's hair. "I've known so little of her love. It's not enough." He shook his head and looked back up at the gods. "It's not enough. You alone have the power to bring her back to me. And if you want me to continue my work here on earth, you will do it."

"Resurrecting the dead requires sacrifice of an equal life."

"You have my father! Is he not of equal value to you?"

Zeus tilted his head slightly, narrowed his eyes, "You would keep your father in the grave to bring back your Grace?"

Ryse swallowed hard. Was he so selfish? Could he sacrifice his own happiness to bring back his father? What would his mother think if she knew he was willing to keep his father in the physical grave in order to have Avery back?

"Yes, he would!" Dynasty ran down the aisle of the temple, black robes flowing around her. Her face was covered in tears and deep hollows under her eyes. Dyna fell to her knees and bowed her face to the floor. "My lords, my masters, I weep at your altar and pray to you as your humble servant. I know my husband would give his life for his child the same as I would. At least his death would not have been in vain. Do this. I beg of you, do this for my son!"

"Mother." Ryse took her into his arms, kissed her wet cheek. He looked up at Zeus and Ares. "Make your choice. You either bring back Avery or you can find some other man to do your dirty work."

Zeus and Ares studied him for a long moment before Zeus answered, "We do not appreciate ultimatums."

"And I will not bow down to gods who do not honor the promises they make to their believers. Either you are benevolent and honor your word, or you are unworthy of my devotion. Now make your choice!" Ryse stood there, one hand on Avery's head, his other arm around his mother, awaiting the decision that would determine the rest of his existence.

Zeus and Ares exchanged a long look. Ryse knew they were communicating. Finally, Zeus approached Ryse and Dyna. "The sacrifice of your father, though his work was not completed, shall balance this scale." He looked at Dynasty, who fell to her knees and bowed her head. "Know your mate rests in the arms of the gods. He has done well in this life and shall take his place among us in the

Heavens. You, my beloved follower, shall remain here with your sons until it is your time to join him."

Zeus twitched and Ryse watched as his eyes began to glow. "We have been summoned. We must go." The god cast a quick glance at Ares, who swallowed deeply. Why the gods were suddenly very stiff and still?

"And Avery?" He queried before they dissipated into mist.

"You will have your Grace. First you must prove your faith. Make a pyre in this temple for the flesh of my son, Troy. Then prepare one to my daughter, Avery. Set her body on fire. Let the flesh go and have faith in the gods. She will rise from the flames—a goddess among immortals."

"You shall have your Grace, my son." Ares said in a voice like breaking glass. "Then you shall fulfill your destiny."

EPILOGUE

AVERY HAD FOUND THE AFTERLIFE. SHE WANDERED AROUND IN THE mist and fog until she heard a female voice singing. Standing in a garden of flowers was the most beautiful woman she'd ever seen. Her long black hair touched the ground behind her, cascading like a waterfall. Her porcelain face was content as she sang to the iris blooms. Avery's presence made the music stop. She looked up and two baby blue eyes framed in thick black lashes captivated Avery, stopping her movement.

"Hello, child," she said, her speech as captivating as her singing. "Are you lost?"

"I don't know," Avery admitted. "Am I dead?"

"Oh, yes. If you are conversing with me, it is certain. You are in the spirit realm of the gods." The woman put down the flowers she had picked and looked long and hard at her guest. "Avery? Why, whatever are you doing in the afterlife?" Concern took over her face and her soft features turned angry. "You are not supposed to be here."

"I don't want to be," Avery said desperately. "I want to go home. I want to be with Ryse."

The angel pursed her lips. "As it should be. I didn't create you just to have you return to me so quickly. No, this will not do. This just will not do." There was only one goddess who had put claim on Avery, one goddess whose brand marked her body, and only one goddess with the power to send her home. Rhea. A sickness bubbled up in Avery's stomach as the goddess pulsed with frustration.

"My sons have not taken care of their responsibilities. It seems I must rectify this situation. You shall be returned to your Ryse. And I shall make sure my children know my vessel is not to enter this realm until it is your due time." Rhea held out her hands to Avery. "Come, child. I would hear the tale of how you arrived here. There is much we can learn from one another."

"And I will get to go back to Ryse?" Avery clarified, not sure she believed this dream she couldn't escape.

"He is incomplete without you. And his task is not finished. The faith shall be restored. The gods once again exalted and loved as we once were. Our people need revival, Avery. And you shall stand beside Ryse as he brings it."

"I need to be with him. He needs to know I'm coming back." Avery was frantic and Rhea gently pulled her close.

"I agree, my child. But I must keep your spirit here for a spell. We shall inform him. Wait here." Rhea disappeared and Avery turned in circles, looking for her.

When the goddess returned she touched Avery's forehead. "You will have but a moment before I retrieve your spirit."

Avery felt her body contort and twist, then fire licked up her spine until she thought there must have been a mistake. Had Rhea sent her to Hades after all?

Avery screamed, her eyes popping open to find Ryse holding her. His face was stained with tears, but he smiled when their eyes connected.

"Avery! My love!"

"Ryse!" She held him close. "I can't stay long. Rhea. It's Rhea."

"No! They promised you would return." Ryse's eyes were wild as he caressed her hair over and over again.

"I will. Trust me, Ryse. Trust in Rhea's promise. Have faith, baby. I'll be in your arms again soon." Avery pulled his head down and kissed him with the passion of woman given a second chance at life. All too soon she could feel her spirit lifting once more. "Take care of my body. I'll be with you again."

"Avery, don't leave me!" He begged as he shook her shoulders. "I need you! I love you!"

"I love you, too, so much even the gods will not keep us apart. Protect me until I return." Avery's spirit lifted and dissipated until she stood once more in the presence of the mother-goddess.

Rhea gave her a knowing smile. "Worry not, I shall return you to your mate in due time." Avery fell into her arms, thankful for her moment with Ryse.

Avery knew she would return to Ryse again. For now, she remained in the realm of the gods to learn from her creator. When she did reunite with Ryse, she would embrace her divine destiny with a new vision.

— —·   ᚼ   ·— —

Ryse bent down to kiss the lips of the sleeping goddess in his bed. She drew breath, her heart beat, and her eyes moved under closed lids. Avery was alive. Her spirit might be in the charge of the gods, but her body was his to protect. Brenden, Dante and Yankee set up a constant guard. Avery's body was in the trusted hands of his Elites. Dyna cared for her attentively, rarely leaving her side.

As for Ryse, faith and hope gave him strength. The gods had made a promise and he knew when the time was right, he would look into Avery's eyes once more and see them full of life.

Until then, he watched over her body and prepared for her return.

Continue Avery's journey with *Divine Judgment*…

ABOUT THE AUTHOR

JoAnna Grace lives in a world of alpha males and strong females where true love conquers all—at least in her books! From the time she started holding a crayon she began to create magical worlds. Living in the real world was never an option. A proud indie, she has published over a dozen novels including The Divine Chronicles series, The Blake Pride series, Riverview Romances, and more. This writer loves to read contemporary, paranormal, and urban fantasy romance novels.

JoAnna's tales are spun at her home in East Texas where she lives with her Prince Charming, three kids, and a few dogs and cats. When not hiding behind the computer screen chugging coffee, you can find her having fun with family and friends, singing, camping, or managing multiple businesses.

Connect on social media!

Like, Follow, Tag Jo, and share this book with your friends.

Instagram @authorjoannagrace
Facebook @joannagraceauthor
Goodreads: goodreads.com/author/show/7173373.JoAnna_Grace
Bookbub: www.bookbub.com/profile/joanna-grace

Make sure you're in the know. Sign up for the newsletter today!
http://eepurl.com/B_DM5

Do you want to help an author? Leave a review
Your opinion matters.
Every review can help.

Bonus images by Meg Murray Designs

www.ingramcontent.com/pod-product-compliance
Lightning Source LLC
Chambersburg PA
CBHW021235250626

47155CB00008B/3024